The
LIBRARY
of
LOST LOVE

About the Author

Norie Clarke lives in a beautiful village by the sea with her husband, son and dogs. When not writing, Norie can be found in her studio at the bottom of her garden playing the piano and trying, not very well, to draw.

The
LIBRARY
of
LOST LOVE

NORIE CLARKE

REVIEW

First published in 2023 by Headline Review
An imprint of HEADLINE PUBLISHING GROUP

First published in paperback in 2024 by Headline Review
An imprint of HEADLINE PUBLISHING GROUP

1

Cataloguing in Publication Data is available from the British Library

ISBN 978 1 0354 0489 6

Typeset in 12.5/14.75pt Garamond MT Std by Jouve (UK), Milton Keynes

Printed and bound in Great Britain by Clays Ltd, Elcograf S.p.A.

HEADLINE PUBLISHING GROUP
An Hachette UK Company
Carmelite House
50 Victoria Embankment
London EC4Y 0DZ

www.headline.co.uk
www.hachette.co.uk

In memory of Jeni A, whose spirit will never be lost.

Greenwich Village, NYC
August 1973

My beautiful Joany,

I know our love too deeply to accept your words this evening. No version of my life could ever be 'freer' or 'simpler' without you.

For me, this is not goodbye, it is simply the end of the beginning of our story. One day we'll find a way back to our love, wherever life takes us.

For ever yours,
Joseph

1

JESS

'How was your date?' Debs calls, when she hears me close her yellow front door behind me.

'Total disaster,' I call back, removing my coat then hunting for a space amongst all the kids' jackets in the hall.

I find Debs in the kitchen.

'Was it really that bad?' she asks, cooking the dinner with one hand while holding eighteen-month Eli on her hip, the sweet smell of caramelised sausages hanging in the air.

'Cricket-obsessed. Bad teeth. Said "yah" a lot. Enough said?'

She laughs at my misfortune and kisses Eli on his plump cheek, an acknowledgement that she's thankful she met Mike at college, and never really had to do the dating thing.

'I'm done with Tinder. There has to be another way of finding someone.' I collapse on to the red chair at the kitchen table and immediately find myself with Toby the cat on my lap, his black hairs clinging to the mustard wool of my jumper.

'Maybe it's not Tinder, maybe you're just not ready yet,' she suggests, reaching into the blue painted cupboard for a tin of beans, Eli simultaneously reaching for her swishing ponytail. Beans found, she hoists Eli further up her hip then tucks her batwing sweater into the front of her maternity jeans, which she's customised by embroidering daisies on to the back pockets.

Just then Mike arrives through the door from the garage. He kisses Debs on the top of her head and places a hand on her bump, takes a moment to feel for any movement, until Debs bats him away playfully with a spoon.

'Still here?' he asks me, jostling my copper curls as he passes.

'I'm working on it,' I cringe, knowing full well I've long outstayed my welcome, even if I have been paying rent, but also knowing nothing vaguely affordable ever comes up on SpareRoom. Only the very best of friends can tolerate a houseguest for a week, and I've been here almost a year, holed up in their box room alongside the growing collection of nursery paraphernalia.

'Not a problem,' he calls, going to the utility room where Debs insists on him taking off his dusty joiners' dungarees and changing into his house clothes, which he does diligently each evening, even putting the dirty items in the laundry basket. Mike is a man-god: handy, compassionate, strong, funny, and he's a great dad; I can only hope that he's lousy in bed, though Debs assures me he's not.

'Jess's date was a disaster,' Debs tells him, when he returns to the kitchen in his joggers and T-shirt, carrying four-year old Ash in a Superman pose.

'Bummer,' he says, and he tosses the local rag, the *Notting Hill News*, on to the table before hurling Ash round the room, divebombing Debs and Eli, causing Eli to shriek with laughter.

'Can't you think of anyone to set her up with, someone we trust, who isn't a total tool?' asks Debs, as she dishes up three plates of food for the kids and calls Jude, their eldest, to come through from the living room.

'Everyone I know is either already shackled or a man-boy,' he answers, taking a seat at the table.

'It's true,' sighs Debs, exchanging a tablet for a dinner plate with Jude, then directing him to wash his hands while putting Eli into his vintage highchair. Watching Debs manage the kids is like observing a master of chess: tiny, seemingly inconsequential moves, all forming part of a master strategy. Debs was born to be a mum, even if we do joke that the only reason she keeps having more kids is so she doesn't have to work; the real reason being that she's desperate for a girl. 'Guess you're stuck with Tinder then.'

'Guess so,' I mumble, Tinder and I having a love-hate relationship.

I was sworn off the app after my ex, Liam, did a runner with my life's savings. Six months later I found the courage to start searching again, more a habit than anything else, and then another three months passed, and I met a handful of guys. But whoever I met, no matter how nice they were, all I could wonder was, *what scam have you got*

5

planned, what signals aren't I reading, how long will it be before you take advantage of me too?

A year on and I'm still wary, but still looking. And even though I'm certain I'll never trust anyone again, I still can't help hoping for my own real life 'meet-cute'. And whilst I'll never be a Hollywood actress in a travel bookshop, or a graduate sharing a car ride from Chicago to New York, or even a bookshop owner unknowingly meeting the man who will eventually break and make her, I'm still hopeful that the day will come, when I'll meet that perfect someone, who makes me feel that one can't exist without the other.

Habitually I pick up my phone and start swiping.

'No screens at the dinner table,' says Jude, sounding just like his mother and looking exactly like his father – carrot-red hair, dark eyes, freckled skin.

'Sorry,' I say brightly, passing Debs my phone when she reaches out her hand, though I really don't want to. Being without it makes me feel twitchy, as if part of me has been disconnected and I might malfunction. Debs puts it on mute and places it behind her on the counter, completely unaware of how I'm feeling, offering me a look that says both 'sorry' and 'thank you for tolerating my children'.

It's only now as she sits down to join her family that I notice she's looking a little peaky; her usual plump, ruddy cheeks have lost their colour and she has heavy shadows beneath her chestnut eyes.

'You all right?' I ask, the kids too distracted by making mush out of their beans and mash to pay any attention to the adult conversation.

'Just a headache. Nothing a good night's sleep won't

fix,' she tells me, rubbing her belly, which is already obvious, even though she's not yet five months gone. 'How was your afternoon shift?'

'Not bad, though Mariko was going on about how she thinks the cinema might be sold.'

'How would she know that?' she asks sceptically. Given the cinema is celebrating its centenary this year, she's probably right to be doubtful about its demise.

'Her boyfriend, Jamal, has a job at I-work. Apparently, they're after new sites, and they're looking to buy out the cinema.'

'Is it for sale?' asks Mike, scanning through the newspaper ads.

'Not that I know of,' I reply, wondering how it is that newspapers are allowed at the table when screens are not.

'Sounds like a lot of old boll . . .' Mike catches himself, 'balderdash.'

'Still, it wouldn't be such a bad thing if it happened,' says Debs, scraping mashed potato from the side of Eli's mouth. 'You could go back to university or film school. Get out of the cinema and into producing, like you always wanted to.'

Debs is right; I have always wanted to be a film producer. But Mum losing her mobility during my first year at uni meant I didn't get my degree, that I had to work full-time at the cinema instead of part-time, and the bigger dream of my own home meant that the moment was never right to go back. There was always the hope that I could return once I was settled and had a little nest egg set aside. But then Liam did what he did and that was that – game over.

'I suppose,' I say, not really sure that going back to uni is on the cards right now, not when my savings pot is still empty.

'It's not as if you meant to end up managing a cinema. And I'm sure your management experience and film knowledge would make you a shoo-in for training.'

'Maybe,' I say, my job being the only thing that's giving me a sense of stability at the moment. It's been the one constant in my life for almost two decades, and a lifeline since Mum died four years ago, that and Debs, who's like the sister I never had. And for all it doesn't really stretch me, and I'm only there because of what happened with Mum, I do enjoy it: the films and the people. 'I'd just like to find somewhere to live, somewhere I can call home before I can think about what comes next. God knows I've outstayed my welcome here, and in four months my room needs to be ready as the nursery.' I keep to myself the anxiety of possibly losing my job and home with nothing in the bank to fall back on.

'How about this then?' asks Mike and he begins reading from the paper. 'Roommate wanted for professional Shoreditch flat. One thousand two hundred pounds pcm. Call Zane.'

I look to Debs with an expression that asks if her husband has gone mad. 'Who puts an ad in the paper?'

'Weirdos and psychos,' Debs says casually.

'Mike, it's the twenty-first century, *the digital era*. Nobody responds to adverts in newspapers.'

'Somebody must, or else why would they print them?'

'Aaah, so the paper can make money,' I say, in a 'duh' sort of voice.

'Jess, not everyone is as addicted to technology as you are. Hold on to your pants but . . .' he pauses for effect, 'some people aren't even online.'

I cock my head to one side and cast him a 'get real' face. As if anyone out there could possibly survive offline.

'I'm serious,' he says.

'Mike, everyone has to have an email address – without one you can't do anything.'

'Not true.'

I look to Debs for back-up.

'Can't help,' she shrugs. 'For once, he's right. Not everyone is online.'

'Bullsh—' I begin, but stop myself when Jude gives me the side-eye. 'That can't be right. How can you do anything without an email address? Utilities – you have to be online for billing.'

'There is such a thing as *the post*,' says Mike.

'Fine, what about setting up a bank account?'

'You can go into a branch.'

'TV licence,' I almost shout, convinced I've outsmarted them.

'PayPoint,' Mike retaliates.

I sit, stroking the cat's silky coat, desperately trying to think of something, but when I come up with nothing Mike says, 'Some people still rely on newspapers to advertise and, believe it or not, there are people out there who answer them.'

'Well, I'm not one of them,' I say fervidly.

'Jess, it's not a big deal,' says Debs. 'When you think about it, someone probably had to speak to someone else in person to place the ad. I reckon you're more likely to

9

meet creeps online, where it's completely anonymous, than you are via the paper.'

'You've probably met at least one percent of London's weirdos and criminals already through Tinder,' laughs Mike.

'Mike!' shouts Debs, causing the kids to look up from their food.

'It's fine, he has a point,' I say, knowing Mike didn't mean to make light of what happened with Liam, not knowing the scar he left me with when he scammed me out of every penny I had, then disappeared, and I was forced to give up buying my first flat.

It wasn't much – only a big room really, at the top of the block across the way from my mum's old place on the estate where Debs and I grew up. The estate is nothing special, three nineteen-sixties four-storey blocks that surrounds a small park where flowers grow, children play and neighbours know each other. And, most importantly, where people still remember my mother. But the flat had a balcony overlooking the grass where Debs and I played when we were little and hung out in when we were teenagers, and was just a stone's throw away from where she now lives on the estate; the moment I stepped through the front door, it felt like home.

I'd been saving towards a place of my own since I was thirteen, tearing ticket stubs and sweeping up popcorn on a Saturday afternoon at the cinema. From as far back as I can remember, Mum drilled into me the importance of owning my own home. She never managed it for herself, having become pregnant at twenty-one. She had to give up training as a dancer and work minimum wage jobs to look after me instead, and rent from the council. This time last year, I was days away from completing the purchase of the flat and moving into it with Liam, imagining how proud of me Mum would be, when he snatched everything away from me: my money, my dream, my trust. In one fell swoop he put my entire life on reset.

'Read the advert again.'

Mike repeats the information for me.

'Four things,' I say. 'One, *roommate* not *flatmate* means sharing a room. Two, Shoreditch isn't my thing, and it's too far from work. Three, I already know that *Zane* isn't my thing, and four, where am I going to get one thousand two hundred pounds a month to spend on rent?' I ask, wondering if it's even possible these days to find a room in the city for under a grand a month.

Debs shakes her head despairingly at Mike.

'OK, how about this,' he says, scanning the ROOMS TO LET column. 'Shepherd's Bush.' He looks up to confirm this is acceptable. I nod, given its proximity to the cinema and Debs' maisonette in Latimer Road. 'House share. Shift worker preferred.'

'I'm sensing ten low-income workers squeezed into three rooms, with one under the stairs, half a shelf each in the fridge with labelled milk cartons, and a bathroom that should come with a public health warning.'

'It doesn't sound great, hun. Pass it here.'

Debs scans the ads, making little tutting sounds as she eliminates them one by one, 'Ooh, how about this one,' she says excitedly, pushing the paper in my direction and tapping the little advert.

11

**LODGER SOUGHT FOR DOUBLE ROOM
ON CHERRY-LINED STREET, NOTTING HILL.**
Female only. £500pcm incl.
Call Joan: 0207 727 9752

'It's close to work, and us,' she encourages, knowing me well enough to know that I'd want to be near to her.

'There must be a catch. It wouldn't be this cheap if there wasn't.'

'It's probably just an elderly lady who doesn't realise the cost of renting.'

'Or a serial killer masquerading as a naïve old woman attempting to lure females,' Mike chuckles.

'Inappropriate,' trills Debs when Jude glances up from his dinner. 'The only way you'll know for sure is to phone and find out.'

'I suppose I could,' I agree, not particularly wanting to leave the comfort of Debs' home and her gorgeous boys who are like nephews to me, but knowing they all need their space back, and I really do need to get back out into the world.

'It might turn out to be exactly what you need to get life back on track,' encourages Debs as I get up for my mobile to call Joan.

2

JOAN

'I'll answer it,' I tell Edward, heaving myself up from my armchair in an effort to get to the phone.

'I can get it,' he says, already on his way to the telephone chair in the hall before I've even managed to straighten up. 'Hello.'

I hurry as best I can towards my son, and gesture for him to hand me the receiver.

'Who's calling?' he asks the person on the other end of the line.

'Who is it?' I ask him breathlessly, taking the phone out of his hand, concerned it might be someone enquiring about the advert, having not yet revealed the lodger idea to him.

'Hello?'

'Am I speaking to Joan?' asks the voice on the other end of the line, Ed having returned to the living room.

'You are, yes,' I reply, sitting on the chair with its built-in walnut table, the worn seat-pad moulded to my shape from years of use. 'To whom am I speaking?'

'My name's Jess. I saw your ad in the *Notting Hill News*, the room to let,' she adds, her inflection rising as if I might need reminding.

'That's correct.'

'Is it still available?'

'It is,' I say, withholding the information that she's the first woman to call. Despite making it clear in the advert that I wanted a female I've had several male callers, all of whom I've had to politely decline despite their own lack of manners. The whole process has made me question if I'm doing the right thing, if perhaps I shouldn't have listened to Pamela after all when she suggested the idea of a lodger over the fence. 'Would you like to view it? It's a lovely room overlooking the back garden, quite peaceful.'

'Can I ask where you are in Notting Hill?'

'Portobello Road. It's not far from Notting Hill Gate station.'

'I know it.' She pauses and I wonder if there's something more I should be telling her. 'Is it just you in the house?'

'Just myself, and Humphrey, my Labrador. I hope that doesn't put you off,' I add, concerned that she'll have picked up on the quiver in my voice and not want to live with an almost octogenarian, let alone her aging dog.

'It doesn't,' she laughs, a light, youthful giggle. 'Is it OK if I come have a look?'

'Certainly, it is. When would suit you?'

'I could head over in about half an hour. I'm not far away.'

'Why not?' I say, surprising myself, and wondering

what excuse I can possibly make to encourage Edward to leave before she arrives.

Humphrey looks up at me from where he's lying on the Persian hall runner, his grey muzzle on his jet-black paws.

'She sounded nice,' I say to him, having given her the full address, hoping I wasn't too brisk. I have a tendency to sound abrupt on the phone, a hang-up from when lines were poor and you often had to shout, and from my days as a piano teacher at Westminster, dealing with parents overseas. Jess possibly doesn't even remember landlines, let alone have experience of using one.

I'm wiping down the black Bakelite telephone and giving some thought as to how to move Edward along, when he calls through from the living room.

'Who was that?'

'The chiropodist,' I fib, amazed at my sudden mental agility.

I return to the living room where Edward is on the two-seater sofa opposite the fireplace, his eyes fixed on his laptop.

'She's had a cancellation and wanted to know if she could pop round in the next half-hour to look at my corns.'

In the mirror above the mantelpiece, I see Edward's face scrunch in disgust, and I delight inwardly at my cunning.

'You might want to make yourself scarce,' I press, checking the clock, which reads just after six. 'She's likely to be here within twenty minutes or so.'

15

Keeping an eye on Edward's movements in the mirror, I adjust my blouse and cardigan, and attempt, with no success, to reposition a curl of fine grey hair which insists on jutting out at right angles to the rest, as it has all my life. Why I bother with such a detail when I have heavy eye bags, deeply lined cheeks and a sagging jawline, I never understand, but still, I do. And then I press my hand over the tiny gold locket I've worn these last thirty-five years, kept as close to my heart as possible.

When Edward fails to move, I check my wristwatch and clear my throat. Humphrey sits alert at my feet, he too, waiting. As we wait, I fight the urge to tell my son that he needs a haircut. Recently he's taken to wearing his wavy brown hair in a longer style near his shirt collar, to the point that it often falls over his face. In my opinion it doesn't suit him; it hides the eyes I love so much, eyes so like his father's.

'I'll get going in a minute,' he says, without looking up from his computer, and I relax, a touch. I plump the cushions next to him on the sofa, smartening the place for Jess's arrival, while thinking how terrible it must be to be young these days, always 'on', never truly being able to switch off. In my day it could take days to arrange meetings, weeks to exchange correspondence; now it all happens in seconds.

'I just need to finish drafting this email . . .' he tails off, his eyes scanning the screen. He hits a button, finishes typing then closes the top before placing it in his bag.

'Everything OK with work?' I ask, directing him towards the hall, glad that he's up and moving, wondering how he keeps up with all his company entails. I've lost count of how many premises he has now, scattered around the city.

'We're expanding again, trying to find new sites,' he explains, stepping into the hallway. 'I'm looking at an old cinema tomorrow. I heard the owner is looking for a buyer. The site would make an amazing space, worth the initial outlay.'

Edward set up his 'co-work space' company five years ago, naming it I-work, which seemed rather appropriate given work is all my son ever does. He told me the idea then – an office space for anyone, with a café and facilities – and I had to stop myself from telling him I didn't think it would be a success. But then the world changed: people started working from home, big businesses reduced their offices, and suddenly everyone was desperate to be surrounded by other people again, even if they were all just staring at their computers. I was wrong; it's been a huge success, the making of him, as he sees it. Personally, I think it will break him if he doesn't slow down, but he doesn't want to hear that; my son's identity is bound to his career.

'Fingers crossed,' I sing, opening the inner door and ushering him into the vestibule. 'How's Izzy?'

'OK, I guess, I haven't seen her recently,' he replies, opening the front door.

'You need to find a better balance: less work, more play.'

He laughs, steps out into the garden. 'Aren't you supposed to give me the opposite advice?'

'I just want you to be happy, that's all. Your job can only bring you so much happiness.'

17

In the fading westerly light, I notice that his brow appears more lined than the last time I saw him, his strong cheekbones more prominent, and his deep brown eyes look heavy with tiredness. I wonder if he's eating enough, if he's looking after himself properly amongst all the busyness.

'You know I'm not the only one who needs more balance – you could do with branching out a bit yourself,' he tells me.

'As it happens, I already have,' I say, deciding now, when he's already out the door, is as good a moment as any to tell him. 'I've advertised for a lodger.'

'You've done *what*?' he asks, reacting as if I've just signed up to a sky-diving course rather than placed an advert for a lodger in the *Notting Hill News*.

'Pamela thought it might be fun to have someone about the place other than Humphrey, someone to have a conversation with over breakfast, or a game of Scrabble with at night. Humphrey's not much of a conversationalist,' I quip, nodding to him snoozing at my feet on the tiled floor of the vestibule.

Ed casts me an unamused look.

'They might liven the place up a bit, help with the bills and chores, that sort of thing. Perhaps some of their youthfulness will rub off on me,' I add.

I neglect to tell him that in the beginning, I'd been as opposed to the idea as he is now, thinking Pamela a fool for suggesting it. Why after almost twenty years of living alone should I want someone in the house? Someone I don't know, who might be messy or noisy or both, or have disagreeable habits. But the more we talked, the more I came round to her way of thinking, that the right person might enhance my life rather than impair it.

'Mum, you're seventy-nine, not twenty-nine. A lodger is likely to be young.'

'Age has nothing to do with it,' I scold, rather wishing he'd hurry along. 'And as Pamela said, if not now, with my eightieth birthday just around the corner, then when?'

He runs his hands through his thick hair and sighs, as if I've done something unspeakably foolish.

'All will be fine,' I say, trying to reassure him, when in truth all the doubts I had when Pamela first mentioned it are beginning to resurface. I crane my neck to see if there are any lone women walking towards the house, a nervous knot twisting in my stomach.

I think of all the young people who stroll past my front windows every day, winding their way towards the market, idly snapping photographs on their phones of the pretty, pastel-coloured houses, all of them mysterious and as distant to me as if they come from another planet. I have no idea what I'd have in common with someone that age, what their lifestyle and routines might be.

'I'm not sure, Mum. You have me, *and* that crazy neighbour of yours, isn't that enough?' He nods his head in the direction of Pamela's house next door.

'Yes, I do, and I'm grateful for you both, but I'd like someone who's here most of the time, not occasionally,' I say pointedly, cross that, just because I'm older, he thinks that a son and neighbour should suffice as company. 'It gets lonely rattling about on my own. A bit stale, if you know what I mean.'

'Wouldn't a book group have sufficed, or a choir, or a simple trip to the shops?'

'I like having my groceries delivered from the shops on the avenue; the drivers bring it straight into the kitchen. It's easier that way. And all I have to do is call if I need something different or extra,' I say casually, even though we both know that I'm no longer comfortable walking up the road to the grocer for a pint of milk or along Holland Park Avenue to the butcher for a bone for Humphrey.

'What about an online group then,' he suggests, ignoring the obvious, as we've always done. 'We could set up the Wi-Fi again. Keep it connected this time. You could get a tablet, or a smart phone.'

'Not on your nelly. I'm perfectly happy with my landline.'

'They have their uses, Mum,' says Ed irritably, which I can't help thinking might have more to do with his desire to be online when he visits – to be able to send emails, not just draft them – rather than anything to do with my wellbeing.

'I've managed this long without one; I'm certain I'll manage another ten to fifteen years without one too.'

'Fine, whatever you want,' he sighs, washing his hands of the matter and turning to leave. 'Just don't say I didn't warn you, when God only knows who walks in through that garden gate.'

My legs feel as if they might buckle when I hear the clang of the gate latch, and I have to pause to catch my breath when I first catch sight of Jess's outline through the frosted glass panels of the inner door. I lean more heavily on my cane, all of Edward's scaremongering rushing back to me. And for a moment, I wish I could go back and undo it all, tell Pamela not to be so foolish, that Edward is right – I am too old for such antics. I try to breathe, the way Pamela attempted to teach me, something about a square, but that I was too proud or stubborn to pay attention to.

As I draw closer to the door, I can make out a silhouette of big hair and a bright yellow jacket, and I'm suddenly even more conscious of not being young, and nervous that we really might have nothing in common. As I fiddle with the lock, my fingers stiff, I try to recall the last time I spoke to anyone under the age of sixty-five, other than Edward and his friend Charlie, and the delivery men, but can't.

'You must be Jess,' I say, having managed the lock, my breathing laboured.

'And you must be Joan,' she says, tucking her phone into her inside pocket, her soft eyes sparkling like polished jade. I'm mesmerised by how vibrant she is. She's like a little porcelain figurine in a shiny yellow puffy jacket and bright blue trousers, with thick, bouncy copper curls that frame her heart-shaped face. I feel staid in comparison, in my box pleat skirt and blouse.

'Won't you come in?'

'Your home is very beautiful, much more characterful than the others on the street,' she exclaims, gazing round the hallway as if she were in a museum, taking in the anaglypta wallpaper and brass and glass lamps.

'Thank you,' I reply, and I wonder if she's being polite,

21

that 'characterful' is just another way of saying 'old-fashioned', that it doesn't quite compare to the houses that have had money spent on them by their wealthy young owners, something I was never in a position to do.

'And is this Humphrey?' she asks, crouching down next to Humphrey, who's meandered through from the kitchen to see who's joined us, his tail swaying.

'It is,' I say, watching him fondly, and I feel my shoulders relax. The fact that Jess should remember his name speaks volumes about her, and that Humphrey seems perfectly at ease in her company gives me reason to feel the same. Humphrey has always been an excellent judge of character.

'Would you like to see the room?' I ask, far less nervous now that we've got past the introductions.

'Yes, please,' she says, getting up from her crouch with perfect ease. I struggle to remember a time when I was so nimble.

'It's this way,' I tell her, leading her up the stairs, clutching the mahogany banister, immediately regretting not suggesting that she go first. I try to ignore my hip, grinding in its socket, and up the pace so she's not left dawdling behind me, but the pain is too great, and I'm forced to ascend the steps at a snail's pace, Humphrey following us at an equally glacial rate.

'I always wanted a dog as a child, but we couldn't afford one,' she tells me, and in the quietness that follows her remark, I wonder about her background and who 'we' might be.

We make small talk as we continue up: how far she's come, the weather, and her work at the Portland Cinema.

'I spent many happy hours there in years gone by,' I say. 'Friends and I would make a night of it, dress up, head out for supper, and then go to the pictures. I knew the previous owner. I think his son owns it now.'

'Clive,' she confirms, which rings a bell.

'This is it,' I say on the half-landing, the door to Edward's old room closed, and showing her into the room opposite. 'It's not much, but it's clean and quiet.'

'Oh, it's lovely,' she says, running her hand over my mother's old pink candlewick and then taking a moment to enjoy the view of the garden from the sash window. There's something in her gaze that makes me wonder why someone so young and beautiful should need a room with a stranger, and an old stranger at that. 'May I take a photo?'

'Certainly,' I reply, and she snaps several shots on her phone of the garden which is unusually large for the road, reaching all the way to the neighbouring street.

'I'm sorry there isn't an en suite. I know they're all the rage these days, but I don't take long in the mornings, and I'd be happy to wait for you to use the bathroom first if you need to get to work.'

'I'm used to sharing a family bathroom, so sharing with one other will be fine.'

'It's just there,' I say, motioning to the door on the landing, glad that the lack of en suite doesn't put her off. 'Nothing fancy, but functional.'

'Perfect,' she says, taking a quick look at the rose-coloured suite, and I hope I've remembered to clear away my ointments and pills, things I could never have imagined needing at Jess's age, knowing nothing of the indignity of an aging body.

23

'Up the half-flight of stairs is my room, and one other . . .' I dismiss this part of the house with a slight wave of my hand. 'Let me show you downstairs.'

'How long have you lived here?' she asks from the bottom of the stairs, waiting for me to join her.

'It'll be fifty years this year. Houses didn't cost then what they do now.'

'No,' she says, slightly despondently, and I think how lucky I am to have been born when I was, when life was more affordable. 'Fifty years is a long time.'

'Almost twice as long as you've been alive.'

'Hardly!' she says kindly.

'This is my sitting room, which you'd be more than welcome to use,' I say, after I've shown her the dining room on the opposite side of the house, and told her of how I grew up just a few streets away in Holland Park.

'Thank you,' she says, taking everything in from the original fireplace with my patterned armchair beside it, to Edward's third birthday photograph, with me on his right, he looking the picture of happiness, his brown eyes glistening like caramels, despite the obvious absence of his father. And I see her eyes sweep over the invitations and cards from days gone by when life was busy and the loneliness of old age unfathomable, and the prospect of losing friends not even a passing thought.

'I like your elephant lamp.'

'It was my mother's,' I tell her as she wanders through to the back section of the room where the grand piano, its cover on, sits unused since my last pupil grew too old for lessons and no one else took her place. As she admires the room, I wonder what she's thinking, unable to see

24

beyond her good manners and youthful enthusiasm, if she's really interested in the house or not. Does the prospect of living with someone almost in her eighties hamper her freedom too much?

'Do you play?' she asks.

'I used to,' I reply too sharply. 'My fingers don't allow it any more.'

'That's a shame,' she says, stopping by the instrument, her fingers tickling the fringes of the shawl that lies over it. 'I always wanted to learn but—'

'The kitchen's to your right,' I say, moving quicker than I have in a long time to usher her away from the piano, and much to my relief she continues round and out of the lounge to the kitchen. 'Do you like to cook?'

'I do, but I don't manage it often,' she replies.

'I'm much the same. Perhaps we—' I'm about to suggest we could cook for each other occasionally, but I'm concerned that might appear too keen, that I've got carried away, so I stop myself and ask instead, 'Would you like a cup of tea?'

'That would be lovely, Joan, if you're sure I'm not keeping you too long.'

'Not at all,' I say, filling the kettle at the sink overlooking the garden, mindful of how dated the pine kitchen must look to her young eye, neglecting to tell her that all I have planned for the weekend is Pamela dropping in this evening for a 'debrief', that plans no longer exist beyond these four walls.

'The garden looks gorgeous,' she says from where she stands at the back door, taking in the borders with the show of daffodils, which I always think look like new-born chicks calling for their mother, even in the dwindling light.

'Why don't you pop out and have a look while I make the tea?'

I watch, while waiting for the kettle, as Jess, followed slowly by Humphrey, takes a lap round the garden. She snaps photos of the herbaceous border and the huge magnolia, bursting with buds, and it amuses me that she deems it worthy of capturing. As she continues, I muse about how I would never have placed an advert in the classifieds in the dead of winter. There's something about the first flush of spring that is capable of motivating and exciting even the most dormant of species into bloom.

When she reaches the bottom, she stands, her hands in her jacket pockets, looking back at the house to the bedroom above the piano room. From what I can tell, she's considering the old place. And I think how lovely it would be to have her here, that all my worries about a lodger were for nothing. I laugh at my stupidity, never learning, even after a lifetime, that my worries are always in vain.

'It's a lovely spot. Hard to believe we're almost in the centre of the city,' I say when she returns, filling the cups, hoping that a mention of the proximity to the West End might aid her decision-making, help her to realise it might not be all bad living with someone ancient. 'I have help with the garden, so you wouldn't find yourself with any outside chores.'

'I wouldn't mind,' she replies, accepting her cup of tea as I gesture for her to take a seat at the table. 'I've never lived in a house with a proper garden before. I might enjoy the odd bit of weeding or mowing the lawn.'

I want desperately to ask where she's been living since leaving home, and with whom, and why it was she didn't have a garden when she was young. But it feels too personal for a first meeting and, not wanting to put her off, I tell her about my daily routine instead.

'I'd be out most of the time,' she tells me, after I've given her a blow-by-blow account of my day, from rising early to let Humphrey out, to my night-time cup of cocoa at nine. 'My hours can be long and late. I wouldn't be too much in your way.'

I resist the urge to tell her I'd like her to be in my way, that the prospect of her being out most of the time is disappointing, that the idea of having her to share my day with fills me with delight, not concern as I thought it might. And for a moment, I wonder if I should look for someone else, someone who would be around more. But there's something so luminous about Jess, so full of energy, that I decide I'd much rather have her around some of the time than someone else all of the time.

'I understand, being young is to be busy. I'd just be glad to know there was someone else about the place.'

There's a moment between us where I feel uncomfortable that I might have let slip that I'm lonely and she, I suspect, isn't certain how to respond. Because why should someone so vital understand loneliness; why should she know what to say to a woman who's already lived her life, when hers is only just beginning?

To fill the gap in conversation, I hurriedly say, 'Would you like the room? I'd be very happy to have you.'

And again, Jess stalls, her eyes looking every which

way but mine, and I fear this time my eagerness really has got the better of me, and I've put her off.

'I'm sure you need time to think it through,' I back-pedal. 'Please, let me know when you're ready. You must have much to consider.'

And then Jess smiles, a radiant smile that lights up her eyes and melts my concerns.

'Joan,' she says. 'I'd love to take the room. When can I move in?'

3

JESS

Mariko and Daniel are waiting for me on the little bench outside the cinema when I arrive to open up the following afternoon.

'Hey guys,' I call, in earshot but still far enough away to appreciate the charm of the old place. Even after almost twenty years of working at the Portland, I still can't conceive of how beautiful the neighbourhood is with its cheerful painted townhouses and elegant shop fronts. Nor can I believe how lucky I am to work in such a cute little building – a semi-hexagonal façade at the heart of a Y-junction. It's a world away from the estate, even though they're less than a mile apart.

'Hi Jess,' says Mariko with a smile, pulling her big headphones down over her black pigtails and looking up from her phone. Daniel, engrossed in his sketchbook, acknowledges me with barely a glance, his scruffy blond hair falling over his face.

'Late night?' I ask him, remembering that he was

29

planning on trying to finish a piece of artwork that he's been working on for months.

He nods his reply, remains seated. Mariko, on the other hand, is up like a shot, smoothing down the short kilt she's wearing.

'How was the preview?' I ask her, unlocking the double mahogany doors, the long, brass handles warm on my palms.

'*So* good,' she says, beginning a monologue about the latest film preview she's been invited to review on her TikTok. She chats at speed about the experience as we pass through the entrance foyer with its central, hexagonal ticket desk and faded Art Deco splendour, down the shallow stairs, the red carpet worn, and into the bar, where the scent of popcorn and polished wood fills the space.

'It's already had my highest views yet, and it's only been up for a day,' she concludes in the tiny, windowless office, crammed with boxes of ticket reels, receipt rolls, and forgotten umbrellas. We drop our bags and throw on our black, Portland Cinema polo shirts.

Daniel, sketchbook in hand, comes inside to set up the ticket desk and open up. Mariko goes to check the toilets and open the doors to the two small auditoriums, while I turn on the lights, popcorn and coffee machines, ready for the first customers of the day.

'I found a new place to live last night, with an older lady, and low rent,' I tell Mariko, when we're both behind the counter, she putting the cups and saucers away from the night before and me replenishing the sweet selection.

'Great, Jess. People do that in Japan a lot. Older people

own their homes so it works out cheaper. They get company, you get a nice place to live,' she says, appearing not to think the decision odd at all, unlike me.

My brain hasn't stopped thinking about it since I left Joan yesterday evening, after we'd agreed for me to move in next weekend, my impulsiveness having got the better of me. I keep worrying that I've made a mistake, that our lifestyles might clash, or that we won't have anything in common. Despite Debs' reassurance, and now Mariko's, I can't quite let it rest.

'Where is it?'

'Portobello Road,' I answer vacantly, thinking about the walk from Debs' to Joan's last night, through the Notting Hill locations where Hugh Grant wooed Julia Roberts. Mum and I stood on street corners for hours when they were filming, Mum desperate for Hugh and Julia's autographs, me entranced by how many people it took to make one film. It was then, watching the camera guys and make-up artists, that I first fell in love with the idea of working in film.

'Is the house nice?' she asks, now topping up the sugar sachets and wooden drink stirrers.

'It's gorgeous, a proper forever home,' I reply, thinking of Joan's road and the pastel Georgian frontages perfectly co-ordinated with the first burst of pink blossom. 'There were flowers and a weeping willow, and a gravel path that led to a front door surrounded by climbing roses.'

'It sounds like something out of a Richard Curtis film,' says Mariko, not altogether approvingly, being much more of a horror enthusiast than a rom-com fan.

'It is very romantic,' I laugh, giving the sweet packets a final straighten. 'There was even a veranda with birds flitting all around. And although inside it was a bit tired, dark wooden furniture and carpet in the bathroom, it felt lived in, you know – her home.' A pang of sadness shoots through me as I think about the loss of the home I shared with Mum for almost thirty years which meant everything to us. It was there that I took my first steps and Mum gave me my first pair of tap shoes; there that she did my make-up for the first time, and made my curls bounce like Mariah Carey's; there that I got my first period, and cried over my first boyfriend, and there that I came home one day and Mum told me she'd been diagnosed with MS.

'She said she'd lived there for half a century and you could feel it in everything, even the patterned carpets,' I say, recalling how Mum's flat, our home, felt when Liam and I had emptied it of everything, down to its bare boards, before we were meant to move into the flat I was buying, and only my memories remained.

'Did you like the lady?' Mariko asks.

'She was lovely. A little nervous, I think, maybe lonely,' I reply, her loneliness being the thing that swayed me, that me living there was somehow important to her, that I might be of use to her.

'So what's the problem?' asks Mariko, opening the doors to the popcorn machine and tossing the puffed kernels vigorously with the scoop.

'I've never lived with someone older. What if it's the wrong decision?'

'Jess, it's cheap, it's close to work and it's gorgeous. If

you don't want it, I'll take it. I'd happily give up my commute from Hornchurch.'

'Point taken,' I say, feeling a little guilty; Mariko spends half her life on the Tube.

'What's the worst that can happen?'

'I lose my job, I need to move out, and end up homeless,' I catastrophise, conscious this isn't like me, that the effect of Liam's betrayal has triggered an even greater desire for some sense of stability in my life than I had before it happened, even after Mum had deteriorated over a decade and finally succumbed to sepsis.

Mariko rolls her eyes, as she's prone to doing, and dismisses my worries with a shake of her head.

When Clive and I first hired Mariko, I found her hard to warm to with all her eye-rolling and opinions. We gave her the job because her knowledge of film was off the charts, and she was super keen to help build the cinema's socials through TikTok reviews. But after a few weeks of her working, alarming our older customers with her spiky black and red hair, strong punk fashion and numerous piercings, that enthusiasm began to feel misplaced, as if she was nipping at my heels for my job, or using the cinema to build her social media presence rather than the other way around. It was only when Mum started to require more care, and I needed more time off, that it became clear that Mariko wasn't after my role; she was just very pragmatic with an incredible work ethic and love of film. If it hadn't been for her covering my shifts in the latter stages of Mum's illness, Clive would almost certainly have needed to find a replacement.

I'm about to quiz Mariko about the rumour she's heard

about I-work, how likely it is to be true, when we hear the voice we hear every Friday afternoon, calling from the top of the stairs, 'Is anybody there?'

The sound would be grating – an aging Janine Melnitz from *Ghostbusters* or Janice from *Friends* – if it weren't for the superstar it belongs to.

'I'll go,' I tell Mariko, who doesn't share the love I do for Zinnia, our ninety-something, New York fashionista. 'Coming, Zinnia.'

'Take your time,' she shrieks, shrill as you like, never shy of being heard.

I find her, a few steps down, clutching the polished handrail with one hand, the other gripping her silver-topped black cane.

'Wow, you look cute today,' I shout, her hearing decreasing by the week.

'You know me – more is more.'

'Our own Iris Apfel,' I laugh, hovering beside her, watching her every step, ready to catch her should she fall.

'I make Iris look dull,' she yells.

'Right, much more Zandra Rhodes,' I say, looking down at her scalp and her shocking pink hair, amazed that it's withstood all the bleach and dye over the decades.

'You gotta have colour.'

'True,' I agree, a lover of colour myself, though Zinnia takes it to a whole new level. Today she looks like a tiny tropical bird in bright yellow trousers, a purple top, lime-green jacket, and lips as red as cherries, with glasses to match.

'And accessories, you gotta have accessories.'

'Gotta love a bangle,' I comment. Zinnia's huge plastic beads and bracelets clatter as she descends the last stair and walks shakily towards the bar.

'And coffee,' she says, pronouncing 'coffee' in the way only true New Yorkers can.

'Is that my cue to make you one?' I ask, helping her on to one of the tall chairs at the bar.

'You know how I like it . . .'

'Strong and black.'

'Like my men,' she cackles, as if she hasn't recited the line every Friday for the last decade.

Over the last ten years, Zinnia has become something of an aging great aunt to us all. She brings us gifts from holidays, tells us stories of her childhood growing up in New York, of her life with her late husband, and how her now single life in London is her 'one last hurrah' to the world.

As I'm making the coffee, Zinnia spreads her copy of the *Notting Hill News* over the counter, giving us a full commentary on everything from the new market regulations to the ever-increasing neighbourhood house prices.

'And this,' she says emphatically, jabbing her finger at the paper. 'Have you seen this? *More* I-works! I ask you, how many rooms full of androids does one neighbourhood need?'

She turns the paper for Mariko and me to look at the headline:

CO-WORK SPACE DEVELOPER EYES NOTTING HILL EXPANSION

'That's what Jamal was telling me about,' says Mariko keenly, scanning the article. 'I told you, Jess, they're looking at here as a new site.'

'What?' yells Zinnia, and I can't tell if she hasn't heard or if she's aghast at the idea.

'Mariko's boyfriend thinks I-work want to turn this place into one of their new locations,' I explain, taking my turn to speed-read the article for any mention of the cinema.

'Poppycosh!'

'It's for real,' says Mariko, going to the bottom of the stairs to tear a customer's ticket. 'My boyfriend heard it from one of their managers.'

'Clive hasn't mentioned anything to me about wanting to sell. And there's nothing about it in the article, just that they're looking,' I try to reassure her.

'Jess, they're taking over the city. The guy who owns it has more money than Musk.'

'Clive wouldn't ever sell to them,' I say.

'That's what you like to think,' she says, tearing another ticket while Zinnia, muttering 'who could believe the state of the world today', folds the newspaper, and makes room for the guy who's just arrived at the bar.

'What can I get you?' I ask, shifting my gaze to discover a customer who's so handsome my breath actually catches for a moment. It occurs to me that the last time I reacted to anyone in this way was the first time I met Liam in the flesh, and I fell into his eyes that were the colour of a turquoise lagoon.

'A popcorn, please.'

'Small, medium or large?' I say, my eyes fixed on his, which are crushingly soulful and brown.

'Large,' he replies, and his gaze moves away from mine, apparently more interested in the cornice work and parquet flooring than me fumbling with the popcorn container.

As I place the popcorn on the bar, I notice Zinnia, none too discreetly, looking the guy up and down over her glasses, from his wavy brown locks to his well-fitted suit, to his brogues without socks.

'What do you make of this?' she asks nasally, staring straight at him as if he were just some regular dude rather than the heart-achingly gorgeous guy that I see.

'Me?' he asks, apparently unfazed by being accosted by an elderly woman who looks as if she's been spat out of a kaleidoscope.

'Yes, you, Jon Snow,' she says, pointing at him, and I giggle inwardly, because now I see exactly who he looks like – Kit Harington.

'What do I make of what?'

She stabs her finger at the article. 'This I-work non-sense, taking over the neighbourhood. This world of robots we're creating, where nobody knows how to talk to each other any more.'

'I wouldn't know,' he falters, his voice low and impossibly husky. 'A meeting was called off; I'm just catching a movie to fill time.'

'Huh,' says Zinnia, still eyeing him up, trying to get the measure of him. 'Well, I guess when you're that pretty you don't need to have an opinion.'

'Zinnia!' I cry, mortified, ready for him to take offence and complain.

'I can only apologise,' I begin, but he laughs it off, paying for his popcorn on his phone.

'No problem at all,' he says, reaching for the tub.

'You know,' I say to them all, trying to keep him at the bar a little longer. 'This place has been part of our community for a century. It's an integral part of the neighbourhood. That's why Clive wouldn't sell, and why his father and grandfather didn't before him. And why I-work would fail even if they did make a bid.'

'Here's hoping,' says Zinnia.

The guy smiles at me in a way that suggests I'm being slightly naïve, but which sends a quiver through my heart regardless.

'Ladies,' he says with a courteous nod, before taking his popcorn and disappearing into the auditorium, leaving me wondering who he is and if he'll be back again anytime soon.

4

JOAN

I've been like a cat on a hot tin roof all morning, waiting for Jess to arrive, unable to sit still or set my mind to a task. I've lost count of how many times I've checked the carriage clock on the living room mantelpiece and pressed my ear to it to confirm it's still working. After a week of overthinking, wondering if I've done the right thing, my stomach is in knots. When she does eventually arrive, wrapped in her yellow puffy jacket and wearing huge purple hoop earrings, I discover she's brought a friend with her, which makes my tummy even tighter.

'This is Debs,' she explains breezily, indicating the ruddy-cheeked, plump girl behind her, her hair pulled tight off her pretty face in a high ponytail, her eyelashes like exotic caterpillars. Humphrey sniffs the bottom of her flared cords and her white plimsolls. 'Is it OK if she helps me bring in my things?'

'Of course,' I say, when in truth I might have preferred a little warning; I can't remember the last time I had anyone in the house spontaneously, other than Pamela.

'Nice to meet you, Joan,' says Debs, extending her hand and shaking mine vigorously, her colourful bracelets jangling. 'Beautiful home you've got.' She casts her eyes around, scoping the place as a tradesman might do. I half expect her to suck her teeth and scratch her head before delivering the bad news.

'Have you much to bring in?'

'Just a couple of car-loads,' says Jess, glancing towards the lemon-coloured car that's parked outside the open gate. At most I'd expected a couple of suitcases and a few boxes, but Jess is pointing at a large estate car with items pressed against almost every window. Despite my desire for company, another knot of anxiety twists inside me, and I find myself reaching for the grab handle at the front door that Edward insisted on me having, even though I'd protested at length.

'Very good,' I smile wanly, my head a little light. 'Would you like a cup of tea before you start?'

'We've Starbies in the car; we grabbed one on the way,' she reports.

'Righto,' I reply, not certain what 'Starbies' might be. 'I'll take Humphrey through to the kitchen and pop the kettle on.'

'OK, Joan, we'll unload,' she sings, her brow crinkling as if I've said something that's confused her, and I hope our start doesn't indicate what is to come – two people speaking entirely different languages.

From the kitchen I hear their merry chatter drift out and in, and their feet on the gravel as they go to and from the car, returning with items that they stack in the vestibule. While my head tells me it's exactly what I need – movement

40

and youth about the place – another part of me feels like an intruder in my own home.

'Joan?' Jess calls from the hall just as I'm sitting down at the table to have my tea.

'Yes?' I answer, and I put on a brave smile and head to find her.

'Is it OK to start taking things up?'

'Certainly, it is.'

The vibrancy of her belongings – shiny suitcases, rustling pot plants, bin liners stuffed full of brightly coloured cushions – makes me feel out of date, out of step with the world, and I find myself wondering if I really have made a mistake after all, if having someone so young in the house will only serve to make me feel older rather than younger.

I start the ascent of the stairs, even more conscious of my rickety frame than when Jess viewed the house last week. She follows behind, carrying a heavy box with another smaller one on top, and Debs brings up the rear with a chair and a denim beanbag.

'Your house is so gorgeous,' enthuses Debs, running her fingers up the dado-rail, and I try to remember when I last dusted it. 'Jess told me you've lived here for fifty years. I can't imagine living anywhere for so long.'

'Time is a curious thing,' I reply slowly, wishing I had something sharper to say that would match their pace. In some ways it feels as if it was only yesterday that Parker and I moved in, straight after our tentative honeymoon in Guernsey, and in other ways as if that was someone else's life entirely.

At the top of the stairs, I pause to catch my breath, aware of the girls behind me, balancing heavy items.

'Whose room is that?' Debs asks when I get going again and she is parallel with Edward's old room.

'It was my son's.'

'And what about up there?'

She motions with her head up the half-flight of stairs.

'Those are my quarters,' I reply, saying nothing further, unnerved by Deb's curiosity.

I open the door to Jess's room where Jess places the box on the bed, and I have to refrain from asking her to move it to the floor, worried that it might mark the candlewick, which is so laborious to clean.

'Joan, the room is even nicer than I remembered,' says Jess, spinning gaily in the space, like a ballerina in a music box. Debs positions the chair and beanbag by the window and studies the garden below. I imagine the two of them sitting there, looking out to the garden, deep in conversation about boys and fashion and all the things I've lost track of over the years, and I hope deeply that I'll allow their youth to rub off on me, and that laughter will find its way back into the house.

'I'm glad you like it. I think it's one of the friendliest rooms, my old guest room,' I say, uncertain when it last had anyone stay in it, and thinking it unlikely that it will ever have anyone other than Jess in it again.

'I'm a bit jealous,' laughs Debs. 'Maybe I could move in too!'

I think she's joking, but one way or another the comment jars with me, and that feeling, of being an intruder, of having bitten off more than I meant to, returns like a sudden cold gust of wind.

'Don't worry, Joan. Debs has a home of her own and three kids. She won't be moving in.'

'Not anytime soon, but maybe when baby number four arrives,' quips Debs, patting her stomach, and I realise now that she must be around five months pregnant.

I find myself wanting to ask if she should be carrying heavy objects, to ask if she knows the risks, but the words fade before I can voice them and, not wishing to sound interfering, I decide to leave them to it.

I've gone through to my chair in the living room to steady my nerves, when there's a familiar knock on the inner door. Humphrey shows no sign of getting up from where he's positioned on the fireside rug, knowing full well, from the four-quaver rap, that it's Pamela. He learnt years ago that it's not worth the effort of moving for someone who doesn't pat him. Pamela is of the ilk who believe dogs are for working, not for company.

'Yoo-hoo. Only me,' she calls, letting herself in, negating the need for me to get up too.

'I'm in the living room,' I call back, when Pamela fails to appear. I have a feeling that she's standing at the bottom of the stairs, scrutinising Jess's belongings.

'So you are,' she says, appearing in the door with a curt little nod that causes her thick, short grey hair to bounce.

'Come in, take a seat,' I say, not that Pamela ever needs an invitation.

'I'm quite happy standing,' she replies, loitering in the doorway.

'It could be a while before they're down.'

43

'They?' she enquires, her eyes peering over the top of her half-moon spectacles.

'Her friend Debs is helping her.' My attempt at casual normality sounds rather forced. 'Biscuit?' I offer, giving her a reason to relinquish her stance at the door.

'Oh, go on then,' she says over-gamely, and she sits down on the sofa, rolling up the sleeves of her thick sweater.

'She has a lot of things,' she says, and then with a wry chuckle she adds, 'we hadn't thought about that.'

'No, but she's young and, like a magpie, pretty things attract,' I muse, the extent of Jess's belongings being one of the few things Pamela and I didn't discuss. Pamela is someone who likes to scrutinise everything, which I always put down to her military upbringing. From the moment I told her Jess had accepted the room she fired question after question at me: 'What is she like? How old is she? Where is she moving from? Why does she need your room? When is she moving in?'

And when I was economical with my answers, not wanting to set myself up for a fall should Jess decide against moving in, Pamela informed me I was being 'very sparing'. I neglected to tell her that was because I knew if I gave her a crumb, she'd take the whole blessed cake.

'How are you feeling now she's here?' she asks, modifying her tone to the one I suspect she used with her patients. People who, unlike her, weren't raised by a brigadier and his wife, trotted round the world before the age of ten, and then sent to boarding school. People who hadn't had self-sufficiency and aptitude drilled into them from birth.

'I feel fine, Pamela. How was your morning?' I reply,

trying to change the subject, not fancying one of her emotional MOTs right now. This newfound fad of everyone wanting to talk about how they're feeling every five minutes is beyond me. It seems it's all they can talk about on television these days.

'Now Joan, don't change the subject. It's a big change for you, after all this time on your own.'

'I'm sure it's the right decision,' I say compliantly, sensing her inching her way towards the topic of me being stuck indoors.

'Good. Because like we said, if not now, then when? You don't want to live the rest of your life alone, do you, or be stuck in the house for evermore? It's recognised medically that loneliness is as bad for your health as fifteen cigarettes a day. Hopefully having a lodger will help.'

Pamela never sits still long enough to entertain the idea of loneliness or boredom or whatever the word is for when life grinds to a halt. She might only be a decade younger than me, but she might as well be half my age. The longest I've known her not leave the house was after having her fourth child who 'put me through the wringer' as she told me some time after, and even then it was for less than a week. Other than that, she's been on the go day after day for the last thirty-five years and, I imagine, long before that. There are days when I envy her confidence, wonder if I'll ever rediscover my own.

'You're quite right. A new chapter is what's needed,' I say, hoping if I say it often enough, I might come to fully believe it.

'Well,' she bristles. 'Hopefully she can fit all of these possessions in her room. The place would look like student digs with a glitter ball hanging next to the grand-father clock.'

The preposterousness of Pamela's comment causes a laugh to burst out of me, which takes us both by surprise. 'She's plenty of space up there. I'm quite certain that the odd extra item here and there won't make much difference. It might be quite nice to spruce the old place up a bit; I can't remember the last time it was decorated.'

Pamela casts her eye round the ornate cornicing, down over the Anaglypta wallpaper, past the gas fire, and on to the brown and orange swirly carpet that Parker and I had chosen when we first moved in, a wedding 'gift' from his parents. I had been relieved to have a project to manage after returning from honeymoon. I'd hoped that choos-ing things together for the house would bring us closer, but Parker soon tired of it and handed the responsibility solely to me, preferring his long hours in the City instead. 'You're right, maybe a freshen-up wouldn't go amiss,' she says, and I push away an unhelpful feeling of offence.

For all I'm fond of Pamela, and can usually find humour in her ways, from time to time her directness can be unnerving. I can remember to this day the first time she knocked at the front door, thirty-five years ago, one child in hand, one on her hip and another on the way.

'I'm Pamela Ashbrook,' she announced, her oldest child trying to hide behind her mother's long Laura Ashley skirt, and I rather felt like doing the same. 'We've just moved into number forty. I need the men to take the gazebo down your side path, they can't get it through our hall.'

And that was that. No, 'pleased to meet you, how do

you do?' or 'would you mind awfully' just, 'I'm Pamela' and 'I need'. She's been the same way ever since. Even while parenting four children *and* running the local GP practice, she's always found time for grand announcements, demands and general interference. It took me several years to realise that under her bluntness was a woman with very good intentions.

We spend the next while passing the time, turning our attention to the birds who are busy building their nests in the garden, and the latest political scuffle, which isn't of much interest to me, having heard them all before, but to Pamela still holds great fascination.

'Joan?' Jess calls eventually, causing us both to turn.

'Come on, I'll introduce you,' I say, bracing myself against the arms of the chair and hoisting myself up.

'Hi,' smiles Jess, cantering down the stairs in her jeans and cropped orange jumper, simultaneously looking at her phone.

'Jess, I'd like you to meet my neighbour, Dr Ashbrook.'

'Pamela,' says Pamela pompously, though I can tell she's trying to be informal.

'Nice to meet you.' Jess shoves her phone into her back pocket and stands on the bottom step, holding on to the curve of the newel post, almost swinging, as if unable to keep still. 'This is Debs, my best friend.'

'Hello,' waves Debs, bounding down behind Jess. She slots her arm through Jess's, standing so close that it looks as if they might be about to run the three-legged race. Pamela and I stand a good metre apart, both stiff as boards.

'Delighted to meet you,' says Pamela with a firm little

47

nod, then she casts her eyes over Jess's belongings as if she's only noticing them for the first time. 'Gosh, what a lot of things you have.'

'I've left quite a bit of furniture in storage,' says Jess, her movement lessening. 'Is it all right, Joan? It should all fit in my room.'

'It's perfectly all right,' I tell her, the remaining bundles now giving me a sense of moving forward, rather than of being left behind. 'Are you winning up there?'

'Getting there, but I can't get any signal. Can I have the Wi-Fi password?'

'The what?' I ask, wondering if I've misheard.

'The Wi-Fi password,' Pamela shouts.

'I'm not sure what that is,' I reply, wondering why she felt the need to shout. My hearing is one of the few things that hasn't been affected by age.

'It's on the back of the internet hub,' Debs explains.

'The internet hub?'

'You know, Joan,' says Pamela, 'the little black box with the blue light that Edward plugged into the phone connection.'

'Oh, that! I put it away,' I say, going to the understairs cupboard. 'The cable kept getting in the way of the hoover.'

'May I plug it back in?' Jess asks, an urgency in her eyes. 'I can clip the cables up, so they don't get in your way again.'

'Whatever you need,' I say, holding open the cupboard door for her to find it. Gone are the days that I can get in to the depth of it myself.

'Thanks, Joan,' she says, backing out again, the 'hub' in hand.

I step back and she jumps up, her earrings swaying and perfume wafting like the smell of candy floss, which takes me back to summer days spent at Coney Island.

'Well, look at you,' laughs Pamela, when the girls have bounded upstairs, two steps at a time, and are out of sight. 'Lodger. Wi-Fi. Joan, what's next? Might we tempt you with a tablet or mobile after all?'

'Steady, Pamela. Let's make sure we can walk before we run,' I say, returning to my chair, only able to recall one time in my life when I felt I had no choice but to be reckless.

Dearest Joany,

I write to you from Vienna, a thousand miles from London, and yet my heart is still there with you.

If it weren't for the photograph you gave me, I'd believe that I dreamt the whole episode of us meeting three days ago. How can it be that before we met, I was able to navigate this journey of life alone, and now find myself lost without a guide?

Yours longingly,
Joseph

My darling Joseph,

I hope your journey to Vienna wasn't too long and that you are enjoying performing in the city. Selfishly I am willing you back, in the hope that seeing you again will cure the pain in my heart I've had since leaving you. My piano professor despairs at my lack of concentration and my desire to play only the romantics: Chopin, Liszt, Debussy, who all transport me back to you.

Please continue to write via Kathleen while you are away, I've been worrying about my parents discovering a letter from you. Kathleen writes to me all the time, so they won't give it a second thought. We could also correspond via the lonely hearts column in the Notting Hill News *to arrange weekly dates. I'll post the first next Thursday when you're back. Look out for JNY19!*

Yours impatiently,
Joany

5

JESS

'How's the first week been at your new place?' Mariko asks me, serving us coffees in the corner seating area as Daniel, Gary the projectionist, Mariko and I wait for Clive to arrive for the staff meeting he's called.

'It's good. Different,' I add, still not quite used to the quiet of the house after the mayhem of Debs' home. 'I like waking up and having coffee in the garden and then taking Joan's dog for a run.'

'Careful, Jess,' chuckles Gary, 'soon you'll be dishing out medicine and viewing care homes.' He stretches his wiry frame.

'She's not that old, Gary,' I say, feeling oddly defensive of someone I've known only a week.

'I think it's great you're both giving it a go. I hope it turns into something long-term for you,' says Mariko.

'Me too.' I keep to myself the fact that it's all still very new, that I'm uncertain about where to dry my laundry, or that I'm over-fastidious about keeping the bathroom clean, and always listening for what Joan's up to so as not to disturb her.

'What are you working on, Daniel?' I ask when there's a lull in the conversation, Daniel, as usual, with his head in his sketchbook.

'I'm experimenting with ideas for a triptych,' he pulls out his phone and shows me several photos of a derelict housing estate on Insta: graffiti on a brick wall, a smashed window, an abandoned kid's bike. 'Just can't figure out the best three to create the right narrative.'

'When you gonna get an exhibition together, mate?' Gary asks, rubber-necking the images.

Daniel doesn't reply and clicks off his phone, all of us aware that his lack of confidence in his work and limited income makes it really hard for him to exhibit. In the eight years that he's been working here, the only exhibition he's done was his graduate show, and that almost broke him. I can remember him barely managing to get in for his afternoon shifts having been up through the nights, agonising over his work, and sleeping in his studio space. Now he lives in his studio, devoting all of his spare time to his urban landscapes, but only ever managing to share them through Instagram.

'How's the house search going?' I ask Gary, knowing that Daniel needs a change of topic.

'We found a place. Now we're trying to sort out the mortgage.'

'Gary! That's a big deal, why didn't you say already?' I ask, knowing just how important finding a place that fits his growing family and all their needs has been. 'Where is it?'

'Chigwell, mate. Just round the corner from where my missus grew up. Four beds. Big garden. There's even a garage.'

'No!' I laugh, thrilled that he'll at last have a garage for his beloved Ford Capri. 'When do you move?'

'Depends on the mortgage. About twelve weeks.'

'I'm happy for you,' I smile.

I'm about to ask Mariko about her latest film review when Clive arrives, skipping down the stairs with his fawn miniature cockapoo, Lulu, tucked under his arm.

'How is everyone?' he asks, pulling up a chair. He parks his shades on the top of his tanned, balding head, and positions Lulu on his knee.

We mumble our replies, more concerned with what Clive is about to tell us than making small talk.

'As you're aware,' he begins, his voice a little breathless, his soft hands clutching Lulu, 'business hasn't been good these last few years. I'll be sixty-five on my next birthday and after thirty-five years of running the place, it feels like time for a new phase in my life, and for the building too.' He takes a deep breath and squeezes Lulu a little tighter. 'So, I've taken the decision to look for a buyer.'

Despite the rumour we've all heard, a stunned silence falls over the table. Clive strokes Lulu repeatedly, Daniel hangs his head, Mariko raises a 'told you so' eyebrow at me; I scold myself for not having taken her seriously.

When I first started working at the Portland, it was normal to have people rattling the doors ahead of time, and queues of people snaking down Portland Place on Friday and Saturday nights. Now we're lucky to have two or three bums on seats for the afternoon screenings, and only a handful more in the evenings. Mariko and I have mentioned so many money-spinning ideas to Clive over the years – using the cinema as a wedding venue, or location set, or holding talks and events, like all the other cinemas in the city do to make up for the shortfall in ticket sales – but he's never gone for any for them. Sitting here now, watching him stroke Lulu repeatedly, I can't help but feel annoyed with him for not trying harder.

'To sell as a going concern?' I ask, even though I'm pretty sure of the answer.

'Not necessarily,' he says, and we all know what that means: our jobs are on the line.

'Jesus, Clive,' cries Gary, running his hand over his buzzcut. 'What the hell, mate? I've got a family to feed, a mortgage to agree.' His strong cockney accent sounds even stronger in anger.

A tiny bead of sweat breaks above Clive's top lip. 'I know, and I promise, nobody will be left in the lurch. You'll all be taken care of.'

Gary swears under his breath before disappearing upstairs for a cigarette. For once I feel like joining him.

'Have you found anyone yet? Has anyone offered?' I ask, tapping my gold vinyl nails on the frayed leather tabletop. It feels as if a rhino has just parked itself squarely on my chest.

'Not yet. But there's interest.'

'From I-work?'

The words feel like poison on my tongue.

He nods with a little crinkle of surprise. 'It's early

stages. They said they'd like to offer; I've given them a month.'

A flurry of anxious looks shoot round the table between the three of us.

'At this stage anything could happen,' Clive continues. 'I-work's bid might not be good enough, there could be competing offers.'

I bite my lip. Mariko fiddles with a stud at the top of her ear. Daniel's head is thrown back, staring at the ceiling, his Adam's apple protruding sharply.

'Does anyone have any questions?'

The three of us mumble that we don't, and Clive releases Lulu, who scampers behind him as he retreats to the office.

At this point in the afternoon, I'd usually be making sure the bar is stocked for the next showing and the toilets checked, but today I haven't the wherewithal.

'Who wants another coffee?' I ask, dragging myself up, feeling as if I've been punched in the gut.

'Triple espresso,' says Daniel flatly.

'Shot of whisky in mine,' says Mariko, and I know she's not joking.

'On it,' I say, trying to sound 'up', knowing, as the manager, that I have to remain positive for the team, despite the fact that I'm freaking out about how I'll be able to pay rent at Joan's without a job, let alone save towards my future.

While the coffee measures fill, I fire a message to Debs, telling her the news.

'How could he do this to us?' asks Mariko when I've made the drinks, the two of them having sat pretty much in silence for the last five minutes, firing off their own messages to friends and loved ones. 'How will I pay my tuition fees, my rent?'

'I can kiss goodbye to my studio and materials,' says Daniel.

'Let's not get ahead of ourselves,' I say, aware that the last thing Mariko needs before the final year of her film MA is to lose her job, but also conscious that if Daniel could find his confidence, he could easily make a good income from his work. 'Like Clive said, I-work might not bid enough, or he might get a competing offer. Anything could happen.'

Daniel gets up, shaking his head. 'Just another faceless enterprise destabilising the neighbourhood.'

'Nothing is decided, Daniel,' I call, but he's already halfway up the stairs with his coffee and not interested in anything I have to say, whether I believe it or not.

When it's time, I get up to pin back the auditorium doors, the straggle of customers who were in there, filtering out.

'Why all the long faces?' asks Zinnia, after I've helped her to the bar and positioned her on a high stool. She's looking particularly natty today in a shiny purple suit, and carrying a huge, bright pink crocodile-skin bag.

'Clive's decided to sell up,' I tell her, unable to compute what I'm saying.

'To I-work,' says Mariko, snapping a bin liner open to clear the litter.

'That's not necessarily the case,' I remind her as she heads into the cinema and I set about making Zinnia more coffee.

'What do you mean, he's selling? Why?' she asks.

'Not enough business,' I tell her, biting my tongue about all the missed opportunities. 'Plus he wants to retire.'

'Retire? Retire from what?' she exclaims. 'He doesn't do anything around here; *you* do it all.'

I laugh, Zinnia having hit the nail on the head.

'And to sell to I-work?' she spits, outraged. 'The generations before him will be turning in their graves.'

'We don't know I-work will get it, that's only one option.'

'We have to do something,' says Mariko, returning with only one popcorn carton and a copy of the *Notting Hill News*.

'What can we do?' I ask, cleaning down the frothing nozzle with a cloth. 'You said it yourself, I-work are loaded. And Clive has clearly made up his mind.'

'We need to find someone who'll buy it as a cinema.'

'How?'

'I don't know. Start a campaign?' she shrugs. 'There must be someone out there with a vested interest in the place – someone who used to work here or has come here for years. Someone who understands that it's part of the fabric of the neighbourhood, *and* who understands the importance of independent cinema.'

'Where would we even start?' I ask, thinking it a bit of a long shot but happy to try anything that might help save the cinema and everyone's jobs.

'You could start by contacting the paper,' suggests Zinnia.

'Right,' says Mariko, clicking her fingers in agreement.

'We could get them to write about how awful it is that in its centenary year it's to close, and that we're searching for an investor.'

'I remember seeing an advert in the paper for stories . . .' I begin, gesturing for her to hand me the *Notting Hill News*, which I spread out on the counter. 'Look. This,' I say, pointing to the little ad:

HAVE A STORY TO SHARE?
WANT TO RAISE AWARENESS?
Contact our local journalists today.
Your cause is our cause.

'That's exactly what you should do,' cheers Zinnia. 'Save Our Local History! Save Independent Cinema! Down with streaming and subscriptions!'

'It might help get more people in the doors, make the place profitable again, which could in turn attract a buyer,' says Mariko, when she sees me looking unconvinced.

'You say it as if it's simple,' I say, loving their enthusiasm but doubting the feasibility of the plan. 'I think it's going to take more than an article in the *Notting Hill News* to turn this place around and fight off I-work.'

'You won't know unless you try . . . and I could help. I've been looking for a sideline, something to keep me busy,' says Zinnia, and Mariko nods her agreement, both of them imploring me to agree.

I think how I'd feel if the old place closed without me putting up a fight, if I lost the semblance of family and home it gives me, and of how many years it would haunt me if I didn't at least try. And I feel something rise inside me, a determination, a steeliness to bring down the opposition.

'Fine, I'm in!' I smile ruefully, knowing how stoked it will make them. 'Let the battle with I-work commence!'

6

JOAN

Jess seems distracted, her attention never far from her phone, as I lay out the Scrabble board on top of the dining room table, Humphrey parked underneath it.

'Is there something on your mind?' I ask, conscious that not only is she preoccupied but that she's also lacking her usual vim.

The first morning she was here I woke to discover a note on the fridge door, 'Gone for a run with Humphrey. Back soon!' and from then on, she's been like a tornado about the place: exercise in the morning, lunch with friends, back late from work. I've caught myself wishing when waving her off that her life wasn't quite so busy, that she might be around more to chat and to brighten my day with her sunniness. So it's perplexing to find her less than her usual bright self, but also gratifying to have her company even if just for a while.

'There's something going on at work,' she says, typing hurriedly on her phone while I deal out the letter tiles.

'If ever you need to talk . . .'

'Thanks, Joan,' she says, putting her phone down and placing her counters on the rack. She places them quickly, apparently in no particular order, while I spend time alphabetising mine, first the vowels and then the consonants.

'Don't you find it hard to concentrate with all that going on?' I say, nodding to her phone, which bleeps again as I place my first tiles on the board.

'I guess I'm used to it,' she replies, mulling over her play, the phone continuing to ping. 'I got my first mobile at thirteen, and I've had a smart phone since I was seventeen.' She lays out her counters, her nails a metallic gold, and takes a long drink of wine.

'What do all the different sounds mean?'

'I've different ringtones for emails, messages, social media, dating apps—'

'Dating apps?' I enquire. 'What are those?'

'You know, like Bumble, Tinder . . .'

I offer her a blank expression.

'Um, like a dating website . . . Match.com?' she asks.

'Is it similar to a lonely hearts column?'

'It's exactly like that!' she laughs. 'Except with a bit more info, photos, and it's much easier and quicker to get in touch. Look.'

She leans over the table with her phone, me inching my tile holder out of view, and flicks through endless photographs of singletons.

'All of these handsome young men are advertising themselves in the hope of finding someone?' I ask, astonished.

'Yup.'

'And does it work?'

'Sometimes,' she shrugs, her tone suggesting she hasn't been too lucky. She pulls back, puts the phone down, drinks some more wine. I play my next move then neaten all the other counters on the board. 'I went out with a guy called Liam for a couple of years, a graphic designer. I met him on Tinder. We were super tight from the start, meant to move in together and everything but . . .' she hesitates. I organise my new tiles, trying to hide my curiosity about what she isn't saying. 'In the end, it didn't work out.'

'I'm sorry to hear that,' I say, having more empathy for her than she might realise. 'Now that I think about it, Edward might have mentioned something about meeting Izzy, his girlfriend, online.'

'It's pretty much the norm these days, though sometimes I wish it wasn't,' she says, and I wonder what this Liam character did to cause her to be so disheartened.

'When I was much younger, a teenager, we met people at the dance halls or arcades. Only people who struggled to meet anyone advertised for someone in the local classifieds section. Although I must confess, sometimes my friends and I used to answer them out of naughtiness,' I tell her, not letting on that the lonely hearts would become such an important part of my life in years to come.

Jess smiles, plays her next word, no doubt amused at the idea of my friends and I writing to strange men for entertainment. I try to remember how I was as a very young woman, going out dancing, or spending time at the arcade looking for Mr Right, but as is often the way, the memory seems to belong to another person now, rather than a younger version of myself.

'Shame the lonely hearts column is a thing of the

past – it might have been fun to give it a go!' she says, bringing me back round to the here and now.

'Oh, but it isn't a thing of the past. I noticed some this morning in the *Notting Hill News*.'

'You're kidding!' she cries, and I get up to go to the hall where I left the paper.

'Look,' I say, on my return.

Jess pushes aside the Scrabble board and I spread out the paper, tapping the lonely hearts column.

'Eeww, look at this one,' she winces, '"MATURE MAN, late 60s, seeks youthful, energetic woman for good times and domestic bliss".'

'It sounds as if he's looking for a cleaner rather than a companion,' I laugh.

'And this one is weird,' she says, stopping her finger on one. '"DOG LOVER seeks female to chase around the park, lick and cuddle".'

'Good grief,' I cry, refilling our glasses. 'I'm not sure they were this racy in my day! What would yours say?' I ask, hoping the wine isn't making me too familiar.

She thinks for a while, running her finger round the rim of her glass.

'I don't know ... *Film Mad Female, 32, WLTM sensitive, loyal, kind guy*. Something like that,' she dismisses, and I wonder how it is that someone so beautiful and full of life could possibly be on her own. 'What about you?'

I sit back down, chuckling. 'People my age don't place ads in the lonely hearts.'

'Sure they do,' she says, tracing a finger down the columns. 'Look at this one, "Young At Heart, 83—"'

'An exception to the rule.'

'Nuh-uh,' she replies, picking up her phone and typing something into it. 'Look. Dating apps for older people: Silver Singles. Our Time. EHarmony.'

'Good gracious,' I gasp. 'Surely not.'

'Why not?'

'Well, love is for the young,' I bristle, busying myself with repositioning the board and counters and taking another mouthful of wine, unable to imagine a version of me now that would even consider, or be capable of, dating.

'Joan! Tell me you don't really believe that?'

'You should give the lonely hearts column a go,' I say, hoping to deflect the conversation away from me. 'Don't you ever wonder what life was like before all this?' I point at her phone. 'How your life would be now without it?'

'You mean being offline completely, like you?'

'Yes.'

'You can't survive offline these days, Joan,' she says, and I notice her body physically tensing at the prospect.

'I survive,' I say, feeling something rising in me, an idea.

'It's not the same for the younger generation, we're hard-wired this way.'

'You can't know unless you try.'

'Are you suggesting I go offline, entirely?' she asks incredulously as I position my next word on the board.

'Why not? You've come to live with me, why not also try living *like* me?'

She takes a moment, her eyes on her tiles, but I know from the nibbling of her bottom lip that she's not thinking about her next Scrabble move; she's considering what I've just proposed.

65

It takes some time, but eventually she raises her soft green eyes to meet mine.

'Fine, I'll do it,' she says, a sparkle to her gaze that tells me she's plotting something of her own. 'But only if you do the opposite.'

'By going *on*line?' I ask, putting down the tile I was contemplating and reaching for my wine glass instead.

She nods.

All of the things Pamela and Edward have mentioned over the years – how being online might enable me to find new friends, reconnect with old ones, and help to discover a fuller, busier life again – pass through my mind. And I think of how the opposite might benefit Jess: more time, new passions, less busyness. Maybe it's the wine, or Jess's spirit rubbing off on me, or a combination of the two, but whichever, I feel a small smile pull involuntarily at the side of my mouth, and my eyes meet hers.

'All right then, I'll give it a go!'

'You're in?' she asks, looking even more stunned than I feel.

'I am,' I reply, and we smile blithely at each other, raising our glasses, neither one of us fully comprehending what we've agreed to.

J022, MEET ME AT THE HOLLAND HOUSE ARCHES,
Friday 7 p.m.
Yours achingly, JNY19

JNY19, ONE EVENING WAS NOT ENOUGH,
Meet me tonight, same place, same time.
Yours passionately, JO22

7

JESS

'You did *what*?!' screams Debs, when I tell her about the switch.

The last thing I did before handing my phone over to Joan last night was to ping Debs a message asking her to promise to come round first thing, as I had to discuss something with her that absolutely 'could not wait'.

'Keep your voice down,' I whisper, not wanting to disturb Joan and her visitors downstairs. I beckon Debs further into my room and shut the door. Despite her outrage she still takes time to admire the room changes: Mum's yellow Anglepoise lamp by the bed, a pink and turquoise rag rug on the floor, my laptop on the table.

'What the hell, Jess. Why would you agree to that?' she asks, positioning herself carefully on a beanbag she re-covered with old jeans years ago.

'I don't know. We'd had a little wine,' I offer sheepishly, flumping on to the other beanbag, still having no idea what came over me. In the harsh light of day, it definitely doesn't feel like one of my better decisions; it's the last thing I need on top of a new living set-up and the uncertainty at work. But despite that, I still really like the idea of Joan seeing what a different version of her life could look like, one with a bit more going on in it. 'Before I knew it, I was increasing the font size on my phone and agreeing to lend it to her, then we ordered her a phone and tablet of her own.'

'Is this for a couple of days, a week?'

'Until her birthday,' I mouth.

'Which is when, exactly?' she asks, unwrapping a banana and taramasalata sandwich, causing me to open the window.

Ever since Debs and I met at nursery she's always eaten odd food combinations – peanut butter and marmalade sandwiches, chips and strawberry ice cream, sardines and lemon curd – though banana and taramasalata is a push, even while pregnant.

'August the fifth,' I wince, a tide of regret washing over me.

Debs lets out a long, low whistle. 'August? Jess, that's four months. How are we meant to chat?'

'On the landline?' I suggest, only just realising that this has a huge impact on her life as well as mine.

'And what about our FaceTime calls?'

'I guess we have to arrange to meet in person instead,' I say, which in fairness isn't that hard given Debs is mostly at home in a rigid routine of cleaning, feeding and bathing small children.

'What about your emails? How are you going to keep on top of those?'

'I put on a "bounce-back" telling people to call me at

Joan's – hardly anyone emails me anyway. Anything for work I can do there.'

'I can't believe Clive is selling, by the way,' she says.

'Nor can I,' I say, that rhino shifting on my chest again.

'How are you feeling?'

'Devastated. Angry. Worried . . .'

'Sounds like a reasonable response,' she nods. 'But maybe this could be your chance to get on to a Producing MA. You've found yourself a great place to live that doesn't cost the earth. Why not give it a go?'

'Debs, I can't wrap my head around the cinema closing, let alone the idea of retraining.'

'Sure, but—'

'And besides, Mariko and I are starting a campaign to keep it open. There's no way it's going to close. Not ever,' I tell her, aware that I'm giving off more than a whiff of denial.

'Just, you know, think about it.'

I think about it. 'I couldn't afford it. Liam took everything. I have nothing to fall back on.'

'He took your money, Jess, that's all. And I know you feel he took your confidence and trust, but bollocks to that. He didn't take your spirit or your drive or your talent. You can't let him hold you back.'

'I hear you,' I reply though I'm not quite there yet. Because for all I don't want Liam to have a hold on me, and for all I loathe him for what he did, a bit of me, the bit that didn't see it coming, still loves the person I thought he was. I can't quite reconcile what he did with who I thought I knew. Until I can figure that out, I'm not sure how I'll ever move on.

'All I'm saying is that you're thirty-two with absolutely no commitments, and trust me, one day you'll realise just how lucky that makes you. It would be a shame to let some moron stand in your way.'

'Right, I hear you,' I answer, when in fact I'm not really listening at all because my mind has taken me to Liam and the confusion I can't unpick, even for someone as drop dead gorgeous as the Kit Harington lookalike, who keeps sneaking into my thoughts.

'And what about everything else, Jess? How are you going to manage? Going offline is major.'

'Joan and I talked about it. I can go to the bank, use cash, buy a newspaper, it should be OK,' I say, though I'm not convinced; even after just a few hours I feel lost, not sure what to do with myself, disconnected from my life. It's a bit like when I fall off the clean-living wagon and I have to wean myself off chocolate and biscuits again, and that's all I can think about for days.

'You won't be able to watch TV or listen to music or podcasts.' Debs makes it sound as if this is the worst of my troubles, when giving up my socials is the thing I already miss, even if it's just looking at Daniel's artwork on Instagram, or Mariko's film reviews on TikTok, the mindless stuff that fills hours.

'I guess I just have to use Joan's radio, or watch the actual television in the living room,' I say, not entirely sure how I'll manage without the option to binge-watch whatever whenever I choose.

'*And* you won't be able to chart your fitness or periods, or buy anything online. Jess, this is your whole life.' I can tell Debs is catastrophising, no longer listening to a word

I'm saying, her imagination having run away with her again as it always does.

When we were little, Debs would lose herself for hours in games of make-believe. She lost whole days to her My Little Pony collection, me bugging her endlessly to come outside and play tig or hide-and-seek, anything that might involve running. Debs was always happier inside, lost in her imaginings.

'I'll just have to buy a notebook, go to the actual shops,' I say, surprised at how lucid I sound despite how weirded-out I'm feeling.

'And what about all your socials? What will you do without them?'

'Debs, I don't know,' I say, her anxiety beginning to flame my own, my chest tightening. 'I'll just have to see.'

'You're mad. And you know the worst bit about it?'

'What?' I ask, wondering what could be worse than losing all my social media feeds.

'You'll never date again,' she says slowly, exaggerat-edly.

'Not true . . .' I lean into her, really whispering this time. 'Joan made me place an ad in the lonely hearts column.'

'Shut the front door!'

'I'm not joking. I wrote it and she called it through on some automated line at the *Notting Hill News*. It was out-and-out weird,' I tell her, recalling how I'd stood next to Joan as she'd dialled the number, looking on in disbelief at how slow her rotary telephone was, and asking myself if I was actually stuck in a dream rather than a state of tipsiness.

'WTF, Jess. What did you write?'

'Please don't make me say it,' I beg.

'Go on! You know I don't get enough laughs these days.'

'Fine,' I agree with a heavy sigh, because she's right, she doesn't have enough fun at the moment. *'Film mad female, 32. WLTM sensitive, loyal, kind guy. Contact CineGirl.'* I mumble it all, as if I've regressed into my thirteen-year-old self.

'Aghh, cringe Jess!' she cackles, loving every minute of my humiliation, which makes me laugh too. 'You're out of your goddamn mind! But CineGirl is cute.'

'Thanks,' I mutter. 'Not that it matters anyway; no one's going to reply, or not anyone worth meeting.'

'You never know. Tinder hasn't found you anyone, maybe this will. Maybe you'll find a good guy this way, rather than the ones you usually meet. No more arseholes, Jess. You deserve that.'

'Right, no more arseholes,' I repeat, wondering if I'll ever meet that person, 'the one' who I can be entirely myself with and trust implicitly, the one who makes me feel that one can't exist without the other. The more I think about it, the more of a long shot it seems.

'Are you sure you want to do this?' she asks after a little lull, probably intuiting that I've enough going on in my life right now.

'I don't know,' I say. 'But if I'm honest, I spend too much time on my phone. Being without it scares me. I'm addicted.'

'So? Phone addiction is a way of life these days. Everyone's addicted. It's normal. It's not as if you're addicted to smack.'

'It's life as *we* know it, Debs. It's not life as Joan knows it. We normalise it.'

'Well, for the record, I think the idea is bonkers.'

'And maybe it is. But maybe it'll make a difference, you know? Maybe, for one, I won't end up getting scammed again.'

'Jess, that wasn't your fault,' she sighs, and I know she's infuriated that I'm turning my life, our life, upside down in part because of Liam.

I shrug.

'It wasn't, Jess,' she presses.

The tightness in my chest increases, and I fight the first sting of tears.

'Anyway,' I say on an outward breath. 'No harm can come from it, and it'll be fun watching Joan discover new things.'

'Yeah, like dick pics, and clickbait and porno flash ads. Great.'

I laugh, despite myself.

'But seriously, Jess, how are you going to look for a job if the proverbial hits the fan?'

'It's not going to come to that,' I say, ignoring the seed of doubt taking root. 'More importantly, I need to figure out how to contact the *Notting Hill News* without my phone, see if they can help stop the place from closing.'

Debs reaches for her phone to look it up.

'Nope,' I say. 'If I'm going to do this, I have to do it properly.'

'Guess that leaves the phone book and the landline then.'

I pull myself up from cross-legged on the beanbag and

offer Debs a hand. 'Let's see if Joan's got one,' I say, and we head downstairs.

'Joan?' I call, knocking lightly on the living room door, not wanting to disturb her.

'Yes,' she calls back.

'Joan, do you have a—' I begin, poking my head round the door to discover Joan with two much younger guys and a little kid on the fireside rug with Humphrey.

'Jess, come in,' she beckons. 'This is my son, Edward.' She gestures to where he's sitting on the sofa.

I start. Knocked by the bombshell coincidence. Because this isn't just some random guy; it's the hottest guy on the planet, the guy from the cinema: Kit Harington.

'Hi,' I say, scooping my hair off my face then straightening my top, wishing I'd given more thought to my Sunday morning outfit. Edward is looking super tidy in a white shirt and low-slung chinos.

'Hi,' he responds, standing up, though he barely meets my eye.

'Hi,' I say again with a nervous laugh, conscious of all the 'hi-ing'. Debs clears her throat in a way that tells me to pull my shit together.

'Do you remember me?' I ask.

'Of course, I remember you.' He says it in such a way that I have no idea if he really does or not, and here I am, my heart working overtime.

'We met at the cinema,' I prompt.

'I remember. Hi.'

'Hi.'

'Edward's considering b—' says Joan.

'Were you looking for something?' he asks, cutting his

75

mother off, a deep frown line forming between his 'kiss me' eyes.

'A phone directory. I've gone offline, or else, you know, I'd use my phone to find what I need,' I over-explain.

A moment hangs between us where he says nothing, probably wondering why his mother invited such a lame-brain to live with her, and I try frantically to think of something to fill the gap other than babbling.

'This is Debs,' I blurt, dragging her closer like a human shield.

He looks at me as if I've just walked into a closed door then, catching himself, he turns to his friend and says, 'This is Charlie and his son, Oscar, who's three.' He gestures at Charlie, wearing khaki shorts, on the pouffe in front of the telly, and Oscar, in matching shorts, on the rug next to Humphrey, tracing his grey whiskers.

'Nice to meet you,' I say, relieved to interact with someone less intense and hot than Ed.

'And you,' says Charlie, getting up to shake both my hand and Debs'.

'Looks as if you're doing what my husband's doing right now – giving Mum a break,' says Debs.

'Mum's doing a weekend shift. Isn't she, Spud?' he asks Oscar, crouching to ruffle his hair.

Charlie is sort of the opposite of Ed in every way: blond, smiley, upbeat, like a good-natured teen in a thirty-something body.

'Ed mentioned Joan had a new lodger.' He throws Ed a look I can't quite read.

'Mum was telling us about the switch,' says Ed, scrutinising me with his deep eyes. 'Whose idea was it?'

'It was mine,' Joan interjects. 'Jess has already given me a little tutorial, and last night I browsed the web for the first time.'

'Browsed the web?' Ed repeats, as if his mother had just told him she flew to the moon and back. 'Mum, you need to be careful, the web's full of exploitation.'

'Oh Edward, you should be pleased. You've been pestering me about it for years. Now when you visit you can stay connected. You'll never have to worry about the lack of signal again.'

'I suppose,' he concedes, and his eyes meet mine, barely guarding his suspicion of me, which somehow makes him even hotter. 'It just seems so out of character, that's all.'

'Jess and I are trying to help each other discover new things, see life from a different angle. She helped me buy some clothes online, I helped her post an ad in the lonely hearts column. She goes by the name of CineGirl. Isn't that super!'

Ed's eyes glisten with delight. 'You've done what?'

'It was Joan's idea, and no one will answer,' I squirm. Joan killing my cool. I wonder how Ed would react to learning I signed his mother up to a dating app.

'CineGirl is like Shopgirl in *You've Got Mail*, which is Jess's all-time favourite film,' says Debs, as if this is something Ed would care about. I'm sure he hasn't the time or the inclination to be watching romantic comedies; he's probably far too busy taking care of himself and wining and dining his girlfriend somewhere different every night.

'It was my mum's favourite film, and mine. We loved

watching it together,' I explain, feeling myself blush, wondering why I feel compelled to share something so personal with him when he's clearly in a different stratosphere to me.

'I think it's a fun idea,' says Charlie enthusiastically, gently guiding Oscar's hands away from Humphrey, who's beginning to tire of the attention. 'No different from online dating really. How's the rest of the swap going?'

'Yeah, you know, I've done easier things,' I reply, underplaying the extent of how difficult it is, that it feels as if half my life is missing; a tad envious that Joan got the better half of the deal.

After we placed my lonely hearts ad last night, Joan went off to bed with my phone and I went to bed with her mechanical alarm clock, listening to it tick-tock all night and wishing that I could watch just enough TikTok videos to ease me into sleep, to escape the reality of the situation. And when the clanging bells jarred me out of sleep this morning, I was reminded instantly of what I'd done, of how I wouldn't be able to check my messages or socials for four whole months, which felt as if I'd been pushed off a very high cliff from which I'm still falling.

'I admire you,' says Charlie. 'I couldn't do it. And I know for sure that Ed couldn't.'

'Hey, at least I'm not finding dates through the newspaper,' he retaliates.

'Mate, at least Jess isn't just working all the time.'

Joan, Charlie and I look at Ed, who's turned his attention to his phone. I wonder about his girlfriend: if she's the perfect model influencer, the trophy girlfriend who can do no wrong.

We wait for Ed to look up.

Eventually he does. 'What?'

Joan and Charlie shake their heads.

'Oscar drew a picture of Uncle Ed the other day,' Charlie says. 'He gave it to me then took it back saying, "Wait, I forgot" then he added in a phone attached to Ed's hand.'

'Ouch,' I wince, feeling a touch bad for the guy, maybe a little glad for the switch with Joan after all.

8

JOAN

The house is refreshingly quiet again after the whirlwind of activity that was Edward and Charlie, and Jess and Debs. Humphrey is enjoying the warmth of the midday sun at the back door and I the rhythm of knocking primulas out of their pots and planting them into the kitchen window box, when I hear Pamela call from over the garden fence.

'Lovely day,' she says brightly.

'Isn't it,' I reply, going over to the gate with my walking stick. We had the gate put in a few years ago, between a small gap in the planting, so that we could hand things back and forth more easily – a washed ramekin dish, seed trays, the odd magazine or two.

'Did you get my message?' I ask her, still unsettled by the turn of events last night, despite me putting my 'best face' on earlier for Edward. Pamela casts me a puzzled glance. 'The one I sent from Jess's phone.'

With furrowed brow, Pamela pulls out her phone from the pocket of her garden apron. 'We had a glass of wine and a game of Scrabble, then agreed to switch lifestyles,' I explain, trying to sound casual, as if it was all perfectly run-of-the-mill when nothing about it feels that way at all.

'Pardon?' she replies, her eyes as sharp as a hawk's.

'Jess and I, we agreed to switch lifestyles,' I repeat, the little knot in my stomach tightening – a knot that questions if I've been too hasty, that it's a decision I might live to regret. 'Jess will come offline, and I will go on.'

'Good heavens!' she exclaims, possibly more astounded than when I told her I'd settled on her idea of a lodger. 'I was only making a suggestion about the tablet last week. I didn't expect you to actually do something about it.'

'In for a penny, in for a pound,' I say, hoping Pamela doesn't pick up on my tightness, which took root almost as soon as Jess and I had agreed the switch.

'Are you ready to try making a call?' Jess had asked, her eyes full of enthusiasm, unaware of how worried I was with her phone sitting in my hand, a riot of colour and symbols, foreign and bamboozling but also tempting and intriguing.

'All you have to do is press the green icon with the phone symbol on it,' she explained patiently, and I did, having had to readjust the distance several times to find my focus. 'Now press CONTACTS, touch SEARCH, and type in who you'd like to call.'

'But I don't know anyone you know.'

'Good point,' she laughed. 'Go to KEYPAD instead.' She leant in closer to me, closer than anyone had been in a long time; her hair, smelling of coconut, brushed my cheek as she showed me where 'keypad' was when I struggled to find it. 'Why don't we start with calling your landline?'

'Good idea,' I said, and I carefully typed in my number. 'Now what?'

'Press the round green button.'

On her instruction, I pressed the button, and almost immediately not only did I hear the dial tone on Jess's mobile but also the BRRING BRRING of my phone in the hall.

'Is that me calling me?' I asked, slightly giddily.

'Seems to be,' she said, jumping up and dashing to the telephone chair.

A second or two later, the cool glass of the mobile to my ear, I heard Jess's voice in the earpiece and also in the hall saying, 'Hello. Joan's phone.'

'It's your phone now,' I teased, and she giggled before congratulating me on using a mobile for the very first time.

And that's when she suggested sending a message, sitting back down next to me, while I marvelled at how she can throw herself back on to the sofa without having to strategically plan her every move. It reminded me of how I used to be, able and agile, always on the go, be it performing, travelling or teaching, before age set in and I realised how I'd taken good health for granted. 'Whose mobile number do you know?'

'I know Pamela's and Ed's.' At this she looked surprised.

'Do you seriously?'

'Certainly I do. Don't you know the numbers of your loved ones?'

'No!' she laughed in amazement. 'How 'bout we message Pamela.'

'But I've nothing to tell her.'

Jess squinted at me as if I've said something farcical. 'What do you mean? You can tell her anything. What you had for dinner. What you're planning on doing tomorrow. What's on the telly. Whatever you like.'

And then it was my turn to squint. 'I wouldn't tell her any of those things, they're not important.'

'It doesn't have to be important, Joan. You're just chatting.'

The lines of my brow deepened. 'You send messages to your friends about what you had for dinner?'

'Sure, look,' she shrugged as if this was perfectly normal, took the phone from me then rapidly tapped and flicked. In an instant she was showing me grids of photos of her meals artfully positioned, like a still-life you'd see at a gallery, with sunny backdrops or subdued lighting, and it was all I could do to stop myself gaping.

'Who do you send this to?'

'Well, someone, or everyone,' she said, sort of baffled by the perceived obviousness of the question.

'What do you mean, *everyone*?'

'All my followers,' she said, and there was a moment when we both looked at each other blankly, the cultural chasm between us as wide as the Grand Canyon. 'This is Instagram,' she explained, pulling me back from a memory of visiting Arizona many moons ago. 'People follow me, which means whenever I post something, they can all see it.'

'What do you mean, "post"?'

'You know, put something out there, send it.'

'Where?'

She hesitated for a moment, thinking. 'Cyberspace, I suppose.'

And there it was again, the silence, the ravine between us.

'Maybe we should go back a step,' she said, when it became clear we had reached an impasse. 'Forget Instagram. I got side-tracked. Let's just send a message to Pamela. No photo. Nothing other than a simple text message.'

'And it will only go to her, nobody else will see it?'

'Yes.'

'Like a telegram?'

Jess looked puzzled.

'Just a message from me to her, with no need for an operator?' I offer.

'Exactly!'

'OK. What shall I say?'

A look passed over Jess's eyes which I suspect was her thinking 'not this again' but kindly and ever so patiently, she suggested, 'How about, *It's Joan, I'm sending a message from Jess's phone.*'

'I should probably start with *Dear Pamela.*'

Jess laughed, not unkindly. 'I don't think she'd expect such formality. *Hi Pamela*, will be enough.'

'Fine,' I said, readying myself for the next lesson. 'Let's begin.'

She talked me through unlocking the phone again, how to open 'messages' and start a new one. I typed in Pamela's number and cautiously dabbed at the letters on the screen.

'There,' I said triumphantly when it was complete. 'What next?'

'You could add a couple of emojis.'

'Emojis?'

'Little characters to show the emotion of the message. For this you might want to show an expression of surprise,' she said, pulling up hundreds of characters for me to choose from. 'And then you could add a couple of little pictures, a mobile phone, a seedling to show a new beginning . . .'

'Oh lovely,' I said, scrolling through the images. 'Pamela loves aubergines and peaches. And perhaps I could put a little waving hand.'

At this Jess suggested I use a different fruit and vegetable, ones with less 'connotations', but I said I'd like to include them, and she shook her head in bewilderment and said, 'O-K then. Press the blue arrow and the message will send.'

And I did, and it sent, and I felt a thrill of achievement race up my spine.

'*Hi Pamela, I'm sending a message from Jess's phone.*' Pamela reads it to me now at the garden gate, as astonished as I had been at my accomplishment. 'Aubergine, peach, waving hand,' she chuckles, her eyes wide.

'She also taught me how to make a call and send an email, amongst other things, and we ordered some clothes and a phone and tablet of my own, though after that, I admit I needed a rest,' I tell her, recalling how I'd been too tired to put up much of a fight about buying something 'online'. I did, however, make Jess promise me that she was 100 percent certain it was safe to use my debit card. Edward has spoken often enough about

85

online fraud for me to be wary; I worry enough just using it over the phone with the local shops. 'I decided if it's not for me, I can always put it back in its box and away under the stairs.'

'Well done, Joan,' says Pamela, flashing one of her wide, toothy grins. 'Just think of all the possibilities. You could join something online, or buy more clothes, maybe even get out and about again. It will improve your mood immeasurably. And think of all the people you could contact. Joan, this is marvellous. Life will flourish.'

'Yes, I suppose,' I say, feeling overwhelmed by all those possibilities, unprepared for any of them now that the wine has worn off.

'Joan, are you OK?' I hear her ask, her voice sounding much further away than it is.

'Joan,' she says again, only this time she is standing beside me even though I didn't notice her come through the gate, supporting me.

Pamela helps me to the bench at the back door, and I feel ancient and stupid. She sits me down then fetches a glass of water from the kitchen.

'You don't do things by halves,' she says, sitting down beside me, no doubt observing my vitals. 'Whatever took you?'

I manage to explain how I felt that Jess could benefit from a change, a slightly slower pace of life, and that I hadn't expected her to then dare me. 'But I could hardly say no, could I?' I say, coming back round to my normal self.

Pamela's silence tells me that she would beg to differ.

'Didn't you think to start with just the basics, the odd

86

text message or phone call, rather than diving in head-first to a full life swap?' She nudges me gently with her elbow.

'I suppose I should have thought of that, but it's a bit late now to back out,' I reply. 'I couldn't bear to let her down, not when the swap will be so beneficial for her. But I can't pretend that I don't feel rather foolish.'

'You've been hasty, Joan, not foolish.'

I cast her a look that tells her she doesn't know the half of it, then hoist myself up and go into the kitchen, returning a moment later. 'Look at this,' I say, handing over Jess's phone.

'That's a lovely photo, Joan.'

'Move further down.'

'"Retired piano teacher, seventy-nine,"' she begins to read, and I blush, regretting the wine. '"WLTM creative, kind animal lover for companionship, maybe more. Contact Ivory Joan."'

There's a brief moment where we sit in silence, Pamela computing, me waiting, and thinking back to last night.

'Don't spend too long online, you'll get square eyes,' Jess had called as I made my way up to bed. I'd laughed at the notion of me being hooked online, but then, tucked up in bed, my eiderdown under my arms, I discovered an entire world at my fingertips. And even though I could go anywhere, see anything, the one thing my mind honed in on was a name. A name from long ago, but one that's never far from my thoughts.

My finger hovered over the screen, uncertain whether to type in the name or not, my chest feeling tight at the thought of what I might unearth. I resisted, and carefully typed in the safe, familiar words of Westminster School instead.

Almost immediately, a great list of items appeared. I clicked on the one at the top, and there, within seconds, as clear as if I were standing in front of the entrance, was an image of the quadrangle with the ghostly limestone of Westminster Abbey looming behind.

Having navigated my way through the 'dropdown menus' Jess taught me about, I found the music section. There I discovered pictures of the orchestra I used to conduct, and children playing oboes, violins and flutes. I scanned every photograph, using my finger and thumb to zoom in and out, in search of someone I used to know, of any staff member from my time teaching there almost fifteen years ago. But there was no one.

Time moves on, I thought, a touch disappointed, but glad of the chance to revisit the old place.

I went further back in my memory to before teaching music, to when Parker and I married, when I did the odd daytime accompaniment gig around my domestic duties, a far cry from the busyness and freedom of my life and career in my twenties. I looked up the places I played during that time: the Cadogan Hall, the Wigmore Hall, and St Martin in the Fields, and some of the people I knew then, now all retired, aging, or dead. It struck me that I could never have imagined then what my life would become – a life full of limitations and ghosts.

I decided not to search for Parker, unwilling or unable to see his face, to see where life took him. And then I paused, the urge still there to return to the name that haunts me, to go back further, to before marriage, to the time when I was happiest and most fulfilled, in New York City.

Slowly, falteringly, I typed, deleting the name several times, aware that my breath was shallow, my heartbeat quickening, concerned that Jess might burst into the room and catch me being foolish. When I was confident that Jess was still downstairs, and with a huge intake of breath, I hit return and clicked on 'images'. My heart sank when I saw no one who immediately resembled him. Because although I haven't seen him in decades, I felt certain that even after all those years, I'd know him instantly.

I tried again, adding his occupation, and within milliseconds a bank of photos filled the screen. And I saw him. Right there. In front of me.

'Oh my,' I gasped, my heart leaping, resisting the urge to shut the thing off immediately.

Half of me wanted to reach out and touch his soft grey curls, the hoods of his eyes, touch every feature that looked as familiar to me now, despite the passage of time, as if it were yesterday, not all those decades ago, that I last traced my finger over his profile and kissed his firm lips. But the other half was terrified, as if he might jump out of the tablet and sit next to me and demand an explanation of why I abandoned him that night and married Parker instead.

And then a feeling came over me I've experienced only once before. It was as if I were a feather spinning in a vortex, and I quickly shut the phone off, barely able to catch my breath.

A roar of laughter from Pamela brings me back to the present, and I realise I'm shaking.

'Joan Armitage, you old rascal! You're on a dating site.'

'Get away with you,' I giggle, feeling a warmth spread over my cheeks, not sure whether to feel ashamed or proud of the profile that Jess set up for me on Silver Singles.

'This is marvellous! Something to really get you out and about.'

'It's not as if anyone will answer,' I dismiss, having only agreed to sign up knowing that nothing would come of it.

'Of course they will! Look at you.' She holds up the photo on Jess's phone next to my face to compare the two. 'Ivory Joan indeed. You'll have them all rushing for you!'

'Hardly. Who'd want to be with an old crone like me?' I say, taking the phone from her, hopeful that no one will reply, though a tiny part of me secretly wishes that one perfect someone just might.

My darling Joany,

I can hardly believe it's been almost five years since we met that beautiful late summer night in London. My heart is even fuller now than it was then despite living an ocean apart for three years.

I know we've discussed it before, but Joany, when you come to Juilliard for the year, won't you live with me? Ever since Peter married Kathleen, I've longed for us to share our life fully together.

I don't want to put you in an uncomfortable position, but nobody in the city would care, and your parents would never find out. Nothing would make me happier, Joany, than to wake up every morning to your beautiful smile.

Write and tell me you will, and make me the happiest man alive.

Always and for ever,
Joe

9

JESS

'Hi. Jess?' asks Cormac, the journalist from the *Notting Hill News*, shaking my hand. 'How are ya getting on?'

'Good, thanks for meeting me,' I answer, as he beckons over the bartender at the Cross, the pub opposite the cinema.

'So, you've a story about the Portland?' he says in his warm Irish accent, after we've got our drinks from the central oak bar and he's leading us to seats at the window. We settle into two high-backed padded benches opposite each other, his long limbs accidentally catching my knees.

'Had you heard of the Portland before now?' I ask.

'Hasn't everyone? It's a landmark around here.'

He takes off his denim jacket, exposing a faded X-Files T-shirt, then sips his beer, foam clinging lightly to his scruffy beard which does little to hide his boyish, wholesome looks. 'What's going on with it? Why are you needing my help?'

I give him the history of the place, how it's been passed

down from generation to generation, how business isn't what it was in its heyday, and how Clive is now looking to sell, with I-work interested in offering. As I talk, he listens, taking notes on his phone but never taking his attentive, blue-grey eyes off mine for long.

'It's been part of the backbone to this community for almost a hundred years. To lose it to I-work, a business with such opposing values, would be a real tragedy.'

I turn my gaze across the road to the cinema doors, the canopy showing film titles and times, but despite Clive allowing me to arrange a special showing of *How to Marry a Millionaire* as a Golden Oldies special, there's still no one in sight. I can just about make out Daniel in the ticket office, with his feet up, sketching. Gary is outside, dragging on a cigarette. And I know that downstairs, Mariko will be beavering away, making sure the place is immaculate despite the lack of customers.

It puts me in mind of when Mum died, when the bottom of my world fell out, and all I had left was Debs and the cinema. I remember Clive telling me to take as long as I needed, and that if I wanted to just come, watch movies and sit in the dark and cry, that was fine by him. And I did, day after day for weeks. Gary gave me countless bony hugs, the smell of his cigarettes that clung to my clothes for the rest of the day oddly comforting; Mariko made me hot chocolates and brought paper towels when my tissues ran out, and Daniel, never one for many words, lent me books of poetry and art, fragments of wisdom that made sense of my grief, that told me I wasn't alone.

And I think too of the good times: Clive's puppies delighting our customers; the birth of Gary's kids and him bringing them in to show them off; Daniel's graduate art show and the reviews the next day that we all pored over together, and Mariko's graduation which Clive and I attended when her parents couldn't make it over from Japan. And all the other members of staff and customers who have come over the years, and though they've moved on they always return, because that's what the Portland does: it draws people in and holds them close.

'I can't tell you how important it is to find someone who's able and willing to bring it back to its former glory,' I tell Cormac, surprised by just how urgent my voice sounds. 'It's too important to too many people to let it fade away.'

'Great,' he says, finishing a note and clicking off his phone. 'There's loads of good stuff there. I can start an article about the impact of the digital era and e-commerce on community identity, all really zeitgeisty stuff. We'll get it in the paper, then share it on our social media platforms, and you guys can do the same. It'll fly, for sure.'

'I appreciate it.'

'It's gonna be fine,' he says, picking up on my worries. 'Everybody loves a good David and Goliath story. There's bound to be some mogul living around here looking for a PR boost. Saving a piece of local history from the big "E-vaders" might just be the sort of publicity they need.'

'Let's hope so,' I smile, drawn in by his infectious enthusiasm and goofy smile.

There's a moment between us where it's clear that we've covered what we needed to, but where neither one of us seems quite ready to leave.

'I should take your number,' he says, breaking the

pause, fumbling a bit with his phone. 'In case I need anything else,' he adds quickly, running a hand over his short, light-brown curls. 'You only gave me the cinema line when you called.'

I explain about going offline.

'Jeez, that's a story in itself! THIRTY-SOMETHING GIRL ABOUT TOWN DIGITAL DETOX,' he says, as if reading a newspaper headline. 'How's that going for you?'

'Pretty badly actually,' I laugh, and he laughs too, tilting his glass towards me in recognition of the challenge, his eyes dancing with warmth and admiration. 'My housemate's phone and tablet arrived yesterday so we put my phone in a box and hid it in the understairs cupboard. I'm telling you, it felt like a funeral.'

'I can imagine. I'd be a feckin' wreck without mine,' he says, turning his over on the table. 'How long's it been?'

'It's only day three. I'm still in the DT stage: headaches, sweats, shakes,' I joke, though the reality of life without my phone really isn't funny. Even the simplest things become hard: paying for things, getting on transport, running without music. 'If I'm honest, I feel a bit exposed without it.'

'I reckon we all would,' he says, holding my gaze, and I notice his eyes are flecked with gold. 'But I guess we all have to get out of our comfort zone if we're going to grow.'

'True,' I say, both of us taking a gulp of drink at the same time, our eyes still on each other.

'Joan? Have you seen what's arrived?' I call from the hall, excited about what I've just discovered in the vestibule, glad to have a distraction from the gnawing irritation of not being able to call Debs as soon as I left Cormac to analyse his every word. I can't figure out if the warmth he exuded was particular to me, or if that's just who he is as a journalist, that it's his job to put people at ease.

'What is it?' she asks, appearing at the kitchen door.

'The clothes we ordered!' I say, lifting the box to show her.

'So soon?'

I take the box to the kitchen table and start prising it open the way I used to on Christmas morning when Mum would pack all my gifts into one enormous box, like a giant lucky dip.

'Check this out, Joan,' I say, pulling a boho paisley dress out of its silk presentation bag.

'I can't wear that,' she says, eyeing it cautiously, the twinkle in her eye telling me that she loves it.

'Sure you can,' I say, and I hold it up to her, cinching in the waist. 'It's perfect for you. And what about this?' I show her the brown fur gilet that I picked out for her to go with the dress. 'I've some chunky wooden jewellery you could wear with it.'

'Get away with you,' she laughs, rubbing her locket, trying to sound dismissive but unable to hide her interest.

I press the garments towards her. 'Try it.'

'Pamela would think I'd gone mad.'

'No she wouldn't! She'd think you were treating yourself. Go on!'

'Oh, all right. I don't suppose much harm can come from it.'

She disappears up to her room to try things on and, without my phone to distract me, for a moment I lose myself in thoughts of Mum. I remember how we used to raid the local charity shops for small items that would transform the clothes we already had, and how we'd come home and rearrange the living room into a catwalk and parade up and down it, just like the fashion segments we used to watch on *This Morning* during the school holidays.

'What do you think?' asks Joan, returning to the kitchen, pulling me out of my memories.

'Joan! You look beautiful,' I say, and she does a funny little twirl, her hand cocked up to the side of her neck as if to show off a cute new hairstyle. 'How does it feel?'

'Freeing,' she says, holding the sides of the skirt out wide.

'It suits you,' I tell her, thinking she looks transformed. 'Will you keep it?'

'Why not,' she says, putting on the kettle. 'It might raise an eyebrow from Edward!'

'Right,' I laugh, trying to sound casual, when inwardly my temperature is rising. 'Perhaps we could go shopping sometime. Try on some stuff together.'

'Yes,' she says unconvincingly, and I wonder, but don't ask, when she last went out to treat herself and for what occasion. 'What did you get for yourself?'

I dig out the purple, orange and yellow bum bag I ordered, not wanting to stretch to anything more with all the uncertainty at work, and put it on.

'Very stylish,' she laughs when I do a little belly dance.

'Thanks, Joan. This has been fun. My mum and I used to love dressing up together, before she passed.'

'You must miss her.'

'More than anything,' I say, accepting the tea Joan's made. 'We didn't have much, but we had each other. That was always enough, even when times got hard.'

I tell her about Mum's illness and having to give up uni to care for her.

'I'm sorry you had to go through that.'

'I'm not. It was a privilege to care for her the way she did for me.'

'It couldn't have been easy though.'

'It wasn't, but the hardest part was after she'd gone . . .' I say, considering whether to tell Joan about Liam when her phone interrupts us.

10

JOAN

'What was that?' I ask, hearing a foreign sound. It's a sort of short sucking noise. For a brief moment I wonder if a frog has crept in from the garden.

'I think it's your phone,' laughs Jess, and it's then I remember I put it in the pocket of my new dress, which feels like the sort of clothing I might have worn, if I'd married a different man and life had taken another path.

'What's it telling me?' I ask, pulling my phone out, rather pleased with its red, drop-proof cover, but mildly irritated too by the interruption; it felt as if Jess was on the cusp of telling me something important.

'It's a kiss sound. You've a Silver Singles message!'

'Good grief,' I say, my heart doing a somersault.

Jess claps in delight. 'I told you someone would message you!'

I try to steady my breathing as I press the Silver Singles icon. Jess leans over me, excited as a puppy with a new toy.

'Click on messages,' she tells me, pointing at the screen.

I breathe out slowly, feeling ever so slightly light-headed, and reposition the phone at the correct distance.

Jess clutches my arm as I read out the message.

Hi Ivory Joan, I'm William, 76, a retired civil engineer living in London with a Weimaraner named Edison.

'Joan!' Jess squeals, smiling broadly, still gripping my arm. 'He looks great.'

We both look at his lean, tanned face with grey, groomed stubble and his hair neatly combed back from his receding hairline.

'He's a bit like Charles Dance,' says Jess, with a 'not too bad' expression. 'You need to reply.'

'No,' I say, rather too quickly, and I wander out front to the veranda.

'Joan,' says Jess calmingly, following me. 'All you're doing is sending a message, nothing else.'

'But what would I say?' I ask, already worrying that it will lead somewhere I'm not ready to go.

'Just start with the simple, small things and build from there.'

'I don't know.'

'Joan, pass it here,' she says, and unthinkingly I hand it to her.

'*Hi William*,' she types, my heart now racing. '*Edison sounds very smart. My black Lab is called Humphrey. What sort of music do you like?* Sound OK?'

I shrug. Not knowing.

'Send,' she sings, and promptly touches the screen with a satisfied tap.

'What now?'

'We wait.'

And we do, sitting in comfortable silence on the swing-seat, watching the passers-by dawdle up the street to the market.

I glimpse at the phone from time to time, wondering if he'll reply straightaway or if I'll have to wait, the way I used to for a letter, or sometimes for a secret message in the classifieds. Fifty years ago, I'd happily wait a week or more for a reply; now just a few minutes seems interminably long.

Another 'kiss' interrupts my musings, and I start.

'I'm a fan of Burt Bacharach. One of my favourites is, "This Guy's in Love with You". Do you like his music?' reads Jess.

'Burt Bacharach,' I say, thinking of his songs, which are a little too popular for my taste. '"*I'll Never Fall in Love Again*" is the track that springs to mind.'

'Joan!' cries Jess, turning to face me. 'I hope you don't believe that.'

The truth is that I do believe it, but there's no use in trying to explain that to someone as optimistic as Jess. The idea of having had a love so intense, so utterly perfect that you know categorically that no one else could ever match it, would be lost on someone so young. So, I play along, 'Of course I don't mean it. That's the great thing about life: chance, the not knowing,' I say, wishing I still believed it.

'What would you like to say in reply?'

'I love Chopin,' I dictate, and my mind wanders to other

101

classical composers I adore, and then the jazz musicians I came to appreciate during my twenties, but I choose not to mention either, that being part of life then, not now. I try to focus on William, 76, civil engineer. *'Which area of London are you in?'*

'Done?' Jess asks, seeming pleased with my effort.

'I suppose,' I reply, thinking the message banal.

And yet we don't have to wait long for a response.

I'm Wimbledon born and bred, home of tennis. What about you?

'Notting Hill,' she types on my behalf, quite in the swing of things. *'Home to the carnival, antiques market, and me, Ivory Joan.'*

I laugh as she sends the message, getting used to it now, rather forgetting that there's an actual man sitting in Wimbledon with his phone sending the replies.

'He sounds really laid-back, Joan. He might make a good first date. Ease yourself in.'

'Never in a million years,' I laugh tightly, one, because I don't imagine for one second that he'll ask me out, and two, because if he did, I'm simply not up to leaving the house.

'Here we go,' says Jess as the phone 'kisses' again, and then she squeals in pleasure.

'What?' I ask, feeling my brow furrow.

'Well, Ivory Joan,' she reads, putting on a silly male voice, *'what say I take you out sometime for a drive in my classic car?'*

And with that, I take the phone and shut it off, alongside any ideas of romance that Jess might have given me.

Holland Park, London
August, 1967

My darling Joe,

*I keep having to pinch myself that in less than a day I will
be with you in New York City. My suitcase is packed and
my tickets ready. All that is left is to say my goodbyes.*

*While I am elated at the thought of living with you
and studying in the city, I am also trepidatious about
withholding the full truth from my mother and father . . . I
can't bear to think about what would happen should they
ever find out about us living in sin.*

Until tomorrow,
Joany

*PS I know I will reach you before this letter . . . isn't it
wonderful that we will no longer be dependent on paper
and pen!*

11

JESS

The scent of roast chicken, crackling and spitting in the oven, has reached every corner of the house by the time I've tidied up and set the table.

'You've been busy,' says Joan, joining me in the kitchen.

'I didn't know how much I could get done without my phone distracting me,' I reply, flicking the tea towel over my shoulder, pleased with my morning's efforts, but still anxious to know what I'm missing on socials, and missing the nullifying effect of my AirPods.

'You shouldn't have gone to so much trouble.'

'It's Easter Sunday, it's not Easter without a roast, and I found a nice recipe in one of your books.'

I spent the first part of the morning looking for a recipe – something I'd usually find on TikTok – in Joan's cookbooks on the shelves beside the cooker: *All Colour Cookbook*; *Book of Home Cookery*; *Dinner Party Cooking*. The tattered, brown, cream and orange spines screamed of the seventies, and I laughed at the images of blancmange, stuffed peppers, and pies that could sink small ships. Among the vintage editions was a copy of *Jamie's Dinners*, so I decided on the safe option of roast chicken with lemon and rosemary roast potatoes, with a French bean salad.

'Left to my own devices I'd have cooked a chicken, too,' she smiles.

'Good, good,' I say, opening the oven door a crack to see if the chicken is almost done. 'Is Edward still joining us for lunch?'

'He should be here in ten minutes or so.'

'Excellent,' I say, hoping she doesn't pick up on the change of pitch in my voice, a change that gives away how nervous I am about her gorgeous son coming to lunch.

I'm heading to unlock the front door when something on the hallstand catches my eye – an envelope, hidden behind a vase of sweet peas from the garden.

'Joan?' I call, my hand trembling as I register that it's been forwarded from the *Notting Hill News*. 'When did this letter arrive for me?'

'Yesterday morning,' she calls back.

For a moment, I forget about the chicken in the oven and sit down on the bottom step, carefully undoing the flap and removing the contents. Inside is a neat little envelope addressed to *CineGirl* and within that a small letter, folded in two. It is hand-written in black ink on cream paper, and before reading any of the words, I can sense the care and attention they've been given.

Dear CineGirl,

I haven't written a letter by hand since my mother last made me write thank-you notes for birthday presents, almost twenty years ago, so I'm not entirely sure where to begin . . .

I see from your advert that you love film. Often at night, when my mind is still occupied, I put on a classic . . . something with Paul Newman, Jack Nicholson or Dustin Hoffman . . . and inevitably I drift off to sleep within minutes. My favourite film has to be The Italian Job. Won't you write and tell me about yours?

Mr PO Box

It's such an honest little note, and so not at all what I was expecting, that I reread it several times.

'Jess?' I hear Joan call, and I'm suddenly aware that I've been staring at the letter far longer than I'd realised.

'Sorry, Joan, back in a sec,' I call, jumping up and placing the letter in the pouch of my hoodie. I open the front door to a rush of bright April light, daffodils turned towards the sun and birds flitting about the feeders on the veranda.

In the kitchen, the chicken is ready, but with no sign of Ed I leave it a little longer in the oven.

'Anything interesting?' I ask Joan, who's looking at her phone at the table.

'It's another message from William.'

I pull out a chair and join her. 'What does it say?'

'He says he's happy for Humphrey to come on the drive.'

'I told you he would,' I encourage, but not overly.

Joan has spent the last few days since William suggested the date, looking for ways to get out of going: being too old, her bad hip, being away from Humphrey, and every time William has come back with a solution: he's old too; he can help her in and out of the car; he's happy for Humphrey to come. Each time they've messaged, I've wanted to ask what the real problem is, what it is that's really holding her back, because for all the fun we've had these last couple of weeks, it does feel as if Joan's still not ready to let her guard down fully, and I'm not comfortable enough yet to encourage her to do so.

I can tell Joan is looking for another reason not to go when we hear Ed's key in the inner door.

'In the kitchen,' Joan calls, putting her phone away in her pocket.

'Happy Easter,' says Ed, looking utterly huggable in a burgundy cable sweater. He hands Joan a wrap of tulips.

'Thank you,' she says, looking surprised by the gesture. She gets up to place them in water while Ed puts his keys on the counter then settles himself at the table, opposite me. 'Jess has cooked a roast chicken. Wasn't that kind?'

'I wouldn't have had you down as a roast chicken kind of a girl,' he says, a tiny flicker of spark in his eye.

'Meaning?' I ask, not sure how to interpret the comment or the look.

'You look more like a "bowl" sort,' he replies, rolling up the sleeves of his sweater. 'You know: noodle salad bowl, falafel and hummus bowl, five bean bowl. All that crazy healthy stuff.'

'Right,' I laugh, getting up to take the chicken out of the oven. 'I guess there's a compliment in there somewhere.'

'It's good of you; I can't remember the last time we did anything for Easter,' he says, sweeping his hair back, exposing his beautiful face.

'My pleasure,' I reply, surprised that Easter isn't more of a thing for them both, knowing how much Mum and I loved the holiday. We'd bake together for days, and Mum would lay out egg hunts in the park where we'd picnic with Debs and her family. Easter always felt like a time of hope and celebration for us, not something to be ignored.

'Leg or breast?' I ask, carving the chicken, which is frustratingly dry.

'Breast,' he says, a rogue smile tugging at the side of his mouth, and I feel heat rising in my cheeks.

'Edward doesn't eat enough,' says Joan. 'He's always been that way. And when he does it's always very healthy: breast rather than leg, boiled rather than roast, no dressing.'

'Really?' I say, figuring it explains his lean bod.

'I don't know how he does it. I've always been one for the unhealthier things in life.'

'It's just about moderation, isn't it?' I offer, placing the breast on his plate.

'You sound like Pamela,' Joan laughs lightly. 'She's always bothering me about healthy eating and exercise. I tell her, I'm too old.'

'You're never too old to look after yourself,' I say, Edward's eyes now on his phone. 'And it's fun to work out, there's something for everyone. We could go for a walk sometime, just a short one,' I add, conscious that Joan doesn't get out much, that she might not be up to any great distance.

'Edward's too busy for exercise,' Joan replies, not responding to my offer, Ed still busy tapping on his screen. 'Whenever I call, he's working. *No time to talk, Mum, I'm busy.* "Fine, fine, a man's got to work", I say.' And then, as an aside she says to me, 'He's got to keep himself "in pocket" for the lady in his life.'

'Right,' I say, glancing towards Ed, wondering how his girlfriend puts up with him being so distracted. Good looks only go so far.

'When he was little, he was on the go all the time. He never seemed to tire. Morning to night, he was always doing something. Even now he's all go-go-go. I don't know how he does it. He barely sleeps.' She reaches for another potato. 'And you know his company is going from strength to strength. They have a huge portfolio. I-work. Have you heard of it?'

In that moment, everything seems to slow, and I'm conscious of my heartbeat pounding in my chest. I put down my knife, wipe my mouth. Ed looks up from his phone, his eyes moving between his mother's and mine.

'I—' I begin but can't find the words.

'What?'

'You—'

'I what?'

'You never said.' I pause and attempt to shake off my daze, trying to remember things correctly. 'That day in the cinema, Zinnia asked you what you thought of I-work. Why, if you own it, didn't you say something?'

'I was just there scouting the place, there was nothing to say.'

'Is it the Portland that you're considering buying?' Joan asks.

'Yes,' I answer for him, and Ed focuses on his chicken. 'And what exactly did you figure out?' I ask hotly, wondering how it is that someone can go from a hundred to zero in the space of a sentence.

'That it's a dated business that was probably once the heart of the community,' he says, matter of fact. 'But now it's fallen on hard times: one, because the place isn't being run properly, and two, because nowhere, even a venue as unique as the Portland, can compete with Deliveroo and Netflix.'

110

'Ugh,' I dismiss, outraged, though I know he's said nothing that isn't true.

'Your turnover's what? About £250,000? Used to be almost seven or eight times that, right?'

I look at him aghast, wondering how he knows.

'It's not rocket science, Jess. It's basic maths. My turnover, on a site like that, would be ten, twenty times that, easy.'

'And that's all that matters to you, isn't it? Money! What about all the people who work there, what about community?'

He shifts a little in his seat, clears his throat.

'Community's changing. People work from home now. They look for community in different places, like co-work spaces.'

'Where nobody talks to each other.'

'Nobody talks to each other at the cinema,' he counters, and I find myself gripping my fork a little tighter. 'It's not easy to hear, but people prize cost and convenience over charm.'

It's then, when I'm aching to tear into him about the merits of art and culture and the shared experience of the large screen, but he's too busy droning on about how 'profits will be huge even after extensive renovations', that I remember when we met for the first time here, at the house, and he spoke over Joan when she was about to tell me he was in the process of buying something. And I realise that he was covering then, too, that it wasn't just at the cinema that he withheld the truth, that he's done it twice, at least.

And suddenly my chest tightens, and memories of the

111

day before I was due to complete on the purchase of the flat flood back to me. Being told by my solicitor, 'the funds didn't transfer, send them again'. My account empty. Liam's phone ringing out, over and over. My head swimming with panic. And then the realisation that the money was gone. As was Liam. As was my ability to trust anyone ever again. And now here's Ed, reinforcing that my instincts were right all along: I can't trust men.

'Would either of you like more chicken?' asks Joan, bringing me back to the present, and I feel guilty that I've been hot-tempered and forgotten my manners, not allowing Joan a word in edgeways.

'No, thank you, Joan,' I answer, my appetite gone.

I glance across the table at Ed, who's wiping his face roughly with his napkin, his eyes cast on his phone. In that moment I no longer see the handsome man with the crushingly soulful eyes; in his place I see an unfeeling capitalist.

I want to tell him how we've started a 'Save the Portland' campaign, that Mariko is using TikTok and her many followers to raise the profile of the cinema, by recreating iconic movie dance scenes with Zinnia in and around the building. It's on the tip of my tongue to say that he should think twice about bidding because her campaign and the article in the newspaper are bound to bring in more interest, that he'll find himself in a bidding war, but I don't; the words catch in my throat.

'I've had enough, thanks,' Ed answers, casting me a hostile look, then pushing back his chair and throwing his napkin on the table.

12

JOAN

'What have you there?' I ask, a short time later when Edward has left, and I've had forty winks in my chair. I gesture to the letter in Jess's hand.

'Somebody wrote to me,' she answers, her soft cheeks flushing slightly.

'From the lonely hearts?'

She nods, taps the envelope gently in her palm.

'I thought someone would,' I tell her encouragingly. 'What did he write?'

Jess tugs the note carefully from the envelope then hands it to me.

'He sounds kind,' I offer, having read it through. She sits down, her eyes forlorn. 'Is this sad face about the letter, or Ed?'

She gives me a look that is only interpretable as 'the latter'.

'I feel silly not to have realised sooner that Edward is trying to buy the Portland. I didn't realise it was for sale. It seems such a waste, all that history. I assumed he was considering one that was out of use, that you'd met when he was seeing a film with Izzy, or Charlie—'

'I imagine it's pretty hard to keep up with all that he does,' she says, her tone a little barbed, not that I blame her.

'Should I talk to him?' I offer, though I'm not certain what good it would do.

'Do you think it would help?' she asks, almost certainly rhetorically, and I shake my head with a wrinkle of my nose.

'I'm afraid my son is rather single-minded when he sets his mind to something, like his dad,' I say, my tone sounding more cutting than Jess's had.

I return to her letter before she has the opportunity to ask me about Edward's father. 'Have you replied?'

'Not yet. I'm not exactly sure how. I think I had a French penfriend once, but that's no help. Do you still write letters?' she asks.

'Not so much nowadays – it seems nobody has the time for them any more – but once upon a time I did; I would write often,' I tell her, immediately regretting their mention, not wanting to return to the memories I unlocked last week. 'I've an idea. Come with me.'

At my father's old desk in the dining room, I open my worn leather stationery box, lifting the hinged section of the small chestnut cabinet upwards to create a wedge shape.

'It was my mother's,' I tell her, gesturing for her to sit at the desk as I draw a dining chair over from the table.

'It's beautiful,' she says, running a painted orange nail down one side.

'Why don't you have it for your room? Now that you

don't have your phone you could make use of all this stationery.'

'Joan, I couldn't.'

'Why not? You lent me your phone. The least I can do is lend you this.'

I watch as she explores the top section, divided into two compartments, and all the pretty notelets from decades gone by. Some are from the seventies with images of flower arrangements and gold borders, and there's a more recent selection too, of plain white cards with dainty pressed flowers.

'These are so beautiful, Joan. Are you sure you don't mind?'

'Not at all. Better that they're used and appreciated,' I say as she sifts through the cards for all occasions that I keep in the vertical slots of the middle compartment.

'You might have to teach me how to use these,' she laughs, pulling out the small drawer that houses a range of pens and ink cartridges alongside a collection of decorative stamps.

'You'll need some blotting paper if you're to use those,' I say, showing her the bottom drawer full of writing papers in different sizes and thicknesses, with envelopes to match, and a collection of handy blotting paper.

'Why don't you choose something suitable for this Mr PO Box?'

It takes a while but eventually she opts for a notelet with a pressed tête-à-tête, and a black rollerball pen.

'How should I start?' she asks.

'How about Dear Mr PO Box,' I suggest, feeling like a teacher again, and she begins writing.

She lifts her pen from the card and ponders something for a while. 'You really have to know what you want to say before starting, don't you?'

'Yes,' I nod. 'And you can't rush something down then delete it if it's not right the way you can with a phone; nor can you write something casually and then throw in an emoji to make sure it's taken the right way.'

'It's hard,' she says, leaning back in the chair and lifting the letter from Mr PO Box once more. 'I genuinely can't remember the last time I wrote one either.'

'Maybe you could open with that,' I suggest, but I can see from her crumpled brow that she's still uncertain. 'Just treat letter writing like any other relationship. You start with the simple, small things and build from there,' I quote back to her.

'OK,' she laughs, and starts writing.

I can't remember when I last wrote a letter by hand either. It feels very strange, an event in itself, and requiring so much more thought than an email or text. Don't you think?

'Beautiful, Jess,' I encourage, quite proud of her. 'What else?'

She doesn't reply; instead she continues to write:

Thankfully my mum never made me write thank-you notes. Instead, she would take a Polaroid of me playing with the toy I'd received, then we'd put on lipstick and kiss the back of the photo and scribble our names with a marker pen. She used to say, 'the present was sent for you to enjoy, not for you to endure writing a thank-you card'.

The Italian Job *is such a great film, though I'm more of a rom-com girl. My favourite has to be* You've Got Mail, *which to me is the perfect blend of symmetry and romance. I guess we're all secretly looking for our own romantic hero/ heroine. As you know from my ad, mine would be sensitive, loyal and kind . . . how about you?*

Yours,
CineGirl

'What do you think?' she asks, handing it to me, having read it to herself several times over.

'I think it's excellent.'

'Good,' she smiles, quite pleased with herself. 'Even my handwriting isn't too bad, given I hardly write anything any more.'

Satisfied with her effort, she addresses the envelope, positions the stamp, blows the ink dry, slots in the letter and seals it with a kiss.

'It's quite fun really, writing to someone you might never meet,' she sings, standing up and stretching, her supple stomach exposed. 'It's kind of liberating to imagine that he could be anyone, anywhere, near or far!'

April 2023

Dear CineGirl,

I know what you mean about writing a letter feeling like an 'event'. It takes time to prepare the stationery, and one's thoughts, to buy stamps and walk to the post box. It feels like being in a different, softer age, which I enjoy.

I don't know You've Got Mail, but I'll find it. I could write a long list of attributes to describe my romantic heroine . . . bubbly, self-assured, kind . . . but then again, what does any of it mean if there isn't that magic spark?

Your mother sounds so youthful. Please write again and tell me about her.

Yours,
Mr PO Box

Dear Mr PO Box,

Sending these letters does feel like being in a different age, doesn't it? I love the scent of paper and licking the envelope, and isn't it fun to choose actual stamps at the Post Office? When I walk to the post box, I think of who you might be, where you are and what you're doing.

Do you believe in 'magic'? I can't decide if I do or not. I want to, but it seems so out of reach, other than in the films I love.

You're right, my mother was very youthful. She was a dancer by training, and loved everything about life. I miss her every day.

Yours,
CineGirl

Dear CineGirl,

My experience of love and magic is that we pick the person who should fit, rather than the one who does. If that makes sense? Maybe that's where we're going wrong . . .

You intimate that your mother passed away, which I am sorry to hear. I hope you'll write and tell me what you remember most about her.

If you don't mind, there's something on my mind I'd like your opinion on . . . recently I made an error in judgement, one that hurt someone else. Do you think I should apologise, or is it better to let things be?

Yours,
Mr PO Box

Dear Mr PO Box,

In my experience the right person often fits us at the wrong time, and the wrong person fits us at the right time. The latter is worse!

I remember everything about my mum; she was a rare gem who lit up people's lives. I live every day trying to emulate her energy and kindness.

We all hurt people from time to time; don't be too hard on yourself. Recently someone was dishonest with me, which I'm finding hard to forgive. The most important thing in life is to be honest, regardless of how difficult that might be. Speak to the person, I'm sure you will both be grateful in the end.

Yours,
CineGirl

Dear CineGirl,

'Sometimes the wrong person fits us at the right time' – I know exactly what you mean. In life, timing is everything.

You are right, honesty is best, even when it's hard . . . sometimes I feel as if I could have been an entirely different person if there had been more honesty in my life when I was young. Perhaps my true self, the person I feel I was meant to be, will eventually find his way out. Life moulds each of us in its own way.

Yours,
Mr PO Box

PS It sounds as if you are already a lot like your mum!

13

JESS

'You should ask if he wants to meet, he sounds completely dreamy,' says Debs, handing back the last letter from Mr PO Box.

'I don't know,' I reply, picking a blade of grass then rolling it between my fingers.

We're sitting in the park at the centre of the estate, on Debs' old tartan picnic blanket, watching Mike, wearing a Coronation paper crown, follow the kids as they find the chocolate coins that I hid this morning. It makes me think of all the other royal events we've marked over the years: from going to lay flowers with our mums at Kensington Palace after Diana died, to sitting on the swings discussing William and Kate's break-up as teenagers, to watching their wedding at Debs' house, our mums and Debs' three siblings all crowded round the telly, cheering and waving flags.

'Are you crazy? Why wouldn't you ask him out?'

'Because what if he's like Liam, on the surface someone pretty perfect, until he's not?' I lean back on my elbows and gaze up. Overhead planes, bound for Heathrow, criss-cross the clear blue sky.

It reminds me of my first date with Liam, the two of us sitting at the top of Primrose Hill, looking out over the city, watching people coming and going as the day wore on, both of us talking endlessly. We watched the planes flying overhead and dreamt of places we might go together one day.

After that day, Liam became pretty much part of me, sitting at the bar of the cinema after work, waiting for me to finish my evening shifts, chatting to Gary and Mariko as if he'd known them for years, happy just being near me.

Debs exhales, reaches for a Corgi shortbread. 'Jess, the odds of what happened with Liam again are infinitesimal. You've got to allow yourself to move on.'

'I know,' I sigh, wishing it were that easy. 'It's just nice having the fantasy of someone for a while, rather than the reality. At the moment this guy seems different from anyone else I've met: self-aware, introspective, sensitive. Why would I want to ruin something so perfect?'

'Jess, no one is going to be perfect.'

'Mike's perfect,' I answer, watching him crouch down beside Eli to help him search through a patch of daffodils.

'Ah, no! He isn't. But he is perfect for me, and this guy might be perfect for you. But you won't know unless you arrange to meet him.'

I stare into the sky a while longer, enjoying the sun on my skin after a long winter.

'Life isn't a movie, Jess.'

'You don't have to tell me,' I say, sitting up and picking at a bunch of grapes. 'But sometimes I wish it were.'

'We've our mums to blame for that, watching all those rom-coms; they gave us a false impression of love.'

Debs is right. They filled our heads with dreams – not that dreams are bad, we just weren't quite set up for reality.

Every Saturday night for years, while Mum was able, we'd pile over to Debs' house where Mum and Debs' mum, Sherry, would load up the latest video they'd chosen from Blockbuster, and we'd all curl up on the sofa and eat homemade buttery popcorn and Maltesers. Mum and Sherry would inevitably sob, and we'd laugh at them, and cringe at the romantic scenes while they swooned. In my mind, when you grew up, everyone bought their own home, worked their middle-class job and got the man of their dreams. It never occurred to me then that Mum had none of those things, and that I might not either.

'If you're not ready to meet someone as perfect as Mr PO Box, why don't you take Cormac up on his offer of going out instead? He sounds nice. Keep your options open.'

'I doubt he's still interested; he hasn't been in touch again,' I say, thinking back to when Cormac popped by the cinema, the day his 'Save the Cinema' article came out in the *Notting Hill News* a few weeks ago. He'd come by in the afternoon, when the films were showing, and we'd all sat around, reading his article and making predictions about who might come forward to rescue us. After a while, the others began to peel away, until just Cormac and I were left, sharing a giggle in the corner, relaxed in each other's company. When he had to go,

I saw him to the door, and under the canopy he asked me out.

'Let me think about it,' I'd said, and I saw him try to hide his disappointment, forcing a smile when I imagine he wanted to sink into his boots. 'It's just, you know, mixing work with pleasure . . .'

'Sure, I get it,' he said, attempting to pass it off as if it were nothing, as if I hadn't just trodden on his pride, however lightly.

'I did say to him to call me, but he hasn't.'

'You haven't exactly made it easy for him by getting rid of your phone.'

'True,' I laugh, remembering Cormac's words of wisdom at the pub, that you have to get out of your comfort zone if you're going to grow. And while I guess he was talking about going offline, the same applies to my relationships with guys. Maybe Debs is right, maybe I should take him up on his offer.

'Is business any better?' Debs asks, stretching to get comfy.

'It's picked up a bit since the article, and with Mariko and Zinnia creating their kooky TikTok routines, we've more followers, but that's about it,' I tell her, unable to hide my disappointment that the interest hasn't been more. Despite Mariko's best efforts, including recreating the *Singin' in the Rain* dance routine outside the cinema, Debs knows that none of it, TikTok or the article, stopped Ed making his offer, and Clive hasn't had any others. 'He said he'll give it a bit longer before deciding on whether to accept I-work's bid; everybody is nervous as hell.'

I'm reaching for another grape, thinking about Cormac

and his easy, slightly innocent Irish charm, which couldn't be more different from Ed's stiff, corporate persona, when Debs grimaces and clutches her stomach.

'Debs?'

She breathes, clutching her side. I look to call Mike.

'I'm fine,' she says, indicating that there's no need to get him.

'You don't look fine,' I reply as she tries to regulate her breathing.

She nods, breathes slowly, begins to sit up straighter. 'Just a cramp, that's all.'

'You sure?'

'I've done this three times before, Jess,' she smiles, relaxing again, returning to her biscuit. 'I'm OK.'

We sit for a while, soaking up the spring sun, watching Mike manage the boys, at least one of whom is always attached to their dad in some way: Eli on his hip, Ash with an arm round his leg, Jude trying to play-fight with him. The man is a child magnet.

'Has Joan decided whether to go for that drive with William yet?' Debs asks, shaking her head at her family's antics.

'Not that I know of. She seems super nervous about it. I keep trying to encourage her but she always has a reason not to.'

'Do you know why?'

'She seems a bit stuck. I've lived there over a month now and I haven't seen her go beyond the front gate.'

'Poor Joan,' says Debs, gently rubbing her tummy. 'It's all so curious: stuck at home; a son, but no husband. I wonder what happened to him.'

I'm about to mention the locket Joan never removes, the lack of photos in the house, and how guarded she can be, when I catch sight of a family of three walking towards us carrying a picnic hamper.

'Isn't that Ed's friend Charlie and his kid?' asks Debs. I strain my eyes to look more closely.

'Right, and I've a horrid feeling that's Ed behind them,' I reply, breathing a little deeper to control the rising fury which still hasn't abated since that fateful lunch with Joan.

'Deep breaths, Jess,' whispers Debs as they approach, me pulling her up.

'What an amazing coincidence,' beams Charlie, putting down the hamper and taking us each by the upper arms, kissing us on both cheeks. Ed loiters behind, looking anywhere but at me. It amazes me that someone as nice as Charlie can be friends with this guy.

'What brings you here?' Debs asks.

'One of Oscar's buddies lives here. We're collecting him for a picnic.'

'Small world,' I say.

'This is my wife, Marina,' smiles Charlie, 'and you remember Oscar.'

'I sure do,' says Debs, going in for a pretend tummy tickle which makes Oscar giggle, then shaking Marina's hand, who is effortlessly blonde and hippy-chic. They exchange pleasantries about Debs' pregnancy, Marina's work as a doctor, and how lucky she is that Charlie, a freelance curator, is able to be Oscar's primary carer.

'And this is Izzy.' He indicates the tall brunette next to Ed, who smiles glassily as if dating Ed has turned her partially to ice. 'Meet Jess,' he says, to Marina and Izzy.

'As in Jess, Jess?' Marina asks, and for a moment I wonder if she's referring to my bust-up with Ed, that he's been telling them about his mother's combative housemate. 'Jess who gave up tech?'

'For my sins,' I laugh, and my shoulders drop, glad that Ed's at least had the decency not to bad-mouth me.

'What's it been now, a month?' asks Charlie.

'Five weeks, not that I'm counting!'

'How's it going?'

'It's getting easier,' I say, not going into the details, aware that I'm in danger of becoming a digital detox bore. After the initial few weeks, I found my groove. I've been doing pretty well this last month without it, even though my fingers are still a bit twitchy. Joan dug out a beginners' piano book, and I've been working through it whenever I have the urge to go online.

'Good for you,' smiles Marina, her attention caught by Ed chasing Oscar by the swings.

'We should really get going,' says Charlie, checking his watch. 'We've a playdate to honour, don't want to leave the parents standing.'

'Of course,' I say, as Charlie beckons Ed to wind up the chase and get going.

'Thank God that's over,' I say when they're gone, slumping back on to the picnic blanket, watching Ed walk away with Izzy by his side, still irritated even after he's left.

'Be fair, Jess. Charlie and Marina are charming, and Ed was really cute with Oscar.'

'Right,' I say, with more than a hint of 'whatever'.

'I get that professionally he's an idiot,' she goes on, 'but even you have to confess he was cute with the kid.'

I ignore her remark, not wanting to admit that she might be right. 'Do you remember when you told me "no more arseholes"?'

She bites into an apple and nods.

'Well, make no mistake, that, right there,' I say, pointing to Ed in the distance, 'is an arsehole of the highest order.'

14

JOAN

Pamela looks a picture of health, sitting on a wicker chair under the magnolia tree, now in full bloom. She smiles that big grin of hers as I bring a tray of tea and two portions of the King's Strawberry and Ginger Trifle, having enjoyed Coronation sandwiches while watching the ceremony on the television.

'I'm awfully glad you and Jess found each other,' she says, standing to take the tray from me. She positions it on the little rattan table as I manoeuvre myself into the low chair, then places a wool blanket over my lap despite the warmth of the spring sun.

'What makes you say that?'

'You seem so much brighter in yourself, and Humphrey looks half his age. It's quite remarkable. And after only six weeks.'

I reach down to scrunch one of his velvety ears, glad that Pamela is considerate enough not to mention his lack of exercise these last few years. He really does have more of a spring in his step, now that Jess has him out with her at least once a day.

'She has done wonders for us; we've been fortunate. I can't pretend I didn't have my doubts. It's rather lovely to have youth and laughter about the place again.'

'I think it was brave of you, Joan. I'm not sure I would have done it,' she says, which from Pamela is high praise. 'Where is she now?'

'Celebrating the Coronation with her best friend's family,' I reply, baffled by how Jess can get up and run first thing with Humphrey, make 'Coronation Cupcakes', and then head out to set up a coin hunt, all before 9 a.m.

'She keeps herself busy, that's for sure.'

'The girl has more energy than a fox in a henhouse,' I add with a laugh, my delight at the liveliness she's brought to the house never waning.

'I still can't believe she convinced you to go online.'

'Nor can I,' I reply. 'If you'd told me before she moved in that I'd have a phone of my own, that I'd be sending messages and emails with ease, and able to shop online and enjoy it, I'd have thought you crazy. And I would never have imagined knowing our local Amazon driver by name.' I smile at the thought of Dren who, despite always being in a rush, still takes time to mention the birds or what's in flower, and something of the flora and fauna of his native Albania.

'And what about William?' she asks, never shy in coming forward. 'Have you accepted his invitation yet? You can't keep him hanging on for ever.'

'I'm too old to be dating, Pamela,' I say, reaching for my bowl of trifle.

Pamela stares at me over the top of her spectacles. 'Joan, I know it's daunting, but you were brave enough to take in Jess, *and* go online. Maybe this is the natural next step, to get out and about again. And it would only be in his car, not really going out at all.'

'Would you?' I ask, turning the tables. Pamela lost her husband, Derek, over five years ago now.

'Maybe. But I've set myself my own challenge. To travel again. Derek and I always planned to set off in our retirement, but, well . . .' her voice catches. 'It wasn't to be.'

'No,' I say, knowing what a hardship it's been for Pamela these last few years. Despite her stoicism, it's taken its toll. To lose her husband at the point they thought their life was about to bloom again was cruel. I felt her sorrow acutely.

'It's been a month, Joan. And you've come this far – why not take one more step, see where it leads?'

I sip my tea, considering how to divert the conversation away from myself and the matter of me being stuck indoors. 'Have you thought about where you might like to go?'

'I've an entire scrapbook of ideas! Maybe we could think about taking a trip together.'

I say nothing. Pamela knows full well that if I can't leave the front gate, I certainly can't leave the country.

'We could visit some of the cities you performed in, meet up with some friends. What do you think? How are you getting on with Facebook and finding old acquaintances?'

'Not so well,' I reply, which isn't exactly the truth; it's more that I haven't wanted to use it. Jess set up an account for me several weeks ago, but the prospect of looking at all those faces from the past, all those memories, left me winded. And now that there are actual 'friend requests' and a message, I can't bring myself to open it. Just the mere thought of making contact with the past leaves me breathless.

'Pass over your phone,' she commands, and before I can think about what I'm doing, I'm handing it to her.

'Let me show you what to do,' she says, navigating through things I can't see, then tuts before saying, 'Look at all these friend requests.'

'I haven't de—' I begin, but before I can get the words out, she's hit this button and that and turns to me saying, 'There, I've accepted those, now let me show you how it works.'

I try not to show the fear that's bubbling up in me, or my hands beginning to shake like the lid on a pan of boiling water. I pretend I can hear what's she saying, despite the sensation of whooshing in my ears, and that I can see what she's showing me even though the garden is beginning to spin. The world feels as if it's about to close in on me when I hear Jess call in the distance, 'I'm back', and I turn slowly, to discover her wending her way up the garden towards us.

'Did you have fun?' I ask, a wave of relief washing over me at the distraction.

'Very much. The neighbourhood's buzzing with excitement. You would have loved it, Joan.'

Pamela casts me a look that asks, 'Haven't you told her yet?'

'I'd better get home,' she says, pulling herself up, her tone implying that she's making herself scarce on purpose.

'Lovely celebrating with you,' I call, Pamela already on her way to the gate.

'I didn't mean to interrupt,' Jess says, folding her limbs into the chair where Pamela sat. She looks like a cat in its basket.

'You didn't,' I reply distantly, still caught up in Facebook and Pamela. 'How was the picnic?'

'Fun,' she answers, drumming her fingers on the arm of the chair for a while as if she has something on her mind. 'Joan, would you teach me some piano?' she asks, and I falter, caught off guard. 'I've been trying from the book on my own, but I'm not getting anywhere fast.'

I consider her request carefully, aware that it might help Jess with her 'life swap' and aid me with mine too. And while the prospect leaves me jittery, I recognise that it might be nice to have a pupil again, something I've missed these last few years.

'Oh, why not,' I yield, when her eyes implore me in a way that's impossible to refuse.

Inside, Jess sits at the piano and I draw up my old teaching stool. I walk her through the basics: the groupings of the white and black keys, the notes' names, the stave and clefs, and before long she is confident with the note values and the position of middle C. It delights me that she takes it all in so easily, and that teaching comes back so effortlessly to me.

'Will you play something?' she asks after a time, lifting a pile of music from the shelves beside the piano and searching through it on her lap.

'I'm far too rusty, I'm afraid,' I answer.

'I'm sure you're not.'

'My fingers don't allow it any more,' I tell her, knowing there's little she can say to that.

'I'll bet they can do more than you think,' she presses, and while I know she's trying to be encouraging, I'd rather she left the matter alone.

Thankfully her enthusiasm is curbed when a collection of old postcards drops from between the sheets of music.

'Are these places you've visited?' she asks, reaching down effortlessly to collect them up, noticing that most of the backs of them are blank.

She hands me the cards and I leaf through them, memories of travelling the world in my twenties as a professional pianist tumbling back to me.

'I used to collect them on my travels, in the days before digital photography, when printing photographs was expensive.'

'You travelled a lot,' she remarks, leaning in for a better look.

'I was a professional pianist. It was one of two passions I've known in my life. I travelled all over the world. Paris,' I say, looking at the image of the Eiffel Tower and recalling my first concert at the Salle Pleyel. 'And Vienna, one of my favourites.' I examine the picture of St Stephen's Cathedral, the memory of eating a glorious ice cream with an old girlfriend on its front steps rushing back to me. 'And New York,' I say, rubbing the black and white photo of Manhattan with my finger, tracing my many journeys through its streets and concerts at its enormous venues.

'And who is this?' she asks, her finger reaching over to a picture of me and my old love, poking out from behind the postcard.

The photograph, taken in Central Park, pulls me away, shrinks the room, and in that moment I am back in New York City, right there in the park. I can see the autumn leaves beginning to turn from glossy red to curling burgundy, feel the temperature cooling, smell the scent of woollen jumpers freshly unfolded after months tucked away. And I can feel not only the change in season but the change between us, too, the concerns I could never put aside, the heat almost, but never quite, beginning to fade.

'Joan?' I hear Jess say, and I return to the room, my hand trembling.

'Just someone I used to know,' I say, covering the photo with a postcard.

I feel Jess's eyes on me.

'I think that's enough for today,' I say, my voice breaking, and I hurry to my feet, closing the fallboard of the piano behind me, before heading upstairs.

Post Card

Toronto, 1970

Joany,

You sounded so down last night on the phone. Please don't worry. Love always wins.
I'll be home soon.

For ever yours,
Joe

Joan Scott

Perry Street

Greenwich Village

NYC

HELLO SPRING!

15

JESS

'This is where you've chosen for us to discuss the media day?' I laugh, as Cormac leads me into Swingers, the crazy golf bar just off Oxford Street. It's not exactly what I was expecting for a work meeting, and it crosses my mind that he might be trying to sway me into going out with him.

'I couldn't help myself. I'm mad for golf. And I thought it might help you take your mind off things. I could tell you were getting a bit nervy,' he says, leading me through the entrance, and down to the courses and street food vendors below.

He's not wrong. My stomach has been doing backflips since one of Mariko's TikToks went viral yesterday and was picked up by national media.

'That video was rad, by the way,' he continues, and I'm reminded of the growing look of amazement on Mariko's face as the views skyrocketed, and all because of her and Zinnia doing a spoof of the *Pulp Fiction* dance in the bar, Zinnia dressed up like John Travolta, Mariko as Uma Thurman, with the banner SAVE OUR CINEMA.

After that, the work phone rang off the hook with people calling to request interviews: newspapers, radio stations, TV channels. Eventually, Cormac came by and suggested we hold a 'media day', which he would manage for us, much to my relief.

'Wanna play?' he asks.

'Yeah, I do!' I smile broadly, casting my eye over everything, from the miniature London Eye to the cute helter-skelter, lit up with lights.

'Let's do it,' he says, clapping his hands.

As Cormac sorts us out with clubs and balls at the kiosk, I feel myself physically lighten, and I'm grateful to him for going out of his way to distract me.

'This is mad,' I shout when we're ready, the music loud, the place jumping with groups of twenty-somethings, hen dos and first daters.

'They sure didn't hold back,' he shouts back, teeing up a shot that needs to curve round a dogleg, and I can tell from his bent knees, squinted eyes and tight grip that while it's just a bit of fun, he still wants to do it well, show off a bit, prove to me that he's got some skills.

'Are you always this competitive?' I laugh, when his putt doesn't go to plan and he groans as if playing the eighteenth at Augusta.

He turns his palms up with a shrug to say, 'What can I do?' 'It's what happens when you grow up with four brothers.'

'Four?' I ask, gobsmacked, unable to imagine one sibling, let alone enough to make up an entire basketball team.

'That's the Irish in me,' he grins, watching me line up a shot. 'How about you?'

'Only child,' I tell him with a fist pump when my putt slows centimetres from the hole.

'Uh-oh,' he smiles cheekily. 'Does that mean you're spoiled, bossy and self-absorbed?'

'Or independent and difficult to pin down,' I say coyly, and there's a moment where our eyes linger, that definitely has nothing to do with work. 'How long have you been in London?'

'Like twelve years or so.'

'You came over for work?'

'That and a girl,' he says, raising a telling eyebrow.

'Ah,' I say slowly, pleased that I've inadvertently landed on the good stuff. 'What happened?'

'What always happens,' he shrugs lightly, and it's hard to tell if it's not a big deal or if he's glossing over something deeper. 'She wanted to find someone with a bigger—'

'Bank account!' I joke and he laughs tightly.

'Something like that,' he says, passing over it. 'You wanna grab something to eat? My stomach's telling me it's chowtime.'

We opt for burgers, big ones in brioche buns dripping with cheese, and take them to one of the seating areas, where we sit side by side on a leatherette banquette.

'Are you going to be able to wrap your jaws around that?' he asks, nodding at the burger in my hands.

'Easy,' I say, and I sink my teeth into it, smearing half of it over my face in the process.

'Nice,' he says approvingly, watching me devour a mouthful. 'How's the no tech thing going?'

'So-so. I've been trying to teach myself piano, gives my fingers something to do now that they're phoneless.'

141

'Cool. What else are you doing?'

'Running, yoga, hula-hooping, anything that doesn't need my phone,' I tell him, trying not to think about running apps, and TikTok workouts and my Fitbit.

'Hula-hooping?!' he says, burger paused halfway to his mouth. 'Isn't that for kids?'

'Not any more. It's a whole new fitness craze.' I smile, doing a little seated, hoop-less demo, which makes him laugh and there's another of those moments between us where we edge dangerously close to flirting. 'Tell me something about your brothers,' I ask, keen to shift us back to safer ground.

'Two older, two younger. Two in Dublin. One in New York. The youngest is arsing his way round the world.'

'You're the middle child?'

He nods, takes a bite of his burger.

'A neglected people-pleaser,' I add.

'Probably not far from the truth,' he smiles, wiping his hands on a paper napkin. 'What's it like being an only? Are you close to your folks?'

I put down my bun, gather myself to tell the bit of my story no one is ever ready to hear. I take my time, more for him than for me. 'I never knew my dad.'

'Where was he?'

'Not sure my mum ever found out,' I say, alluding to the fact that I was conceived after one too many cosmopolitans. All Mum could really remember about the night was a packed suitcase in a hotel room with flight tags on it, and a Spanish-sounding name she remembers being tongue-tied by all evening. *Which didn't exactly narrow it down to where he was from*, she used to say, and we'd look at the map on the kitchen wall and pick out all the Spanish speaking countries in the world and imagine who and where he might be.

'It's just you and your mum then?'

'*Was* just me and Mum. She died four years ago.'

'Crap,' he says and this time it's him who puts down his burger. He looks at me in an entirely new light, almost as if I'm someone different. 'I'm sorry to hear that.'

'It wasn't easy,' I say, trying to laugh it off but failing.

'What happened, if you don't mind me asking?'

'She got sick when I was about twelve. MS,' I say, not wanting to get into the full details of how we had seven good years, followed by almost a decade of decline, and then a cruel, untimely end. 'I ended up being her carer.'

We sit quietly, my childhood sitting between us.

'I'm not sure what to say,' he says, dazed by this revelation.

'You don't have to say anything. It's what it is. She got unlucky, that's all,' I say, because that's what my NHS therapist taught me, that it wasn't personal, even though it felt like it was for a long time.

'What was she like?'

'Vivacious, creative, a dancer,' I tell him, no three words ever enough to capture her essence. I think about the words I used to describe her to Mr PO Box, 'a rare gem', 'energetic', 'kind', and I think of him too, despite Cormac's company, of what he's doing, and weirdly I feel a bit jealous of whomever he might be with. 'It was cruel, what happened to her. Really cruel.'

We're quiet for a moment, Cormac probably wondering what to say, me remembering Mum as she was – a

143

mum who learnt all the Spice Girls routines with me in the front room – and how she became – entirely bed-bound. Two polar versions of herself, one easier to remember than the other.

'What about your folks? What are they like?' I ask eventually, when the moment of reflection has grown too long.

'Mum's a teacher. Dad's a surveyor. Pretty boring stuff.'

'Sounds secure, stable,' I say, not knowing that feeling, but wishing I did.

'I guess I take it for granted,' he says a touch guiltily.

'Don't feel bad about that. Stability is the least we should expect of our family. You shouldn't notice it; it's only when it's gone that you do.'

'Hence why the cinema is so important to you?'

I don't reply, both of us knowing the answer, and for a moment our eyes flicker in the semi-darkness. It's only when I remind myself that we're here on business, not pleasure, that I look away.

'Jeez!' I say, shaking it off, things getting far too intense for a miniature golf bar. 'Let's get some drinks in. Hit me with how to deal with the media stuff tomorrow.'

Dear Mr PO Box,

I'm sorry I've been quiet for a while. My best friend suggested we should meet, and I've been thinking about asking, but it doesn't feel like the right time, yet.

I know what you mean about life moulding us. I often wonder how I, and my life, would have turned out if my mum hadn't become sick . . .

I found myself thinking about you this evening, what you might be doing, and with whom. And an irrational feeling of envy, that you might be with someone else, came over me. Why is it that I should not want you to be with someone else, and yet not want to meet you myself? Isn't that odd?

Yours truly,
CineGirl

PS Did you manage to speak to the person you hurt?

16

JOAN

'He's here,' Jess calls, hearing the toot of the Ford Zephyr that I've just seen pull up outside. The sight and sound takes me back sixty years.

'Righto then,' I call resignedly, raising myself from my seat in the living room, feeling as if a balloon is about to explode inside me. Despite my numerous protestations, neither William, Jess nor Pamela were prepared to let our meeting lie. In the end it was agreed that Jess would come along as our chaperone, and now here I am, feeling as if I'm walking to meet my maker rather than a perfectly respectable gentleman.

'I've locked the back door. Make sure you wrap up warm,' she tells me, already halfway out the front door to meet William, Humphrey trotting behind her.

Jess had Humphrey up early this morning for a run, before making sandwiches and filling the old flask which I used during my teaching days, and generally busying herself with the day ahead. She chattered merrily, enthusing about the experience of a 'classic car tour round the city', and being 'excited about seeing more of Joan's London' and organising everything but my handbag, while I did everything and nothing, going from one thing to the next forgetting immediately what I was doing.

It takes me several minutes to put myself together, my shaking hands making it difficult to do up the buttons of my jacket and put on my gloves, my mind too muddled to think what I might need. And when I am eventually ready, I feel uncertain on my stick.

'You all right?' asks Jess, returning.

'I haven't done this in a while,' I say breathlessly, taking a seat on the phone chair, feeling the same sense of panic that set in the last time I left the house. I'd attempted to walk to the Avenue to get a bone for Humphrey and been overcome by the pace of the city, the throngs of people rushing in a hundred different directions, none of them seeing me, most of them too absorbed in their phones to notice the elderly woman clinging to the far side of the pavement for fear of falling on to the road.

It took me over an hour to work my way back that day, my limbs trembling, my chest tightening, an alarming sense of disorientation setting in. When I eventually reached close to home, Pamela saw me from her front garden and brought me the rest of the way, reassuring me I'd had a panic attack rather than a heart attack as I'd feared.

'Just be yourself, Joan. You'll be fine,' reassures Jess.

'It's been five years,' I manage, and I catch the look of confusion on her face.

'After my last private piano pupil went off to university, I was hit by a dreadful low,' I start, not mentioning why or just how dark a place it was, as if every cloud in the world had descended on me. 'I was getting a little better in myself when the world shut down,' I add, remembering how much easier it was when everyone else was stuck at home, that there was no shame in it any more. 'The weeks rolled past, then the months. Before I knew it another three years had passed. Other than Pamela and Edward, and Humphrey, I've been stuck at home all this time on my own.'

Jess pauses for a moment then offers me her hand.

'Step by step, Joan,' she says, with no look of judgement in her eyes, guiding me up. 'You've got me now.'

Together we walk to the front door where Jess locks up and I adjust my eyes to the glare of the day.

She takes my arm. 'Let's start with the front gate.'

'Yes,' is all I can manage, the balloon inside me feeling dangerously close to bursting.

'Ivory Joan?' comes a voice when we reach the gate, and I look up to see William, more handsome in the warm sunlight than in his photo, a kind, guiding arm outstretched.

I nod.

'A pleasure to meet you,' he says.

There's something in the kindness of his tone, the softness of his eyes, and the slight smell of chamois leather that confuses me for a moment. For a second I am back in 1962, on the arm of my love about to go for a drive in his Ford Club Victoria.

'Humphrey is already settled in the front,' he says, when I do not immediately respond. 'You two ladies can take the back.'

'Humphrey,' I say, the name triggering me back to now, knowing Humphrey doesn't belong in 1962. 'How kind of you,' I manage, now at the car door, which is open, the black bench-seat shining in the morning sun.

'It's my pleasure,' he says, and he takes my cane, hovering beside me in case I should fall, which feels like a very real possibility.

'There,' I say, when I'm in the back seat, rather incredulous that I've made it.

'All set?' he asks, and, on my acknowledgement, he closes the door tight.

Jess busies herself with plugging in her seatbelt and attending to her hair, which shines a glorious copper in the sunlight, giving me the chance to study my new surroundings: the thin, stylish steering wheel, the walnut trim on the black dashboard, and the polished chrome of the door handles. Rather than feeling overwhelmed and panicked as I expected to, I feel altogether different, cocooned in something familiar, an environment that brings back nothing other than happy memories.

'Ready?' asks William, starting up the engine, the familiar growl making the hairs on my arms stand on end.

'Yup,' sings Jess.

'I believe I am,' I smile, the balloon in my chest slowly deflating, ready for my first trip out in years.

'Where to, Ivory Joan?' asks William, through the rear-view mirror, and I giggle, wondering if he knows my name is just Joan.

'I hadn't thought,' I reply, rather dazed at the thought of having to make a decision. There are so many places I haven't seen in years, it's impossible to know where to start.

'How about we drive through Hyde Park?' Jess suggests, when I struggle to decide. 'You could show us where you trained. The Royal College of Music, right?'

My face must give away my puzzlement at how she knows because she laughs and says, 'You have your diploma on the wall next to the piano.'

'Of course, silly me,' I laugh, shaking off the confusion. Jess is a regular visitor to the piano these days and I her less frequent teacher.

'Behind the Albert Hall?' asks William.

'Yes, just off Exhibition Road,' I tell him.

'I know it well,' he says as he manoeuvres the Ford out of the parking space and drives towards Pembridge Road. 'My wife, Sylvie, used to love the Proms. We went to the Last Night every year for decades.'

'It's a magnificent tradition,' I say, not wanting to jump straight into asking about his wife, conscious of what he might ask in return. 'As students we were given free tickets to stand, right up the top. I couldn't tell you how many concerts I attended during that time.'

'Makes you proud to be British,' he replies. 'We used to take a picnic and sit in the park beforehand. There's nothing quite like it anywhere else in the world.'

'I'd have to agree,' I say as William indicates to turn on to West Carriage Drive, which will take us through the park, across the Serpentine, and on to Exhibition Road and the museums. It feels at once familiar, run-of-the-mill and at the same time electrifying, as if I've been transported into a whole new world, full of items from the future – grown men on scooters, people of unspecified gender, and vehicles that are fast and sleek.

'How long have you lived in London, Joan?' William asks.

'All my life, bar a time in New York after college,' I say, immediately regretting the mention of the Big Apple.

'What took you there then?' he asks, and I'm relieved that his question coincides with our arrival at the college.

'This is it,' I say.

William slows to allow me a closer look at the majesty of the red-brick Victorian building.

'Magnificent architecture,' he remarks, glancing at its splendour while keeping an eye on the road and mirrors.

'And yet when I was eighteen, nineteen, I'm not sure I noticed,' I say. 'We took it all for granted: the park, the building, the Royal Albert Hall and all the experiences that brought us, and the museums right on our doorstep. How lucky we were.'

'What is it they say, youth is wasted on the young?'

'George Bernard Shaw,' I confirm with a faint laugh at how right he was.

'Where next?' Jess asks when it becomes clear that William can loiter no longer, a lorry looming behind us.

'How about we head down to Westminster? I can show you where I taught, and where Edward went to school,' I suggest, rather more in the swing of things now.

I sit back and drink in the beauty of the city as William drives past Harrods, Hyde Park Corner and down to Buckingham Palace, complete with a commentary on various engineering projects he worked on during his career.

'Give a wave to the King,' Jess cheers as we circle round the Queen Victoria Memorial outside the palace, and along Birdcage Walk, all the way to Parliament Square. It feels rather strange to be hearing 'king' again after so many years of having our queen.

'When did you work here?' William asks as I stare out of the window, bamboozled by the busyness of Westminster.

'I started in the late eighties when Edward, my son, was quite young.'

'Is it just the one you've got?'

'Yes,' I tell him, my throat tightening. 'Do you have children?'

'Three kids, eight grandchildren and a great grand-child on the way.'

'Goodness,' I reply. William pulls up by the ancient arched pend that leads into the school's quadrangle.

'Excuse my French, Joan, but bloody hell, that's a school?' exclaims Jess.

'Fancy, isn't it?' I laugh when I see the incredulity on her face.

'It makes my school look like something out of the Eastern Bloc. Fancy doesn't cut it. This is seriously bougie.'

'Bougie?'

'Bourgeois.'

'I can't argue with that,' I say, drinking in all that sur-rounds it – the Abbey, Parliament and Big Ben. 'Sometimes I questioned whether I might prefer to teach children whose parents couldn't afford lessons, but it wasn't viable at the time.'

'How long did you teach here?' asks William.

'Over twenty years.'

'And Ed came to school here?' Jess asks.

'On a scholarship,' I say and then change the subject, not wanting to discuss being unable to afford the fees and where that might lead. 'Shall we head elsewhere?'

'It's your tour, Joan,' says William, and I suggest we might head north, along Horse Guards towards Trafalgar Square and on to Covent Garden and then Soho, a thought springing to mind of a place I haven't seen in too long.

As we traverse the maze of streets, I point out the venues I performed in before motherhood, before life took its course, when life was still exciting: St Martin's, West End theatres, the Royal Opera House at Covent Garden.

'How about we head along Frith Street,' I suggest, shooing away a flicker of uncertainty, and William turns on to the far narrower street, the four-storey Victorian apartment blocks looming down on us.

'I might just pull over for a minute. Nature calls,' says William and he pulls up outside Ronnie Scott's to visit a pub across the road 'to use the facilities'.

'Does this street hold a particular memory?' Jess asks when William has nipped across the road, and I am quiet.

I clutch my locket, holding it tight.

'The man in the picture,' I say, the words barely forming.

She listens.

'Joseph,' I add, realising this is probably the first time I've said his name out loud in almost four decades.

I press a finger to the window, like a marker in time.

'This is where we met,' I whisper, and my surroundings fade as I'm transported back to that night, sixty years ago, the sound of Joseph's languorous guitar playing seeping into my mind. I see him walking towards me for the first time as if he were right here in front of me, his presence filling the room despite him not being a big man. It was as if we were two magnets, involuntarily pulled towards each other, the force far stronger than either of us could resist . . .

Dear CineGirl,

Please don't worry. I think your instincts are correct: when the time is right to meet, we will know.

I can only imagine how losing your mother felt, and how the experience altered you. I hope one day we can talk about that in person.

I don't think it's odd at all that you should want to meet but choose not to. Initial steps are always hard, even when they're towards something we desire. Recently I've been thinking about something I've always wanted, but I've no idea where to start.

I still haven't found a moment to speak to the person I hurt, but I will, when I find the right moment.

Yours truly,
Mr PO Box

17

JESS

I'm thinking about Joan, feeling proud of her efforts yesterday, and wishing I could send her a quick message to check on her, when Cormac arrives for our media afternoon.

'I haven't seen the place this busy in a long time. Your suggestion of a free afternoon viewing has definitely worked,' I say to him, placing my hand on the arm of his plaid cotton shirt, my stress falling away as I kiss him lightly on his soft, bearded cheek.

'We just need to remind them what they've been missing,' he says, as we head downstairs where customers are milling around, reading the Upcoming Showings leaflets, admiring the vintage film posters and sipping coffees which Mariko has been making continuously since the doors opened a half-hour ago. Zinnia, unable to sit at her usual spot at the bar, casts an approving eye over proceedings from her position in the corner.

I take the ticket needle from Clive, who dashes to answer a phone call from Capital Radio. 'If it wasn't for Zinnia and

Mariko's amazing videos, I doubt we'd ever have the *Guardian* writing about us, or Clive talking to Capital Radio, or London Live coming over this afternoon.'

'That's the power of social media,' Cormac grins.

'This is my favourite quote,' says Zinnia, snapping her newspaper into position, her bangles clattering. '*The duel between old and new, past and future, is nowhere better exemplified than in Notting Hill, where the charming Portland Cinema is at risk of closing to the soulless Goliath, I-work.*' She reads some more of the article before delivering the final sentence emphatically, '*Liberate the Portland Cinema or risk losing community for ever.*'

'Wow!' I say, still amazed that the story has generated national interest. 'Surely there has to be someone out there who will come forward now to take it over as a cinema.'

'That's the message you need to put out when you speak to London Live,' says Cormac. 'Really play on people's passion for history and sentimentality, show how the community is getting behind you, how it can thrive for another hundred years, at least.'

'I'll try,' I say, my stomach doing backflips at the prospect of being interviewed on television.

Thankfully, the next customer to walk down the stairs is Debs with Ash and Eli. I wrap myself around her far tighter than normal.

'You OK?' she asks, clutching my arms and scrutinising my eyes.

'Petrified,' I laugh. 'Cormac's set up a TV interview.' I nod to where he's standing chatting nineteen to the dozen with Zinnia.

Debs gives him the once-over then offers me a look that says, 'cute'.

'Not appropriate, but I know what you mean,' I tell her telepathically, through wide-eyes.

She gives me a sly wink and a grin before taking off after Eli, who's ransacking the sweet selection.

I chat to a few more arriving customers before a woman in a red blazer with gold earrings and a blonde blow-dry descends the stairs, followed by a guy carrying recording equipment.

'Jess?' she asks, reaching out her hand. 'I'm Olivia, from *London Live*.'

'Nice to meet you,' I say, shaking her hand, hoping she won't notice mine is a little damp.

Zinnia, sensing my nerves, takes the ticket needle from me and sits on the seat at the bottom of the stairs to tear tickets, while I take Olivia to meet Cormac.

'Oh hi, nice to meet you,' Cormac says brightly, eagerly shaking her hand. 'What's the plan?'

Olivia talks us through how she'd like to set up outside and briefs me on the questions she'll ask, and while I see her mouth moving and I hear the words, little of it actually goes in. She's asking me to get myself ready, 'a little pressed powder to reduce shine if you have it', when Zinnia calls over,

'Jess, look, Kit Harington's here!'

I turn to discover not just Ed but Charlie and Oscar, too.

Of all the moments . . . I think.

Charlie offers me a wave and makes towards Debs and the kids who are slurping milkshakes through straws at a table, leaving me no option but to talk to Ed.

158

'What are you doing here?' I blurt, my nerves overriding my manners.

'Charlie wanted to bring Oscar to the *Peter Pan* viewing.'

'And you thought that's something you'd like to do too?'

He doesn't respond, casts his eye round the bustling bar instead.

'Business is strong,' I say bullishly. 'We'll find someone to take it over as a cinema.'

He nods in a way I can't read, probably calculating just how much more he'd have to offer to successfully compete with another bidder. He's about to say something when Cormac calls:

'Jess, you're up,' and he comes over to us, touches me calmingly on the back, oblivious to Ed.

'Good luck,' says Ed quietly, in his usual detached way, the merest crumple of his brow suggesting he might just be worried after all.

18

JOAN

I made a little bet with myself that Pamela would be round at some point to interrogate me about the drive with William and, true to form, she raps on the inner glass just before 3 p.m.

'How did it go?' she asks, before I've had a chance to shut the door behind her.

'Come in, Pamela,' I say, taking my time, refusing to be hurried. After the events of yesterday, I'm in no rush to do anything.

'So, tell all. How was it? How did it feel to be out in the city again?'

'It was all very pleasant,' I confirm, hanging my stick on the side of my chair and catching my breath. 'And I admit, I did enjoy being out in the car.'

'Good!' she cheers, pleased for me. 'Where did he take you?'

'Oh, around,' I say rather coyly, settling back into my chair. I can tell from Pamela's pinched expression that she's frustrated with my lack of information.

'Did you like him?'

'He was a gentleman,' I say, not having made any more of an assessment than that.

'And you'll see him again?'

'Pamela,' I laugh. 'I've barely had time to think, let alone plan our future together!' I don't let on that I've been preoccupied with Joseph since arriving home and haven't given much more than a moment's thought to William, despite the many messages he's sent.

'A second date doesn't mean writing your life away.'

I shake my head despairingly.

'Well, maybe Jess will encourage you to see him again, if I can't,' she adds.

'I'm not sure Jess is too concerned with either my relationship or one of her own at the moment,' I say. 'I've a feeling there's some unresolved history there.'

'Meaning?' she asks, quickly taking the bait of distraction.

'She mentioned an old boyfriend a while back. I'm not sure, there was just something in the—'

Before I can finish my sentence, Pamela has reached into the pocket of her blouse, dug out her glasses and is now tapping furiously on the screen of her mobile phone.

'What's her surname?' she asks, her eyes fixed on mine over the top of her spectacles.

'Harris,' I reply. 'What are you up to?'

'I'm going to google her, to see what we can find.'

'Pamela!' I scold, my tone implying that she shouldn't, though quietly I'm as intrigued as she is. For all Jess's bubbliness and zest for life, there's part of her that feels off limits, and though I tell myself to respect her privacy as she has mine, it's impossible not to be curious.

'Aren't you inquisitive to know more about the person sleeping under your roof?'

I don't answer, but allow her to pull up the velour pouffe and take a seat beside me.

'Jess Harris,' she says as she types, her eyes squinted, peering intently at the screen.

A bubble of curiosity forms in my stomach, and I lean in.

'*Jess Harris Official Website for Recipes, Books, TV Show and more*. Not her,' she dismisses, scrolling further through the results. '*Jess Harris – Cambridge University*, *Jess Harris Facebook Profiles*, we could probably find her there—'

'That's her,' I burst, catching sight of a lovely headshot of her in the Google image section, her copper curls glossy, her make-up heavier than she needs, and a gold lamé turtleneck shining gaudily.

Pamela clicks on the picture and reads, '*Jess Harris, open brackets, @ The Only Jess Harris, close brackets. Instagram photos and videos*. Visit.'

She taps again and a whole page dedicated to Jess appears in front of us.

'*What's Up. It's Jess. Cinema manager, wannabe film producer, fitness freak.*'

'I remember her showing me this,' I say, catching sight of the artfully positioned plates of food.

Pamela scrolls through the photos, pictures of everything from the outfits Jess wears to the food she eats, even her walks with Humphrey. In the most recent photographs, before she gave up her phone, I catch glimpses of the house in the background: the wardrobe in her room, the kitchen table, even Humphrey's bed.

'That's her friend, Debs, you remember,' I say, looking at the two of them pouting at the camera, dressed up to the nines, a sixties maisonette in the background.

'And this must be where she works,' comments Pamela, tapping on a picture of Jess smiling underneath a cinema canopy, her arms spread gaily.

'And the gym where she exercises.' I point to a photo of Jess in her workout gear, her arm round a friend, both of them glowing with sweat and beaming.

'She certainly looks to have a full and busy life, no signs of heartache,' says Pamela, and I can't disagree. Seeing her life laid out in front of me makes me consider my own, how a life that started with such daring and determination has amounted to so little.

'Yes,' I say, reaching for my glass of water, not wanting Pamela to notice that something has been piqued within me.

As I'm ruminating over how limited my life has become, and how days like yesterday need to become more frequent, Pamela clicks on a photograph of Jess lounging on a purple sofa.

'Some things aren't meant to be . . .' she reads from the comment that accompanies the image. And then she reads the replies that follow beneath.

'"Sorry to hear what happened with Liam. Something good will come of it", "His loss, your gain", "Bast**d".'

Pamela and I exchange wide-eyed looks.

'I wonder what that's about?' I say.

Without answering, Pamela pulls up another page and types in 'Jess Harris Liam', then scrolls through various dead ends before saying, '*Jess Harris on Twitter. Love this guy @LiamAnderson*' and she clicks on the link which brings up a photo of Jess and a young man standing in the snow, kissing.

'@ Liam Anderson,' ponders Pamela, lost in the digital maze, tapping the name in blue, which leads to the message 'user not found'.

'Oh well,' I say, assuming that's the end of it, but Pamela keeps going.

'Jess Harris. Liam Anderson,' she types, then flicks through pages of search finds until she happens upon something else, 'Bingo!'

'What have you found?' I ask, feeling a touch guilty, as if I were rifling through Jess's belongings in her room.

'It looks like an old Instagram account she shared with her boyfriend,' says Pamela. '@HarriSon-Scored,' she reads, laughing at the way they've blended their surnames to create a username, and the photograph they've mocked up of the two of them standing with Harrison Ford between them.

Pamela scans through countless photos of Jess looking cosy with Liam: nights out at restaurants; posing on a pebble beach; the two of them ten-pin bowling; everything that goes to make up a normal life.

'On December the third last year, Bella Fields wrote, *Jess, is it true? Did Liam scam you out of your flat deposit?* To which Jess replied, *Fraid so. Just hanging in. Hoping the pain won't last for ever.*'

164

Pamela and I take a moment to fully digest the comment.

'Poor thing, she did mention they were going to move in together,' I remark, understanding now why Jess hadn't been keen to explain what had happened between them, and why someone so young and beautiful ended up needing a room with someone like me.

'What a dreadful betrayal,' reflects Pamela, removing her glasses and moving to the sofa.

'But what I don't understand is why anyone would want to make their life public like that.'

'My daughter likens it to a diary of pictures, a way of documenting your life.'

'But why show everyone? Diaries used to be private – several of mine had locks and keys so my mother couldn't read them should she find them.'

I attempt a little laugh, as if I were joking, but it rather catches in my throat.

Pamela casts me a surprised look. 'I never knew you had secrets to keep!'

'How are your travel plans coming along?' I divert; the last thing I want is for Pamela to start diving into *my* past.

'Good. I've been looking into a trip to New York City,' she says, immediately forgetting about Jess and Liam, and my secrets. 'It was top of Derek's travel list, so . . .'

'He had good taste,' I remark buoyantly, sensing a shift in Pamela's spirit. 'It's one of the best places in the world.'

'Of course, I forgot, you spent time there. Don't you have an old friend who lives there? There was a message on your Facebook, *Hello from NYC*—'

'Just an old acquaintance or two, no one special,'

I interrupt, wondering if she senses the fib, not wanting to be reminded of the message I can't bring myself to open.

'Why don't we go, Joan? You and me. You could show me old haunts, catch up with faces from the past. It would do us both good to get away.'

'No thank you, Pamela. The prospect of flying frightens me now,' I say, hoping she doesn't pick up on what, or whom, is the real reason behind my fear.

19

JESS

'Save the Portland Cinema from the clutches of I-work, and save our community,' I watch myself say on Mariko's phone, before the camera returns to the reporter who wraps the report.

'Agh, Jess, you were amazing!' squeals Mariko, turning off her phone and giving me a hug, and everyone whistles and applauds round the bar.

'None of it would have happened without your and Zinnia's TikTok content, or without Cormac managing the whole thing,' I say, going round to sit next to him at the bar, my bare arm touching his.

'Let's hope it gets us the outcome you deserve, and you all get to keep your jobs,' he says.

'I'm so going to build on this, see if I can start earning some money off my socials, and continue to help promote what's going on here,' says Mariko, brimming with excitement.

'And hopefully it means you can keep your studio,' I say to Daniel, who looks unusually lit up.

'A customer saw my sketchbook, we got talking, showed him my Insta, he offered me an exhibition.'

'What?' I ask. 'Who?'

'His name's Charlie something. He gave me his number.'

'Charlie? As in Ed's mate Charlie?'

Daniel looks at me blankly.

'Never mind,' I say, realising that's not the important part. 'Daniel, that's incredible! Are you thrilled?'

'Sure,' he shrugs, which for Daniel is as good as a sofa dance.

We're chatting about Gary and how he can hopefully continue with his mortgage application, when Clive comes out of the office.

'You'll never guess what's just happened,' he says theatrically, Lulu jumping up at his ankles. 'Someone just called, expressing an interest in bidding.'

'Already?' I exclaim.

'He said he saw the six-thirty news. He used to visit when he was little, now owns a hedge fund, has great memories of the place. We're meeting tomorrow.'

'Oh – my – God,' I say slowly, almost melting into my chair in relief. 'That'll wipe the smile off Ed's face.'

'Can you believe the balls on that guy?' says Mariko. 'I mean, coming in on the day we're trying to save the place *from him*.'

'I'm sure he did it to make me crazy, to throw me off track. Arsehole,' I say, my skin prickling at the thought of him.

'Only because he's threatened by you,' says Mariko casually, helping herself to a carton of popcorn.

I look at her doubtfully.

'Why else would he come?' she shrugs. 'If the media day didn't worry him, he wouldn't have shown up.'

I look to Zinnia for clarity, who's been uncharacteristically quiet. She pulls a 'she has a point' face.

'For sure that's the reason,' says Cormac, giving me a little side nudge and a smile that tells me he's proud of me. 'The man knows he's in trouble. Mess with Jess? I don't think so!'

20

JOAN

'You look worn out,' I say to Jess when she arrives home and finds me in the kitchen, where I'm preparing a late supper of a piece of shortbread and a glass of sherry. Her face, naturally pale, has lost all its colour and her eyes look heavy.

'It's been a long day,' she says, running her hands through her curls then tying them up with the scrunchy she wears like a bracelet. She nods to the bottle of sherry. 'May I?'

'Certainly!' I reply, glad that she'd like to join me.

'Have you recovered from yesterday?' she asks, pulling out a chair at the table.

'I certainly slept soundly,' I say, unsure if she's referring to my revelation about being stuck indoors so long, my meeting William, or my mention of Joseph.

'He was easy company,' she clarifies unaware.

'I hope I didn't put him off with my upset outside Ronnie Scott's,' I say, even though I can tell from his messages that I didn't.

'I doubt he noticed.'

There's a pause in the conversation in which I suspect Jess is wondering how to ask about Joseph.

'You're probably curious what it was all about,' I say tentatively, bringing a plate of biscuits to the table.

'I am a little.'

I sit at the table, offer her some shortbread.

'Joseph, Joe, an old flame, was playing there the night we first met,' I begin, cross with myself for referring to him as an 'old flame' when he was so much more than that.

'He was a musician too?'

'An American jazz musician. He was playing with a band I forget the name of.'

'Did you hang around afterwards to meet him?'

I laugh at the idea that she has me pinned as some sort of groupie. 'I was there with some friends from music school, Kathleen and her fiancé, Peter, a fellow American musician. Peter and Joe were good friends. He introduced us after their set.'

'Was it love at first sight?'

I feel my cheeks flush. 'I suppose it was,' I answer, recalling how mesmerised I was by his thick dark hair which sat around his collar, his dark, sensuous eyes, and the way his entire face transformed when he smiled, lighting up the room.

'What was he like?'

'Gentle, big-hearted, a surprising lack of ego for a person with such talent,' I say, none of it adding up to the sum of the man, or able to capture the feeling that when we met it was as if our souls touched.

171

'Did he ask you out?'

I ponder this question for a moment, trying to remember the sequence of events that led to us being together: the four of us sitting round a table in Ronnie's, the two of us locked on each other's eyes, Peter and Kathleen forgotten; and then driving through the city at night in his car, talking endlessly, extracting everything we could from each other until we parked up, and he kissed me. The softness of his lips and sweetness of his breath left me so light-headed he had to prop me up, and then when we all returned to the flat where Joe lived with Peter, we shared beer from a bottle before collapsing on the sofa and falling asleep side by side.

'I'm not sure he had to ask me out,' I answer eventually. 'The bond between us was so apparent from the beginning that we just fell into being together. From that first night, we were inseparable.'

'How long were you together?' she asks, and I sip my sherry, the rose tint of my memories beginning to fade.

'Over ten years.'

'That's a long time, Joan,' she says, her eyes on mine. 'What happened?'

I hesitate, my memories sharpening. It takes all my effort for me to continue.

'It was complicated from the beginning. Joseph's family were Jewish, mine were Catholic. My family didn't approve of relationships outside the church.'

'But still you managed for ten years?'

I push back my chair and go to the understairs cupboard, returning with a shoebox of old clippings, covered in a thick layer of dust.

'We decided to keep our relationship a secret, knowing my family would disapprove,' I tell her, taking off the lid and digging out a collection of lonely heart ads, items I haven't dared look at in years. 'It wasn't like these days when you could send messages to one another and nobody knew. We had to use our imaginations. In the first two years, when he was living in London, we would send coded messages to each other through the classifieds, so we could make arrangements to meet without anyone knowing.'

'Really?' she asks, no doubt finding the idea of someone as old as me being involved in a clandestine relationship unimaginable.

'I was JNY19 and he was JO22. Joany, that's what he called me, even though everybody else referred to me as Joan. I suppose it was a little bit like texting now.'

I hand her a couple of adverts which Jess reads aloud, transporting me straight back to almost sixty years ago.

JNY19, MEET ME AT OUR FAVOURITE SPOT,
Tuesday 7.30 p.m.
For ever yours, JO22

JO22, MY HEART ACHES FOR YOU,
Friday 9 p.m.? Usual place?
Always yours, JNY19

'Where was your favourite spot?'

'A bench under the arches at Holland House,' I say, remembering all the times we met there, eking out every minute of dusk that we could before I had to dash home.

'And what do the numbers mean?'

She handles the clippings as if they were artefacts in a museum.

'Those were our ages when we first met.'

'How often could you post one of these?'

'The paper came out, as it does still, every Thursday.'

Her brow wrinkles in confusion. 'But what happened if you both posted and the plans conflicted, or the plan didn't suit?'

'Then we would turn up, or not, and the other simply waited,' I answer, remembering several instances when I sat waiting for him, often under the arches, uncertain if he would appear or not. 'Once, one muggy summer's evening, I sat for three hours reading a book and watching the peacocks on the lawn, and just as I got up to leave he arrived, drenched in sweat, having walked almost ten miles from where his car broke down to reach me.'

Jess's eyes light up at the romance of it all.

'There was a lot more trust then, a lot more patience,' I go on. 'And when you weren't in each other's company, that was that; you couldn't communicate every second of the day. It made things slower, yes, but also more exciting, I think.'

'I feel that about the letters from Mr PO Box,' she says slowly. 'They give me something to look forward to.'

'Exactly,' I say, glad that our experiment is beginning to pay off in some way, even if it is as simple as developing more patience. 'And we weren't limited to the lonely hearts column — that was mostly for meeting over the first two years — we also had Kathleen, who forwarded letters for us so my parents wouldn't become suspicious, and when Joseph moved back to America, he set up a postal subscription for the *Notting Hill News*. And there were the occasional calls from phone boxes, often, it felt, in the rain, and we also made plans when we were together.'

'It sounds like a lot of work.'

'I suppose it was, but it wasn't all that hard really, we managed quite well. When Joe was back in New York, we'd arrange our schedules so that we could meet in different places around the world, far away from the eyes of my parents. In the end we even lived together in New York for five years without them knowing.'

'So what happened, why did it end?' Jess asks, twiddling with the stem of her glass.

'My parents found out. Someone they knew saw us in a hotel bar in New York, and they made me choose — Joseph or them,' I say, my voice trembling, trying in vain to push away the painfulness of the memory of my mother confronting me over the phone. No matter how much time passes, the shame of lying to my parents never fades, nor their disappointment, nor my utter devastation at having to choose between them and Joe.

I brush away a tear that brims over my eyelid and down my cheek.

'You chose your family.'

I give the merest of nods, unable to go any deeper into the memory, to explain why I chose as I did.

'Did you ever see him again?'

'Just the once, a lifetime ago, you might say,' I reply, gathering myself, dabbing my eye with a hankie from the sleeve of my new dress. 'But he wrote often, and he continued to post adverts in the classifieds intermittently. I never did stop checking the column every Thursday. Up until our switch I was still doing it. He even placed one the day before my wedding.'

'You're kidding?' she says, her eyes full at the drama of it all.

'It's in here somewhere,' I say, carefully going through the contents of the box. 'Here.'

I lay it on the table, my fingers shaky, not having looked at it in decades. It's worn now, a little dog-eared, the paper discoloured and fragile, much like its owner. But even so, the memories flood back to me, the torment of it all, how utterly conflicted I was.

JNY19 DON'T GO TO THE CHURCH
Come here instead.
Please, I can't live a life without you.
Your beloved, JO22

'He really fought for you,' whispers Jess, reading the advert and reaching out her hand to mine.

'He really did,' I whisper back, another tear slipping down my cheek, wishing that I could rewind the years and my decision, and be back with him again.

Dear Mr PO Box,

I hope we have the chance to talk about my mum too. More than anything I wish I could have one more day with her. She always used to tell me that whatever you want in life, go after it. Take her advice and be bold. Life won't come to you.

Yours truly,
CineGirl

21

JESS

Of all the places Cormac has taken me over the past month, a cheese bar in Covent Garden has to be one of the weirdest, and that's including our date grooming dogs at a shelter, and a 'splatter paint room' experience. But it's great, like a sushi restaurant, just with cheese.

'You've outdone yourself,' I laugh, as we take a seat at the conveyor belt.

'I have to find something that makes up for my deficit in the looks department.'

'Cormac,' I reprimand, having talked about his self-deprecation before. For all it's true that Cormac isn't classically good-looking, his old-school charm and gentle manner definitely make up for it.

'Jess, I'm no Henry Cavill. I gotta work harder than most if I'm going to punch above my weight.'

'Not true,' I laugh, amused at his idea of what he considers desirable. 'Plus, you're the perfect gentleman,' I say, because it's true. Whenever and wherever we've gone, he's never once been late, always seen me home, and never tried to do anything I wasn't ready for.

'Do "gentlemen" usually end up with the girl?'

'Sure they do. The good guy always gets the girl in the end.'

'Name me three films where that's true.'

'*The Notebook, Bridget Jones's Diary, Titanic,*' I fire off.

'Wow, that was fast,' he says, flashing me a smile. 'But I haven't seen any of them, so you could just be making it up.'

I screw my face up and throw a balled-up napkin at him.

Our eyes meet, the way they did at Swingers, so I change the subject to work.

'Did I tell you that the guy who owns I-work told me we don't stand a chance?'

He reaches for a plate of blue cheese and fig, shakes his head, 'No.'

'It kills me to say it, but I reckon he might be right,' I go on. 'Things aren't looking good, nothing's come yet of the other buyer.'

I watch the conveyor belt of cheese samples slowly trundle past us, wondering if he's as conscious as I am that I'm purposefully sticking to talking about work.

'You don't know that. There's still time for us to find another buyer.'

'You sound like Zinnia,' I say, reaching for a plate.

I spent the afternoon going through the accounts for the last month, and while it felt over the last few weeks that business was up, in truth it was simply the free promotions we'd run, trying to generate interest, that brought people in. Now that the hype has died down, we're back to how things were. Worse than dead. Zinnia told me to stay positive, that potential investors don't just buy things on a whim, that there's still time for the other interested party to step up or for someone else to come forward.

'Zinnia is wiser than she looks.'

'I hope so,' I smile, keeping to myself the thought that I often think she has a face that looks a lot like Yoda.

'And besides, you can't give up, you love that old place,' he says, reading a message that's just pinged through on his phone. I try not to show my irritation, now hyper aware of how distracted everyone is by their phones, how fragmented conversations are, and that for years I was one of the worst culprits.

'Maybe that's the problem. Maybe I need to let go,' I say, wondering if I ever could, why I find change so difficult.

'And do what?'

'Before Mum got really sick, I was studying film. I always wanted to be a producer. Debs thinks I should go back. Maybe she's right. Maybe I do need to start thinking about an alternative.'

'I'd stick with the cinema if I were you. I'm convinced we can turn the place around. It's just a matter of time.'

'We haven't much time left, Cormac. It's been over a month, and Clive is getting restless; we all know he won't resist I-work's bid for ever.'

'Just give it a bit longer?'

'I'm not sure how much longer I have. I'm thirty-two. I'm getting old!'

'Oh yeah, I see that!' he laughs, his eyes twinkling. 'The grey hair, the wrinkles, the hunched shoulders.'

'You know what I mean,' I laugh back.

'You've plenty of time, Jess, you just have to have faith,' he says, his expression intensifying, his eyes lingering on mine again. 'The Portland is lucky to have you. As would I be . . .'

His gaze flits between my eyes and my lips, and a butterfly flits through my stomach when I realise that this time, he definitely wants to kiss me.

'Well, like I told you before, I'm difficult to pin down,' I say, and I break the look, turning my attention back to the conveyor belt, questioning why I can't just allow the charming Irish guy to kiss me.

I split pretty quickly after that, telling Cormac I needed to get back to check on Joan, which wasn't true, I just needed to get out of there. When I return home, I see Joan's light on in her room and, with my fingers restless, I sit at the piano and sift through a pile of Joan's old teaching books.

I'm attempting some scales when I hear keys in the front door.

'Oh, it's you,' I say, when I find Ed in the hall, not sure who else it would be.

'Hey,' he says, with a half nod, the edge that's usually present in his voice missing. 'You OK?'

'Fine,' I reply, surprised that he should ask. 'Just doing some piano practice.'

'Cool. I'm going to . . .' he tails off, points to the dining room.

'Sure,' I say, not exactly clear what he's referring to but more than happy to leave him to it.

I return to the piano and work through more scales and some exercises Joan recommended. I'm about to turn my attention to some pieces when Ed comes in.

'Sorry,' he says, doing that thing where you try to pretend you're not there so as not to bother the other person. He rummages in the drawers of the old bureau.

'Looking for something in particular?' I ask, wondering if Joan is cool with him going through her things.

'Just something to help me—' he answers, cutting short what he's saying when he happens upon something of interest.

I keep half an eye on him while going through a pile of music Joan laid out for me.

I'm flicking through the pages of *It's Easy to Play Beethoven* when one of Joan's lonely hearts adverts flutters on to the keyboard.

CONGRATULATIONS, JNY19
On the birth of your child.
I hope motherhood brings you great happiness.
Can we meet again?

The clipping intrigues me, and as I set it aside, I wonder when Joan and Joseph met after their break-up and what was said. A memory of Liam, of us picking out a purple sofa together for the flat before our break-up, jolts unhelpfully into my mind. I try to push away the regret of

182

choosing not to look for him when he took off, to confront him, to say all the things I needed to say.

I position the music on the stand, open to *Ode to Joy* and tentatively begin picking out the melody.

'I'm not sure that's the best choice of—' Ed begins but is cut short by Joan shouting from above, followed by the sound of her heading downstairs, agitatedly calling my name.

22

JOAN

Every note Jess plays pierces my heart and penetrates my mind, like salt on broken skin. Anger at not being able to move quickly enough to stop her wells inside me, and when I do eventually enter the piano room, I'm so overcome with emotion that I shout, 'Stop that. Stop that, now!'

And without thought, I reach for the music and tear it from the stand, almost catching Jess on the cheek as I do so.

'Mum!'

I turn to find Edward, his eyes deep with shock.

'Joan?' Jess looks at me like a wounded foal.

'Forgive me,' I say, dazed, walking away, immediately regretting my outburst but my blood still fizzing.

In the hallway, I clutch a baluster and attempt to slow my breathing, wishing again that I'd paid more attention to Pamela when she'd tried to teach me her method.

I'm gathering myself, preparing to ascend the stairs, when Edward comes after me.

'Mum, what the hell?'

'I couldn't help it,' I say defensively, holding tightly to my locket.

I feel as if he wants to say more, but he doesn't.

It's then that I notice Jess at the living room door observing us both. I wonder how it must look, what her thoughts are.

'Forgive me, Jess. I'm just a little tired,' I tell her.

'I understand,' she says quietly, not entirely convincingly.

23

JESS

'Are you OK?' Ed asks, when Joan has returned upstairs.

'Uh-huh,' I reply, though in truth I'm unnerved, uncertain what just took place. 'Do you know what that was about?'

He nods contemplatively. 'I do.'

'But?' I ask, sensing he isn't going to tell me.

'I think it's for my mother to say, not me.'

'Got it,' I reply, shifting uncomfortably, not sure what's left to say.

'I'd better be going. Early start and all that,' he says kind of nervously.

'Sure, I'll lock up behind you,' I say, and I see him out, watching him walk to the gate, and for a second, a very brief second, I forget all the crap between us.

With Ed away, I head straight up to bed, but as I step on to the middle landing, a shaft of light, coming from the room opposite Joan's bedroom, catches my eye.

'Joan?' I ask quietly, surreptitiously tiptoeing up the small run of stairs towards the light.

I rap my knuckles gently on the door and call for Joan again. When there's no answer, I gently inch it open.

With the door just wide enough, I pop my head round and discover a room frozen in time.

On the back wall is a pine cot with a pink canopy, all perfectly made up with white sheets, patchwork quilt and a pink bunny rabbit still with the label on its ear. A nursing chair sits by the old fireplace, and a pine changing table by the side of the window, overlooking the street. The room is spotless, not a fleck of dust anywhere, as if it's been sealed off from the rest of the house.

I'm about to push the door further, when the sound of the landline ringing downstairs causes me to jump, and I quickly switch off the light and draw the door closed, rushing to answer the phone before it wakes Joan.

'Are you sure you're OK?' I ask Debs, when she and Mike are back from their late-night dash to St Mary's Hospital after Debs developed blurry vision and started vomiting.

'They told me it's perfectly normal, that I just need bed rest,' she says, positioning herself on the sofa, the kids sound asleep upstairs, Mike not far behind.

'How are you going to manage to rest with the boys to look after?'

'Mum's back from her holiday in the morning. She'll take a load off. It'll be fine.'

'I'll do whatever I can.'

'Thanks, Jess,' she says, rubbing her bump, and watching me. 'What's up with you?'

'I don't know,' I reply, not sure what I'm feeling these days.

'Cinema?'

'Yeah, that and Cormac . . .'

She doesn't say anything, waits for me to say more.

'We had a moment . . . I think he wanted to kiss me.'

'Not before time!'

I laugh. 'I dodged it.'

'Do you know why?'

'Nope.' An unhelpful image of Ed in the hallway flits into my head. 'Maybe because of the stress at work. Sometimes it feels as if I'm treading water against a growing tide. Why can't I just move forward: change my job, kiss a guy I'm into? It's not like me. Sometimes I feel as if I've become stuck, like Joan was.'

'Did you ever think that you might still be grieving?'

'I'm not sure that's it . . .' For once it feels as if Debs is off track.

'And still processing the shock of what happened with Liam?'

I sit on that for a bit, as difficult as it is.

'You probably don't want my opinion but, for what it's worth, I think until you've put that to bed, you're going to struggle to move on.'

The prospect of confronting Liam cuts too deep to contemplate, so I shift my focus to Joan instead.

'I discovered the room opposite Joan's bedroom is set up as a nursery,' I tell her, leaving out the part about Joan being upset with me at the piano, figuring Debs has had enough drama for today. Quietly I wonder what it was all about, when the piano became something other than Joan's passion.

'Really?' she asks, her eyelids growing heavy. 'That's weird.'

'Isn't it? The door is always shut, but tonight it was ajar with the light on; it was like a museum, a nursery from decades ago.'

'You think it was Ed's?'

'It didn't look like it had ever been used. And it was pink.'

'Poor Joan,' Debs says. 'Maybe she had her heart set on a girl.'

'Maybe,' I say, my mind drifting to what might have happened to Joan in the past, the parts of her life she hasn't told me about. 'She mentioned the other day that she gave up the man she loved because her family disapproved of him.'

Debs snuggles deeper into the sofa. 'I knew she had a story.'

'They had a secret way of messaging each other, through the lonely hearts column. She was JNY19 and he was JO22. Isn't that romantic? He sent one the night before she got married, asking her to change her mind.'

'That's so heart-breaking,' Debs says sleepily.

'Isn't it?' I say, aware that she's barely listening now. 'I got the impression she still longed for him.'

'You should look for him,' she murmurs, almost asleep.

Though Debs' eyelids are closing, her suggestion makes me think, and before I know it, I'm reaching for a pen and paper and composing a lonely heart advert, to Joseph from Joan.

189

June 2023

Dear Mr PO Box

Today has been one of those days where everything goes wrong . . .

I realised that my work is in very real trouble and likely to close, I'm in denial about an old relationship, and to top it all off my landlady tore into me over something I don't understand.

I heard somewhere that happiness is found in healthy work, home and relationship, but what happens when none of those things are right?

In the height of all of this, I found myself wishing we could meet. Would you like to?

Yours truly,
CineGirl

24

JOAN

William is waiting at the bottom of the steps to Tate Britain, red rose in hand, when my taxi pulls up, my heart thumping hard in my chest.

'Joan,' he says, after he has made sure I'm safely out of the cab. He presents me with the flower and kisses me once on each cheek. 'What a pleasure it is to see you again.' He smiles affectionately, as if he's known me all his life. The anxiety of my first trip out alone in years fades, and I feel quite bashful, uncertain why I've waited a month to see him again.

'Shall we go in?' he asks, offering me his arm.

'Let's,' I answer, and I link my arm in his, and together we slowly ascend the wide steps that lead to the classical portico of the entrance.

'Isn't this magnificent?' I gasp as we step into the rotunda with its glorious gallery and dome.

'Breath-taking,' he says, and we stop to turn slowly, gazing upwards.

'It makes me rather dizzy,' I confess, and he squeezes

my arm a little tighter, and places his hand over mine. And I must admit that it's rather nice to be made to feel special, taken care of, though with that comes a certain sadness, a realisation that I've spent half my life without that feeling.

'Didn't you mention you lived in New York for a time? You must have enjoyed the galleries there.'

'Oh, I did,' I enthuse, both of us sauntering through to a long gallery full of Henry Moore's sensuous sculptures.

Memories flood back to me of Saturday afternoons at the Guggenheim and entire days spent wandering the Met with Joseph, hand in hand, followed by long meals, lost in conversation, in the Village restaurants, and wine-soaked evenings in jazz venues across the city.

'What took you to America?'

'A relationship, and my career,' I answer, reminding me of the very different conversation I had with my parents when I told them I wanted to move to New York. I mentioned only the part they wanted to hear, that I'd been accepted to Juilliard to continue my piano studies and to teach. I said nothing of my plan to live with Joseph, that I'd applied to Juilliard primarily to be near him. 'My beau was a jazz musician, a native New Yorker. Opportunities for him were greater there than here.'

'And for you?'

'I studied for a year and taught, then performed all over the city and world. When money was tight I would work as a class pianist at the New York City Ballet.'

'How marvellous,' he says, looking at me in wonder. 'I'm afraid I can only dream of such talent.'

'It's natural to want what we don't have,' I say, referring to talent, skill, but finding my thoughts wandering back to Joe. I force myself to stay in the present. 'New York City was my big adventure. What about you?'

'My life has been rather dull in comparison,' he confesses. 'I trained here in London as a civil engineer; I met my wife, Sylvie. We never left. My passion has been for family, and classic cars.'

'Both noble pursuits,' I say, and while I'm intrigued about his wife and family, I choose not to enquire.

William pauses to admire Moore's *Family Group*. 'How does one man imbue so much soul into bronze?' he asks.

I move further on, towards his more abstract work, unable or unwilling to admire the piece.

'Is there anything you still want for, Joan?' he asks, joining me by a reclining figure.

'Goodness, that's a question. I'd need to think,' I say, somewhat under the spotlight. 'What about you?'

'Nothing,' he says, not requiring any time to consider. 'I'm a man of great contentment. Of course, I miss my wife, but the past is the past. I have my home, my family, my passion. Perhaps, if pushed, I might say someone to spend my days with, a companion.'

'Yes,' I say, wishing I shared his contentment, his satisfaction with life, his ability to leave the past behind.

'A companion,' I continue, trying it for fit, wondering if companionship could ever be enough after knowing the love I knew.

I couldn't relax after William's mention of contentment and companionship, and I spent the rest of our time together preoccupied. Having taken coffee and cake in the gallery's café, we parted, William, I suspect, thinking about our future, me thinking about my past.

The taxi couldn't speed me home fast enough, nor my legs hasten me up the garden path quickly enough, to reach my chair and tablet, where I could resume the search for Joe that I abandoned all those weeks ago.

My hands shaking, I return to my original search of 'Joseph Blume' and, once more, his image appears in front of me.

As I look at the image of him centre stage, playing his guitar. I wonder about all the years we missed together, what sort of life he led that left his skin so soft and unlined, and I wonder too if we'd stayed together, had I not abandoned him, how we would have aged together; if the passage of time might have been kind to us both, rather than only him.

I click on the 'visit' tab below the image, having adjusted to the older man he is now, rather than the man I knew then, a man who was always so innovative and ahead of the trend, a man whose energy and spark shone from his eyes like stardust. The tab leads me to an article from 2011 about the Village Vanguard, a venue that became like a second home to Joe.

'Twelve years ago,' I say quietly, a quick calculation telling me that the photo is of him aged seventy-one at the time, not an old man by any standards. I skim-read the article about the iconic venue to see if there is any mention of him, other than the caption that accompanies the picture, but there isn't, so I move away, typing in 'Joseph Blume Jazz Guitarist' instead.

There are plenty of mentions of his name, but nothing concrete, such as a Facebook or Instagram page. And I look at further images, but none more recent than the one from 2011. In turn I find articles, documenting Joseph's career, his great skill, his life spent travelling every corner of the globe, enjoying a freedom I never knew.

A cloud settles over me, and difficult memories flood back: I remember how the agony of lying to my family about Joe never quite left me. Even on the happiest of days spent together, there was always that gnawing sting that I couldn't shift. And then there were the conversations between the two of us about our future and how we both envisaged it, me wanting family and he only his career.

More than anything I wanted a family of my own, but Joe didn't. We spoke about it for years, but I could never sway him. He thought it would be selfish, a touring musician's life isn't set up that way, but I knew children were the one thing in the world I wanted more than Joe himself.

When my parents discovered the truth of our relationship, my mother promised that, if I gave Joe up, she'd help me find someone 'suitable' whom I could build a home with, and a family; I knew what I had to do, that it wasn't fair to either Joe or me to live a life of compromise.

And even though I was certain I was doing the right thing, I will never forget the sheer agony of the moment we parted, how his eyes pleaded with mine . . . it was just before the clock struck 8 p.m. on 5th August, my thirtieth birthday. We were standing on the Radio City Music

Hall roof, a place we frequented with friends who were employees, about to attend a concert, when I told him, 'Joe, I have to leave. I have to go back to England. I know it seems unfathomable now but, I promise, your life will be freer and simpler without me.' And with that I ran, winding my way down seemingly endless flights of stairs, like a feather trapped in a vortex, Joe calling my name behind me. With every step I took downwards, it felt as if a small piece of my heart broke away from me.

Every birthday since has been a cruel reminder of my decision, another year spent without him.

And then the worst strikes me: what if, like so many of those I have known and loved, he has passed?

'Joseph Blume obituary,' I whisper as I type, barely able to press search.

When I do eventually bring myself to look, it is clear immediately that he is gone.

For a moment it feels as if my own spirit has left me.

I click on the link.

There on a chapel of remembrance site are four simple lines:

JOSEPH BLUME, AGE 80,
OF GREENWICH VILLAGE, NYC,
PASSED AWAY PEACEFULLY
ON AUG 22ND 2022

And once again, I am without him.

Dear CineGirl,

I frequently have days when nothing goes to plan. Just the other day, I planned to apologise to the person I offended and instead managed to upset them once again. Some days I question how it is that I have reached the age I am and yet still struggle to have true connections with the people I love the most.

Wouldn't it be great if there was a formula for happiness! The most I know is that it must come from knowing one's self first, and from freedom. You strike me as someone who knows themselves well, but perhaps there is something you need to let go of? Usually when we pull too tight, the knot of life grows.

I often find myself wishing to meet you. May I suggest Monmouth Coffee, Borough Market, this Thursday at 3 p.m.?

Yours truly,
Mr PO Box

25

JESS

As I wait for Mr PO Box in the coffee shop opposite the entrance to Borough Market, the Shard towering behind, I try to distract myself by reading my three-line advert in the *Notting Hill News*, to Joseph from Joan, over and over:

JNY19 SEEKS JO22
To reminisce and possibly
Rekindle romance

I nibble the edge of a nail, worrying I've been too impulsive in placing it, anxious about how Joan will respond if Joseph replies, or if he'll see it, if he still has his subscription.

'Can I take this seat?' someone asks me, bringing my attention back into the café. They gesture to the classic French bistro chair tucked neatly under the small round table.

'No!' I say, almost pouncing on it, a clear indication, if I needed one, that I'm seriously nervous about meeting

Mr PO Box. Debs couldn't believe it when I told her he'd agreed to meet, and now, sitting here waiting, I can hardly believe it myself. I haven't managed to eat a thing all day.

'I'm waiting for someone,' I explain, trying to gather myself, closing the paper and folding it in half until it will fold no further.

'Anything else for you?' asks a waiter a little after, the clock above me reading 3.14 p.m. I order another coffee, wondering if he's decided not to come.

If I had my phone, I'd be messaging Debs, who'd send me platitudes about how any man on the planet would be lucky to have me, and how of course he's going to show, he's probably just stuck on the Tube. But I haven't got my phone, so I watch people coming and going through the green-steel and glass of the market hall entrance instead, which does little to soothe my nerves.

I'm wondering if I've got the wrong place or time, or if he's got cold feet the way I almost did, and wishing I had my socials to distract me, when I notice, across the street, Ed.

'You cannot be serious!' I whisper, pressing myself up against the exposed brick of the café wall in the hope that I'll somehow morph into it.

But my plan fails. He sees me. Comes over.

'What a coincidence,' he says, not unpleasantly, fid-dling with a cufflink on his pink shirt.

'What are the odds?' I say, feeling a smidge less annoyed by him than I have these last two months.

'Would you mind if I joined you?'

'I'm waiting for someone,' I answer, but he sits down anyway. My eyes flicker towards the door, looking for anyone arriving who might be Mr PO Box. It doesn't help that I've no idea who I'm looking for: tall, short; black, white; able or disabled. I wish I'd thought to ask for a clue.

The waiter comes over, asks for Ed's order. I tell him he's not staying, making it clear to both the waiter and Ed that I'd like him to go, but he doesn't.

'Are you waiting for one of your lonely hearts?'

'Not that it's any of your business, but, yes, I am,' I say, still glancing over his shoulder, worried that Mr PO Box won't see anyone sitting alone, and leave.

'First time you've met him?'

'How do you know that?'

He gestures from my hair to my shoes. 'If it was a third date you'd be in jeans; second date, maybe a skirt, or trousers that show off your waist; but you're wearing a dress, and you've spent time on your hair, so my guess is a first date.'

It surprises me that he should notice so much about someone he finds more irritating than a trapped fly.

With no comeback, I fidget with the newspaper, running my hand firmly over the folds.

'Are you still mad at me?' he asks.

'Of course, I'm still mad at you!' I stage-whisper. 'You're single-handedly trying to close a workspace that my friends and I love, and in doing so you're killing part of our community.'

'I get it, I do,' he says, and there's a moment where I could swear he feels bad. 'But maybe it's time for a change, to focus less on work.'

I baulk at the hypocrisy. '*You're* telling me to focus less

200

on *my* work? This from the man who does nothing other than work!'

'I understand what the place means to you, Jess. I've seen that. But losing the cinema doesn't mean losing your support.'

'This isn't just about my friendships, Ed. You're destroying a piece of history. You can't get that back. Once it's gone, it's gone. And the community won't thank you for it. They'll boycott the space.'

'If the community still wanted the cinema, your media campaign would have worked. But it hasn't, so . . .' he shrugs, as if that's that. No more to be said.

'Someone else has come forward, someone who'll run it as a cinema,' I say haughtily, even though I know the interest has come to nothing and that Clive is keen to accept Ed's offer.

I sit back, fold my arms and stare at him, having just figured something out.

'What?' he asks self-consciously, as if he might have something in his teeth.

'The cinema isn't the main thing that bothers me about you, nor your deep-rooted self-importance, or total lack of self-awareness.'

'Oh really?' he says, his head cocked to one side, as if to encourage me to say more.

'What really bothers me is your dishonesty.'

A tiny crease forms between his eyes. 'Meaning?'

'The day you came into the cinema to scope it out. The day we met at your mum's house. On both occasions you had the chance to tell me what was happening, and you didn't. That's what bothers me most about you. You lack sincerity, candour, authenticity. You don't know who you are.' I sit back, a smug smile on my face, pleased that I've nailed my feelings.

For a split second, I see a flash of something in his eyes, of being rumbled, maybe, but then it disappears in a blink.

'What about the man you're meeting today, the man who writes you letters, does he have all those qualities?'

'He's searching, self-analysing, trying to find his true self. And I know he is sensitive, loyal and kind, attributes you will never have.'

'Well, I'm glad you've got that off your chest,' he says, looking slightly crestfallen, looking too as if he has something else he wants to say, but decides not to.

'Me too,' I say staunchly, though inwardly I feel a smidge guilty for being so harsh, that really I'd like to know what it is he can't bring himself to tell me.

'I guess I should go,' he says, not immediately leaving, a dumb silence falling over us.

I think to take back some of my words, to ask what he's left unsaid, but before I can he gets up, smiles kind of sadly and says, 'Goodbye, Jess. I'm sure he'll show up, eventually.'

June 2023

Dear Mr PO Box

What happened today? I waited for you at the café for an hour. I hope you're OK.

While I was waiting, something terrible happened. The person who is trying to buy out the place where I work, came into the coffee shop and insisted on sitting with me. I spoke unkindly, which left me feeling bad and, I assume, him too.

What makes it worse is that he actually said something that made sense, similar to what you said about letting go. He suggested it was time I made a change in my life, just as my best friend has done so often. The truth is that I, like you, have wanted to do something for many years but have never found the right time, or courage, to pursue it. I worry I've become stuck and haven't the strength to pull myself out.

You spoke about struggling to make true connections with the people you love, and I feel the same way about my passions. For some reason I hide from them. Why is that?

I hope you're OK. When you're ready, please write again. I'd miss you if you didn't.

Yours truly,
CineGirl

26

JOAN

The restaurant, on the corner of Westbourne, looked so inviting from the outside with its pale grey façade, awnings the colour of lemon mousse and planters, but inside it looks more like my school gymnasium: cork, parquet and metal, making it cold, and the noise, even at lunchtime, bounces off every surface.

'Is it just me or has food changed?' I all but shout at Pamela. The two of us are raising the average age of the clientele considerably. We're surrounded by people Jess's age, almost all of them equally fit and healthy, in clothes more suited to exercising than dining. And everyone leans in, huddled together, as if they can't get close enough which, given the noise, might be true.

'It's Australian cuisine. Sarah recommended it,' Pamela laughs.

'It's confusing,' I rebut, trying to make sense of the language, 'bowls' or 'plates', 'sides' or 'add'. The 'burgers' I understand, but it's been a long time since I could manage one all to myself, and the 'classics' are anything but: 'knuckle sourdough' and 'green kimchi' are lost on me.

As I muddle my way through the menu, Pamela talks at me about the wedding of her youngest, Sarah, and a story about one of her five grandchildren, though which one I couldn't say, such is her habit of talking at a million miles an hour about them all.

'What are "hotcakes" and "gravadlax"?' I ask.

'Pancakes and smoked salmon,' answers Jess, joining us. She hangs her cardigan on the back of the wooden chair, and piles her hair on top of her head as she does when she's about to head out for a run. I wonder when eating out became akin to an Olympic event.

'Uh-huh,' I reply, turning my attention to the drinks menu, which is equally bamboozling. *Turmeric and tonic soda, black sesame oat latte, hot chocolate with Pump Street.* It's more tiring than going out to lunch should be, and certainly not as I remember it being, but still, I'm grateful to be out, conscious that without Pamela's initial idea for a lodger or Jess answering the advert, I wouldn't be here at all.

We eventually order, me selecting the safest option I can find, the chicken schnitzel and a tap water, Pamela finding a tuna salad, and Jess going all out with a buckwheat bowl, whatever that might be.

'So, come on, Joan, tell us everything. How was your date? Are you and William an item?' asks Pamela once the waiter has left us.

'Steady on,' I reply, not entirely sure how to respond. These last four days I've been entirely lost to Joe, not that any of them know, and lunch certainly isn't the time to tell them that I oscillate between heartache and denial almost as often as I breathe in and out.

'He's been messaging A LOT,' embellishes Jess, who graciously seems to have forgiven my outburst at the piano though I'm conscious I owe her an apology. 'And they're going to Brighton next week. Imagine. Joan on the beach!'

'We're going to try and walk some of it, up my daily steps,' I add, showing Pamela the Fitbit Jess lent me on my wrist. Jess smiles proudly at me, knowing the difference I've made already to my fitness simply by taking short daily walks with her. My walking stick has become a thing of the past.

'How marvellous,' says Pamela enthusiastically, and I admire her magnanimity, knowing it's not always easy when new people enter friends' lives, particularly when you've been their main support for so long. 'What's he like?'

I think for a moment before answering, the waiter delivering our food at just the right moment. I square up my plate as he leaves, delighted that the schnitzel looks as I'd hoped rather than zhuzhed.

'He's a kind man, uncomplicated,' I tell her.

'He's a classic car fanatic,' chimes in Jess, as if this might help Pamela to paint a mental image.

'He's a retired civil engineer,' I say, feeling this tells her something more about his stature, his discipline and fastidiousness, than the cars. 'Restoring cars seems to enable him to still utilise those skills.'

'He sounds like a catch,' chuckles Pamela, and I ponder that thought while slicing my chicken, knowing that he should be. After all, a good solid family man was the thing I thought I wanted all those years ago. But, like so many things in life, when presented with the option, the reality doesn't quite marry up with the dream.

'And what about you, Jess, how was Mr PO Box?' I ask.

'Who's Mr PO Box?' asks Pamela.

'Jess's lonely heart admirer,' I explain, watching Jess for tell-tale clues as to how it went.

'He didn't come,' she says, casually reaching for the salt. I can tell she's putting on a brave face.

'He stood you up?' asks Pamela.

'I'm sure there's a perfectly sound explanation,' I say, trying to counter Pamela's abrasiveness.

'Or he might just be leading you on,' presses Pamela.

'Pamela, what would possess someone to spend months writing letters and then not turn up?' I demand, feeling quite protective of poor Jess.

'Maybe he came, took one look at me and ran,' says Jess.

'Nonsense!' I say, not believing for a moment that she could think that about herself, which is so out of character. 'Perhaps nerves got the better of him, or something came up, or maybe he simply muddled the details. If you'd had your phone, he would have contacted you to explain. You just have to use that newfound patience of yours and wait for his next letter to arrive.'

'Where were you meeting? Couldn't he have called there?' asks Pamela unhelpfully.

'You're right, he could have,' says Jess.

'Maybe he isn't who he says he is,' continues Pamela, to which both Jess and I shake our heads despairingly.

'The worst of it is that, while I was waiting, Ed came in and we fought again.'

'Oh Jess, I'm sorry,' I say, reaching out my hand to hers. 'Pay no attention. He has a lot on his mind at the moment.' She eyes me sceptically. 'I'm not trying to make excuses for him, but I promise, Edward has a good heart. Did you know that he collects Oscar from nursery once a week to let Charlie get on with a few extra things? And he's been a good, helpful son to me over the years,' I say, not adding that I haven't exactly made it easy for him to be more.

'You should come on our trip,' Pamela chimes in. 'Take your mind off things.'

'Where are you going?' Jess asks, and I can tell from her tone that she's surprised this is the first she's heard of it.

'New York,' trills Pamela, as if it's a done deal.

'The two of you?' she asks, perplexed.

'Yes,' says Pamela, and this time I don't disagree. Having discovered Joe has passed, I'm no longer quite so anxious about the idea. And with only one other contact in the city, I'm coming round to the idea that it might not be so frightening a prospect after all.

'Joan, there's someone with the same surname as you in the paper,' Jess mentions, scanning the paper at the kitchen table.

'Oh really, who's that?' I ask, coming over to join her.

'Look, Parker Armitage,' she says, pointing to an advert in the Deaths column.

The room narrows as I read the three short lines:

PARKER ARMITAGE
Peacefully at home on Monday
Funeral details to follow

'Joan?' Jess asks, as I fall into a seat.

'I'd better call Edward,' I say, a hollowness creeping through me.

'Why don't you take a moment first?'

'Yes,' I answer quietly, the years peeling away in my mind, while Jess gets up to make tea.

I recall the day I landed back in England and my parents meeting me off the plane. They took me straight home where I stayed in my room for weeks, the quiet of their anger, the disappointment that filled the house too heavy to bear. I thought my torment of leaving Joe would eventually subside, but it never did, so when my mother told me we were going to Surrey to meet a young man, I hoped it might help me move on, move past the anguish I couldn't shake, the sorrow that filled my body as if my blood had been replaced by sand.

I remember little of the drive, or arriving at their elegant home, but I do recall the five of us sitting in their beautiful sitting room, the double doors wide to a sweeping lawn, surrounded by open countryside, sipping tea and talking about everything other than the fact I'd been living in New York for five years with the man I loved most in the world. Somehow my parents had been able to pass the incident off as 'a simple fabrication', and Parker's parents had been more than happy to matchmake their aging son with a woman of 'good stock'.

After a time of saying nothing, Parker arrived. We

were introduced and shook hands and were allowed to take tea on the terrace, where we too spoke of nothing in particular, other than the weather and birds.

By some process of parental hastening, all of which I was numb to, we took several days out together – a cathedral, a palace, a garden – and within a few months of meeting, Parker proposed.

Our wedding was everything you'd expect: the preposterous white dress, bridesmaids I barely knew, a church, three-tier cake, more flowers than was sensible. But after the 'excitement' of the wedding, the honeymoon and moving into our home, the cracks became many and wide. I began to wonder if I should have insisted on spinsterhood, or a life without my family, but the daughter in me couldn't do that; I was determined to make it work for my parents, and me.

I'm not sure how long it takes for Jess to bring the tea, lost as I am in my memories. But when she does return, the past starts tumbling out of me.

'The reason I was short with you, when you were playing *Ode to Joy*,' the words catch as I speak them, and I hope that she hears the note of apology, 'was because I had a daughter, named Joy. She died when she was just a couple of days old.'

'I'm so sorry,' whispers Jess, quietly dropping to her chair.

'Parker couldn't cope; he left us when Edward was two. I had to raise Edward alone, give up my career, grieve and hold down a teaching job all at once. It broke me for a long time. And Edward and I suffered because of it. Her passing is something we've both always been too afraid to discuss. A gaping wound in our relationship we can never recover from.'

Jess shifts in her chair.

'After Joy's death, I never played piano again for pleasure, only to teach. It was the one piece of me I could sacrifice for her.'

'I had no idea,' she says, reaching her hand out to mine.

I open my locket to the tiny photograph of Joy, the only one I have; we both stare at it, as if all the world was in it.

'You couldn't have,' I say. 'Nobody knew the full story of Joy other than Parker. And now he is gone too.'

27

JESS

I know it's bad news the moment Clive tells me, 'Staff meeting at four p.m.', but for the sake of the team I remain upbeat.

'He'll just be giving us an update,' I say, followed by, 'maybe another bidder came forward, it could be good news.'

What I definitely don't say is, 'I've a horrid feeling this is it, the end of the road.'

And I'm right, though it kills me.

'I've decided to accept I-work's bid,' says Clive, the five of us standing in a circle in the café, like mourners round a grave. 'The other interested party has formally dropped out.'

Nobody says anything. The quiet hangs heavy. A tear escapes the corner of my eye, one I can't be certain is of sorrow or anger or both. Anger that I saw Ed just last week and he didn't tell me Clive had accepted his bid, anger that he's seen this through to its bitter end, sorrow that I'm losing the most important thing in my life, second to Debs.

'We managed to agree a price which will enable a few months' severance pay for each of you, enough to keep you going while you find new work.'

'When do we close?' I ask, the words barely forming, hardly believing it's come to this.

'Next month.'

'Next month?' cries Gary, sounding as wounded as I feel.

Daniel breaks the circle, walks away, no doubt wondering how he'll complete his work for the exhibition without wages for materials. Mariko goes to make coffee.

'I'm sorry your campaign to find another buyer wasn't successful. I-work's offer was too good to refuse. I've my retirement to consider. I hope you'll understand.'

'I've my family's home to consider,' mutters Gary, returning to the projection booth.

'I understand,' I say, though I'm not entirely sure I do. I think about Clive's family, the generations before him who poured their hearts into this place. It feels to me as if Clive has taken the easy route out.

'I knew this would happen,' says Mariko, handing me a latte, when Clive has retreated to his office.

'I didn't want to believe it,' I say, my stomach tight.

'What will you do?'

I shrug, uncertain. 'I guess if we're getting a few months' pay, I'll find something,' I say, though I've no idea what. The prospect of being without the cinema feels as if I'm being smothered, preventing me from thinking beyond the here and now. As I fight that sensation, a thought of what Mr PO Box said about letting go floats into my mind. It looks now as if I have no choice but to do so. 'What about you?'

'Guess I'll hound some cinema managers, keep trying to build my followers some more, hope someone will hire me on the basis that I'm a good marketing prospect. Failing that, I can always be a barista.'

'Things will turn out for the best,' I say, Ed's comment, annoyingly, pushing into my head: *Maybe it's time for a change, to focus less on work*. 'Perhaps it's a blessing in disguise.'

'Maybe,' shrugs Mariko, not buying it. 'Or maybe it is what it is: a goddamn kick in the teeth.'

I'm sitting on the bench outside the cinema, seeing the neighbourhood and all its charm differently now, as if I'm in a bubble and it is not, everything as normal but now just out of reach, when a familiar figure, tall and easy, walks towards me.

'Cormac,' I say, as he stoops to kiss me on the cheek. 'How are you?'

'Good,' he says, sitting beside me, his hands in the pockets of his short suede jacket. 'How's you?'

'Been better.'

He cocks me a quizzical look.

'The cinema's closing next month.'

'You're kidding,' he says, turning fully towards me, his eyes full of shock and concern.

'I wish.'

'But all that interest we generated,' he shakes his head trying to fathom the news. 'It wasn't enough to bring someone else forward, or to make Clive reconsider? How is that possible?'

'The other party didn't come through; it was only ever I-work.'

'I don't get it. Clive could have had you run the place, made all the changes to make it profitable again, *and* earn a tidy pension each year.'

'Right, I know, but he's done. He doesn't want the responsibility any more.'

Cormac leans back with a puff of resignation, flicks away a message on his phone and tucks it in his pocket. 'It's a whole lot of history to throw away.'

We both sit quietly for a while, reflecting on the change and drinking in the gentle busyness of the neighbourhood: shop workers bringing in an A-frame; a group of women enjoying an early drink; a small dog barking on its lead.

'It's probably not the best time to ask,' he says, breaking the peace, 'but I actually stopped by to ask if you'd like to go out again. Maybe catch a show together?'

Perhaps it's the shock of the news, or the comfort of his steady presence in the absence of everything else, or of Mr PO Box suggesting I need to let go . . . but whatever the reason, when I look into his eyes, so full of goodness and hope and optimism, I finally let him draw me in and allow him to gently kiss me.

28

JOAN

'Beautiful spot for a send-off,' says Jess, handing me a glass of white wine and sitting down next to me on the bench in the Surrey hotel garden.

'It's very Parker,' I comment, regarding the manicured croquet lawn and majestic oak trees, with a pristine golf course beyond. 'One of his golfing cronies told me they played here most days after his retirement.'

'Huh,' says Jess with an inflection that suggests *how tedious*, and I laugh, because she's not wrong.

Looking out over the gardens, I try to imagine how my life with Parker might have turned out if the worst thing in the world hadn't happened. Over the years, I haven't allowed myself to think about it, the mere thought of another version of my life feeling as if I was dishonouring Joy, but, sitting here now with Jess, I allow my imagination to roam.

I imagine how our family might have been. Four instead of two. More than likely a move to the home counties that I wouldn't have wanted to make, miles away from everything I loved in the city. Me being the home-maker, the hostess to Parker's bosses and clients at the bank, the organiser of holidays, school sports days and festive celebrations. A chill runs through me when I think of how bored I would have been, how void of spirit, that for all the strain of teaching and being a single parent, it suited me far better than the person I would have become if Parker hadn't left. And when the children were grown, what then? Cruises with friends as bored as us? Attending concerts with a husband who had no inter-est in being there. A life lost to primping the house, and preening myself, and golf.

'How are you feeling?' she asks, and I take a long drink of wine, to wash away the daymare.

I breathe deeply, staring straight ahead. 'Relieved,' I say bravely, and without guilt. And I wonder for the first time if Parker knew, deep down, that his decision to leave us was for the best, that I never was, nor ever could have been, happy with him. It pulls a little that I'll never have the opportunity to ask.

From the corner of my eye, I see Jess nod slowly.

'I'm relieved that this isn't the life I led.'

She scans the lush, kept grounds in front of us. 'It couldn't be any further from your life in Notting Hill if it tried.'

'No,' I say distantly, my only regret being that Edward missed growing up with a father.

From the corner of my eye, I see him walking towards us, a glass of beer in hand. He looks handsome, smart like Parker in a well-fitted suit, his beautiful eyes hidden behind dark glasses.

'How are you holding up?' Jess asks, putting their grudge aside. I'm glad of her support; I can't imagine how I would have managed this day without her.

He pulls over a wooden lawn chair, removes his shades. I can tell from his blotchy face that he's been crying, and I want desperately to hold him, to tell him everything.

He sits down. Clasps his beer. Stares into the distance. 'I'd been searching for him,' he begins, catching me unaware. 'Online. For anything at the house. But I came up with nothing.'

'Why didn't you say?' I ask, knowing the answer full well.

He looks at me as if to ask if I'm joking, as if he could ever have asked me about something so deeply buried.

'I can't believe this is it,' he says. 'That the door is shut for ever.'

Neither Jess nor I say anything. There are no words in the world that could ease his pain now.

'Why did he never reach out?' he asks, his voice as raw as I've ever heard it. 'Was it me?'

'No! It was never you, Edward,' I say quickly.

'You then,' he says, as if there can be no other explanation.

'It wasn't me either, Edward.'

He pleads with his eyes for more, an expression I've seen before which knocks me sideways.

'When you were little,' I begin, gathering myself, knowing as hard as it is, I owe him an explanation, 'I told you he left because of work, which was true because that's what he threw himself into. As the years passed, that story took root because that's all we had, but the truth is that work was his coping strategy to manage something he couldn't ever face. Your father worked his life away because he couldn't come to terms with the loss of your sister, of Joy.'

Edward rubs his hands down his face, revealing eyes brimming with tears.

'Oh Edward,' I say, wanting to wrap my arms around him but not knowing how. I can't remember the last time we hugged, or how it felt to hold him. 'I tried for sixteen years to make him part of your life. I wrote to him every Christmas and birthday via his mother, but he never replied. Neither one of us knew where he worked or lived, she had to wait for him to contact her. I know that she tried, that she felt ashamed of his behaviour, that she wanted above all else, for us all to be a family again. When she passed, just after your eighteenth birthday, that was the end of the road. My belief is, the reality of seeing you grow and change, would only bring home to him the sorrow of never being able to see Joy do the same.

'Ultimately he didn't want to be found. We never even formally divorced. He just disappeared from our lives, I imagine in the hope of forgetting. It was only because of Jess seeing the death announcement in the paper that we found out about his passing at all.'

'I guess I should be thankful for this switch of yours after all,' he says to Jess through a half-laugh, tears tumbling down his cheeks.

There's a little moment between them when their eyes meet tenderly, when I wonder if they might be able to put their troubles behind them.

'What's going on here then?' comes a voice from behind,

and I turn to find Charlie, always a breath of fresh air, strolling towards us.

'Joan,' he says, stooping to kiss me on the cheek, so demonstrative in his ways since he was a child. Even as a teenager he would offer me a cuddle, which always made Edward's and my lack of affection feel all the more acute.

'Jess,' he says, greeting her with a squeeze as she rises a little from the bench. 'How is Debs? She must be due soon.'

'Not long to go now,' Jess answers.

'And how's the lonely heart search going?' he asks, dragging a seat over next to Ed, rubbing his back then offering a grip of support round his shoulders.

'I've been exchanging letters with someone, actually,' she says, her cheeks blushing slightly. 'We're hoping to meet soon, talk through the things we've been writing about – the loss of the cinema and what to do next. You know.'

'It must be a blow to have to say goodbye to the old place,' says Charlie, in that way he has of making something difficult or painful sound light, but not frivolous.

'It would have been easier if I'd been given a heads-up,' she says, though I can tell from her look of contrition that she knows now is not the right time to be angling for a fight with Edward.

'I should have said when I saw you at the café,' he admits, and it throws me for a moment, it being so unlike my son to accept fault.

'Thank you,' says Jess, possibly as taken aback as I am that Edward has as good as apologised. They hold eye contact, his drawn to hers in a way that takes me right back to that first night at Ronnie Scott's, the night I met

Joe, and my heart throbs both for them and the lost hope of seeing him again.

'So, what next?' asks Charlie, clapping his hands, inadvertently breaking the moment.

'I was just about to suggest to Ed that we need to spend more time together, to be more open with one another,' I say, composing myself, knowing that if I say it in front of his best friend, Edward will have no choice but to agree; that the wound between us, that I'm so desperate to mend, might have a chance to start healing after all.

Joan, I've been thinking of you and your son
today. I hope it wasn't too difficult. William

     Thank you, William. It was both an end and
      a beginning, far more than I anticipated.

I'm glad to hear that. Would you like
me to come by, take you out for dinner?

       That's a very kind offer, but not
        tonight. It's been a long day.

But we're still on for tomorrow,
our trip to Brighton . . .?

I'll pick you up at 9 a.m. as planned?

Hello?

Joan, are you there?

29

JESS

It's oddly cathartic removing the film posters from their glass frames, rolling them up and wrapping rubber bands around them for the final time.

'You could sell those, set up a side-hustle!' calls Zinnia, arriving at the top of the stairs.

'I might have to!' I laugh, even though it may not be far off the truth. I escort her down the stairs and as I do, the memory of the first time we met comes back to me: Zinnia arriving at the bottom of the stairs, more able than she is now, wearing a yellow cape and gigantic hexagonal sunglasses, with a jade-green suit beneath.

'I've come to see Ingrid,' she'd said, her voice like a cheese grater, as if she were meeting Ingrid Bergman in person.

'She's in Cinema Two,' I told her, playing along, and she'd smiled through those bright red lips and told me, 'We'll be friends, you and me,' and she was right. Every week since, sometimes more, we've 'shot the breeze' and 'put the world to rights', laughed and cried together.

When Mum died, Zinnia cooked me countless slow-cooked casseroles, most of which I cried into rather than ate but were appreciated nonetheless, and on Zinnia's ninetieth we drank so much sake that we laughed until we wept. It hits me, this could be the last time I ever see her. Someone who's been part of my life for over a decade will be gone.

'Is it really free entry?' she asks, flicking the cream feather-boa she's wearing today over her shoulder. I can tell she's gone to town on her outfit for the occasion: boa, sparkly gold jacket and red velvet trousers – very Hollywood.

'First come, first served. Take your pick of films.

'We've each chosen our favourite,' I continue, swallowing hard, trying to push down my emotions, fearful of what might happen if I don't. 'But I've chosen *Casablanca,* just for you.'

'An all-time classic,' she tells me, as we walk towards the bar, where I help her on to her stool for the final time.

'There isn't enough romance these days,' she says. 'In life or the movies.'

'No,' I sigh, thinking how right she is.

'Don't be afraid to open your heart again, Jess. You'd be amazed the difference it makes,' she says, taking my hand and patting it. I want to be all strong and 'I've got this', when in truth I feel myself crumble, and it's all I can do to breathe deep, and compose myself, knowing that something has to give.

The next while is spent busily dealing with customers, each with a story to tell: 'I'm devastated it's closing'; 'I came every Saturday night when I was a teenager'; 'I watched every showing of *Titanic* for two weeks straight.' One customer suggests boycotting I-work, 'Start a picket,' she cheers triumphantly, and I laugh, when actually I'm wondering where all these people have been the last few years, when sales were plummeting and business was poor. I want to ask all of them, 'How many subscriptions do you have? How often do you order in compared to eating out? What do you do for your community?' But I don't. I simply smile and shrug, knowing their sense of loss doesn't compare to mine.

When the last customer has made their way into the auditorium, all of us collapse at the bar, a weary, contemplative hush falling over us until Clive says, 'I really am sorry, you know. I don't want to let the place go either, but nothing is for ever, even when we want it to be.

'This place made me,' he continues, unusually melancholy. 'I used to sneak in and watch *Saturday Night Fever* and *Cabaret* when my father thought I was upstairs doing homework, and everyone who's worked here over the years has shaped me in some way. All of you have contributed something to my life.'

Gary gives him a manly pat on the back. 'I don't know what my life would be without the old girl,' he says. 'It's the only place I've worked since I began as an apprentice at sixteen. I've known it longer than my wife!'

We all laugh at that, but when the laughter fades, the sense of loss remains.

I want to say something about how they all supported me through losing Mum and then Liam, but aware that might be too much of a downer, I share my memory of my thirtieth birthday instead, and how we all dressed up for a private viewing of *The Rocky Horror Picture Show*.

'You looked knock-out that night,' I tell Mariko, remembering how she managed to put a punk-twist to stockings and suspenders, with a red and black corset and mohawk to match.

'You were the first thing close to family that I felt away from home,' she says, holding back a tear, and I reach over to her, never once having seen Mariko cry. 'Life won't be the same without you.'

'But we'll keep in touch, right?' asks Daniel, his brow etched with worry.

'Of course!' I reply. 'We've got your exhibition to go to for a start.'

'About that . . .' he says.

'Daniel?'

'There's a problem with the venue. Burst pipes. Water damage. I'm not sure what exactly. Charlie's trying to come up with an alternative, but for now it's on hold.'

'It'll all come good, mate,' says Gary, giving him a side-hug. 'Life has a way of working out.'

'How about you, Gary?' I ask. 'What are you going to do about your new house?'

'We've decided to stay put,' he shrugs, matter-of-fact. 'What we've got isn't big, but it's home.'

'Glad to hear it,' I say, though I can tell he's disappointed. 'And Mariko?'

'Jamal thinks he knows of a management job that might work for me after graduation so . . . we'll see. What about you?'

I pause for a moment, uncertain what to say, worried that if I speak I'll burst into tears. So I shrug, offer a 'what will be' smile, and hug each one of them instead.

I wander home a different way, passing the I-work on Westbourne Park Road and without meaning to, I go in. Inside, a hundred people stare at their laptops, head-phones on, all of them supping coffee. There's nothing bad about it, but equally there's nothing good about it either. It's just a whole lot of nothing that lacks soul.

I sit down on a hard plastic chair, next to someone watching a movie on his computer. I want to take off his headphones and tell him there was a place down the road where he could chat with staff, meet other customers, watch a film on a huge screen and sit in a squishy chair where thousands of others have sat before him, and eat popcorn made with real butter that tastes of a childhood he probably never knew. But I don't, knowing it would be lost on him.

As I'm scanning the room, devoid of much sound, smell or visual stimulae, I catch sight of someone familiar. Ed.

He's busy, talking to an employee who's taking notes on a tablet. And it hits me that what he said in the café that day, is right. It's OK to focus less on work. Mariko and Zinnia, Daniel and Gary, and Clive, the people who really matter, they'll still be in my life without it. All the other stuff, the customers I never knew, the cleaning and ordering, the admin and scheduling, none of that mat-ters. Life moves on. Things change. It's just that I haven't figured out how to move or change with it.

As I'm heading out, Ed looks up, catches my eye. And

for a short time we just stare at each other, both of us still, until he raises his hand, a slow, tentative acknowledgement. I don't wave back but I do give the tiniest nod, and despite myself, the merest smile, too.

'Hey, Jess. You all right?' says Mike, answering the door, my legs having unintentionally carried me to their house, my key left at home. He looks me up and down, my hair limp and clothes sodden from the rain that I hadn't noticed until now.

'Debs home?' I ask, dodging his question, and he opens the door wider in answer.

'In the nursery,' he says. 'I'll get towels.'

I head up to the box room at the top of the stairs, now unrecognisable from the time I spent in it.

'What the hell, Jess?' says Debs, attempting to get up from where she's reclining in her nursing chair; cot parts, tools and instructions strewn around the room.

I put out a hand to stop her trying to move with her huge belly and swollen hands and legs. She gestures to Mike, now standing in the door frame, to hand over the towels. 'And grab her my dressing gown,' she instructs.

Having brought me the robe, Mike heads downstairs to make us all a brew, while I strip off my wet clothes in the nursery. It's clear that Mike has been busy clearing and decorating, and he's built the changing table, which is now set up in the corner by the door.

'What's going on?' Debs asks, when I'm snug in her thick terry-towelling robe with dry socks, and I'm sitting with my back against the wall.

'The cinema closed today.'

'Aw, hun,' she says, her face crumpling.

'Sorry, matey,' says Mike, arriving back with the teas.

'How does it feel?' asks Debs.

'As if I've lost another part of me. First Mum, then Liam and the flat, now this.'

Debs and Mike exchange a look of sadness for my troubles.

'But I'll get through it,' I say, buoying myself. 'Move forward. It's probably time I started looking for a new job.'

'Or, not to sound like a broken record, maybe you could apply for a producing course instead,' says Debs.

'Still skint.'

'You'd find a way.'

'Maybe,' I say, knowing that I need to but not knowing how.

I set about helping Mike build the cot, with Debs pointing at screws and Allen keys we can't find in the jumble of parts on the floor.

'Did you ever get to the bottom of Joan's mysterious nursery?'

I tell her all about Joy, and Parker leaving Joan after their daughter's passing, and how Joan now seems to be moving forward in her life, despite her sorrow, unlike me.

'Did you place the lonely heart for her in the end?'

I nod. 'Haven't heard anything back. I've checked every Thursday for the past month.'

'And you've told Joan?'

I don't answer, reach for a nut instead.

'Jess, you have to.'

'There's no point until I hear back from him,' I tell her, though my conscience is pricked.

'Is she still seeing William?'

'Not sure. He came looking for her the day after the funeral, but she was out.'

'And what about you and Cormac?'

'He kissed me,' I mumble, an Allen key in my mouth, my body, like a game of Twister, now straddling bits of cot.

'He did?' she asks, her eyes lighting up. 'Are you together?'

I shrug, remove the key, don't bother telling her that we've seen each other a couple of times but haven't gone beyond first base. 'He's exactly what I need – stable, supportive, chilled but, I don't know, something's missing.'

It occurs to me that the problem might not be so much Cormac as me.

'What about Mr PO Box then? Does he have something missing?'

'I wouldn't know. He stood me up, and Ed showed up in his place.'

Debs' mouth falls open.

'What?' I ask, trying to hold a cot end and side at right angles.

'Your mystery lonely heart stood you up and your arch nemesis came in his place?'

'So?' I frown.

'Ah, duh, Jess. Doesn't that remind you of something?'

'What?' I ask, for once having no idea what she's on about.

230

'The café scene in *You've Got Mail*, when Kathleen Kelly's adversary shows up instead of her mystery email writer?'

'Debs, life isn't a movie, remember?' I laugh, loving that's what she got out of my strife. That in the depths of my confusion she can still find the romance in it all.

June 2023

Dear CineGirl,

I'm sorry that I put you in an awkward situation. It was not my intention. I promise to explain what happened very soon.

As for the things we hide behind . . . I've hidden for years from the thing I wanted most, and now it's too late. I urge you not to do the same.

While I'm unable to meet at the moment, please know your letters mean everything to me; I would be lost without them.

Yours truly,
Mr PO Box

Dear Mr PO Box,

You can't know how much it meant to me to receive your letter this evening.

Everything is changing and I feel completely lost, even more so than when my mother died.

It's an odd feeling to miss someone I've never met. But I do miss you.

Yours truly,
CineGirl

30

JOAN

'Joan,' says Jess, turning off the hoover at the switch on the wall to grab my attention.

'Yes?'

'I need to talk to you.'

Jess's face is quite solemn, and I wonder what else could have been piled on to her plate on top of the loss of work and ailing love-life.

'What is it?' I ask, when we're both sitting in the living room. Me in my chair, she on the edge of the sofa, her hands neatly clasped in her lap.

'I did something I probably shouldn't have,' she confesses.

'Oh?' I say, curious to know what it could be. 'I hope it wasn't illegal.'

'No,' she laughs, which lightens her mood a little. 'But I have taken things a bit far.'

'Go on,' I say, a nervous flutter passing through my stomach, sensing it has something to do with me.

She pauses. Takes a deep breath. 'I posted an advert in

the paper.' Another pause. 'In the lonely hearts.' She glances up, with a look that questions if I've figured out where she's leading. But I haven't. I already know she posted a lonely heart; I helped her, all those weeks ago. She inhales again. Positions a cushion on her lap. 'To Joseph,' she says, gripping its corners.

Now it's my turn to pause, not quite making sense of what she's just said. And then it hits me. She's sent a lonely hearts message to Joe on my behalf.

'I'm so sorry, Joan. I got carried away. After you told me about your notes in the classifieds, how Joseph tried to win you back right up until the night before your wedding, I was left with a sense that you wanted to see him again. I know I shouldn't have done it, but I felt so compelled; I couldn't resist.'

'Oh, Jess,' I say, laughing lightly at the twist she's created for herself.

'Forgive me,' she implores. 'I just got so caught up in the romance.'

'I hate to disappoint you,' I say, preparing to tell her about Joe, not entirely sure that I can bring myself to voice the news I've kept to myself these last few weeks, knowing it would make it all too real, that I've have no choice but to accept the truth and devastation that would bring.

'What?' she asks, her eyes searching mine.

There's something in her look, so hopeful and idealistic, her heart clearly set on finding him for me, that prevents me telling her about his passing.

'Are you furious?' she presses when I hesitate over what to say next.

'Not at all,' I laugh, and I lean in to her confessionally.

'Do you remember that I told you we saw each other once?' Jess nods. 'It was *after* Parker and I were married.'

'You did not?' she says, her eyes now twinkling with curiosity.

Her eagerness to find out about my romance makes me giggle, and I'm thrilled that at last, so many years later, I can actually share it with someone rather than keeping it locked away in my memory vault. It almost makes the pain of losing Joe more bearable.

'He was here in London, performing, and he posted a classified. Parker and I were in a difficult place at the time. We'd been trying for a baby for over a decade and having no luck. His work was increasingly pressured. I was often bored, most of my work having fallen away. When I saw Joe's advert, I thought, what harm can it do? It had been so many years, and Parker and I were established, despite our difficulties, that I never imagined for a moment that the passion would still exist with Joe.'

I swallow hard, remembering our meeting, particularly cruel now that he's gone.

It was at a concert at the Barbican, where I watched him play from the stalls, I cloaked in darkness, he bathed in light. I was close enough to see his chest rising and falling, close enough to familiarise myself with his body and face, but far enough away not to inhale his scent or touch the skin on his arms that flexed as he played, though I wanted to.

My hands grew damp as I sat at the bar, nursing a vodka and orange, waiting for him to join me after the concert, and when at last he arrived, my heart seemed to physically grow inside me. I trembled as he leant in to kiss me on the cheek, every hair on my body standing on end as I inhaled his scent, completely unaltered by the passage of time.

We sat for what felt like several minutes before either of us spoke, our eyes searching, shining, our breathing shallow. It was only when he spoke that I realised we were instinctively holding hands.

Shall we stroll? he asked, and I agreed. He carried his guitar case on his back, I carried the burden of guilt.

At first the conversation was cordial, both of us navigating new territory, neither one of us certain if the other was feeling the same ache, the same longing to be physically intertwined, until Joe stopped. Dead in his tracks. And turned to me.

Without hesitation he kissed me, a deep, passionate embrace that burst any uncertainty of what either was feeling.

My hotel is just round the corner, he said.

Yes, I answered, not needing him to elaborate further.

I'm ashamed to say I didn't think of Parker once as we hurried along the pavement, hand in hand, running towards that hotel room . . .

We parted hours later, me then thinking only of Parker, and the excuse I would have to make, though it turned out he'd left a message on the answerphone to say he'd sleep at the office.

'Months and years passed after that meeting. We wrote, a lot,' I tell Jess. 'But then there was Joy . . .'

I get up, go to the understairs cupboard and return with a storage box of unopened letters. 'He wrote faithfully every month for years. But after Joy, I never opened another. I couldn't bring myself to feel anything other than heartache. Over the years his letters have lessened in their frequency; now it's just a card or two a year.'

'Joan, there are hundreds,' says Jess, when I lift the lid.

A wave of grief hits me when I realise, I've received his last.

'And all in calendar order,' I say, trying to sound bright. 'I've been careful to keep them organised, and away from the light.' It is like a library of letters, I realise now. My library of lost love.

'What stops you from opening them?' she asks, gently leafing through the assortment of envelopes in which Kathleen forwarded them. Even after moving back to America herself when Peter retired from his orchestral post, even after Parker had left and my parents had both passed, even after she and I had long stopped seeing each other, she continued to act as our go-between.

'Habit, I suppose,' I say, though I know that's not entirely true.

Jess nods knowingly, holding the latest, which arrived almost a year ago now, gently in her hand. I think of the obituary, which had been dated August 2022, and wonder if he'd known he was close to death when he wrote.

'My mum made little videos for me throughout her life,' says Jess, 'but mostly towards the end, when she knew she was dying. I discovered them when I was clearing out the flat. I couldn't watch them for a long time; it was too painful, too raw.'

She sits quietly reflecting, running her fingers round the edge of the unopened envelope.

'In the end my therapist suggested I watch them. To

hear Mum's voice again. To face my fears. She told me that I wouldn't be able to move on until I did.'

'And did you watch them?'

'Yes.'

'Did it help?'

'Absolutely.' She hands me the letter. 'Maybe it's time you did the same, hear Joseph's voice again.'

I take the letter from her, hardly able to refuse it after what she's just told me. I admire Kathleen's beautiful penmanship, and the dazzling airmail stamp of a Blue Jay.

'Go on, Joan, at least open the outer envelope.'

'Oh, go on then,' I say, knowing nothing bad can come from that.

I run a knife under the seal and reach in for the contents.

Inside is a pale pink envelope. My breath catches at the sight of Joe's handwriting, so stylish and unchanged even after thirty-five years, unlike my own which has become spidery and erratic.

'You can do it, Joan,' encourages Jess when I turn it over to look at the seal.

I know it's foolish to be fearful of opening a letter but every fibre in my body tells me not to, that if I do, it will release a flood of emotions that may drown me. But Jess's eagerness makes me reckless, and soon I have sliced it open and am reaching for the contents.

But inside the envelope isn't just a letter; inside is a rush of Joe's scent that takes me straight back to that night, thirty-seven years ago, to the man I adored more than life itself, and the room begins to turn.

'Joan?' asks Jess, when I freeze, the letter half in and half out.

'I can't,' I stammer, clumsily pushing myself up to flee, the letter falling to the floor in my hurry.

My Dearest Joany,

Of all the letters I've written to you over the last sixty years, I believe this to be the most important. Allow me to tell you three things:

1) *I have lived at the same address since the day you left in the hope that one day, I would answer a knock at the door and find you here.*
2) *I have travelled the world and found you in every corner, and played music woven with the sorrow of losing you.*
3) *I have imagined your life to be one of sacrifice and compromise, and you probably believe mine has been one of freedom. But let me assure you, any freedom was lost the day you left. I too have lived a life of compromise; I lived without the woman I loved.*

I planned to propose that night at Radio City. I wanted to marry you, to give you the children you so desired. My dream was the fulfilment of your dream.

I still have the ring. I hold on to it in the hope that I can give it to you some day. Until then . . .

For ever yours,
Joseph

Dear Joseph,

*My name is Jess, and I live with Joan, someone
I believe you know well. I discovered your
address in a letter you wrote to Joan last year.
I hope you won't mind me writing.*

*The reason for the letter is that I think Joan
would like to see you again, but, for reasons I'm
unsure of, she's holding back.*

*If you'd like to see her again to reminisce,
I know she'd be thrilled to see you.*

Please write back, even if it's just to decline.

Yours sincerely,
Jess Harris

31

JESS

From the kitchen, I hear the post drop through the letter box and I hurry through to check if there's anything for me. Every morning for the last two weeks, since the cinema closed, my morning ritual has been the same: Run. Shower. Post. My runs have taken me all over London, my feet pounding the pavement to quiet the pounding in my brain of what to do next with my life and how. My showers have been long, planning how to fill empty days, and how to pay the rent that Joan so kindly offered to let me off paying, which I was too proud to accept. The highlight of most days has been the sound of the post on the tiled floor of the vestibule, bringing hope of either Mr PO Box or Joseph.

This morning, as I open the inner door, I see immediately, amongst the dull brown envelopes of the bills, a familiar cream one.

My heart plummets, and when I pick it up I see my own handwriting. Where I had written Joseph's New

York address, there are now two dark lines, and the words RETURN TO SENDER scrawled diagonally over it.

I imagine the person who lives there now, hastily scribbling on the envelope, probably thinking they were doing someone a favour, not realising they were actually creating a dead end.

Humphrey emits a little whine from where he's lying in his bed.

'I know,' I say, going through to him. 'I don't want it to be the end of Joan's love story either. But he hasn't answered my advert, and the letter's been returned. What more can I do?'

The two of us wander through to the piano, where I sit on the stool, my eye drawn out to the garden, summer sun falling on the dry grass. I wonder if there's an avenue I've missed. Humphrey paces the room as if trying to figure out the impossible: how to find a lost love.

As I practise my scales, I think about Joseph's letter, and of how I've kept my reading of it a secret from Joan. I wonder if I should tell her, if I should try again to have her read it, if she'd really want to know that the man she loved most on earth regrets not marrying her, that he had planned to propose . . .

From the corner of my eye, I catch a glimpse of the understairs cupboard. Desperate to go online to do my own search for Joseph, I get up from the piano and go to it. But as my fingers clasp the handle, I imagine Joan's disappointment if she knew I'd broken our promise, and my own disappointment, too.

I guess it only leaves one other option, I think to myself, heading upstairs to get dressed so I can nip to the news-agent to buy a copy of *The New York Times*. I figure the only way I have left to find Joseph is to place the JNY19 SEEKS JO22 ad somewhere he might be more likely to see it.

I'm standing in my bra when I hear a voice call from the hall, 'Hello?'

My heart skips, knowing instantly that it's Ed.

'Anybody home?'

There's something about his presence in the hall and me in my bra that makes me freeze. I hope, illogically, that if I stand still long enough, he might disappear.

I listen carefully, trying to trace his path through the house.

'Hello,' he calls again. This time his voice is closer, and I hear him mounting the stairs.

'Mum? Jess? Where are you?' he enquires, even closer now.

I grab my T-shirt from the bed just as there's a knock at my door.

'Just a minute,' I call, hurriedly throwing on my top.

'There you are,' he says, when I open the door. He's looking relaxed in a faded T-shirt that hugs him in all the right places, and jeans. In his arms is a wrap of pretty pink larkspur.

'Hey,' I reply, shoving my hands deep into the pockets of my trackies, embarrassed that he's found me again without make-up or my hair done. I nod to the flowers. 'Joan's not here. She's out for the day with Pamela.'

'Actually, I brought them for you,' he says, directing them towards me. I make no effort to remove my hands from my pockets. 'Mum told me you weren't doing so well.'

'What's it to you?' I shrug, squeezing past him and heading downstairs, surprised and vaguely flattered that he should care.

'I was concerned,' he says, following me.

I scoff at his blinding lack of self-awareness, irritated. '*You* were concerned,' I say, rounding the bottom of the stairs. 'The man who closed the Portland, a one-hundred-year-old cinema. The man who put us all out of a job. *You're* concerned about *me*?'

He stands quietly, absorbing my anger.

'You should go,' I say, heading into the kitchen.

'Let me put these in some water,' he says, continuing to follow me. He fills a vase, removes the wrapping, even trims the stems, then places them on the table. 'For you,' he smiles.

Part of me wants to thank him, but I don't.

'Mariko says hi,' he continues, casually putting on the kettle. 'You know she's working for me now at the Westbourne site.'

'I heard,' I say, mellowing slightly, glad that Mariko isn't out of work, that she's got the managerial role that she deserves, even if it isn't at a cinema, which I know she'd prefer.

'She's like a pocket-sized drill sergeant. I've never had such a well-trained, disciplined group of staff.'

'I'm happy for her,' I say, wanting to ask him about Daniel, if Charlie's come up with an alternative space, but I can't.

'How about you? Anything in the pipeline?'

'A few things,' I say, which is an out and out lie, but I've no intention of letting him know that every job in

245

film that comes up has at least five hundred applicants, that I haven't been short-listed for anything.

I busy myself doing things that don't need to be done: replacing Humphrey's water; filling his food bowl and sweeping the kitchen floor.

Ed hands me a cup of tea. I put the broom aside and wander out to the garden.

'How are you?' I ask, unable not to consider his grief.

He takes a seat next to me on the bench by the back door. 'I'm busy, which helps. And I've someone who's helping me through.'

'Good,' I reply, remembering Izzy, and wondering why, after all these months, he's never brought her to the house. I run my finger round the rim of my mug. 'It must be tough.'

'Everyone loses someone, it's part of life.'

'Right,' I nod, and the day Mum passed away flashes back to me.

She'd been in hospital for weeks with sepsis, growing weaker and weaker as each day passed. When the doctors told me she was near the end we made the decision to bring her home, to allow her the comfort of her own bed, to be surrounded by all the people and things she loved.

The night before she died, we'd had a movie night with Sherry and Debs, all four of us bundled up on her bed, watching *The Notebook* and weeping inconsolably at the end as Noah utters to Allie, 'Goodnight, I'll be seeing you,' and they both slip towards heaven; our tears not for their glorious romance, but for the loss of love we knew was coming.

Sherry and Debs left that night saying they'd be round in the morning to help, but when I woke next to Mum

246

the following day, she was gone, and I wished in that moment that I, like Noah and Allie, had gone with her. We lay there together for several hours before Sherry and Debs arrived and took over the practicalities, none of which I can remember, only that they were there and that had made all the difference.

Ed sips his tea, gazes into the garden. 'Did your lonely heart show up in the end?'

There's something in the way he phrases, 'Your lonely heart', that isn't quite right. It's as if he's not really referring to the person I was meeting at all, but to my own loneliness; my own brokenness. I wonder if he feels broken too.

'Nope. We're back to just writing.' I wrap my fingers tighter round my mug.

'But you're crazy about him, right?' he asks, looking at me.

I pause, puzzled, scrutinising his face. 'How do you know that?'

He shrugs. 'I could tell by the way you reacted to me that day at the café. You were obviously disappointed.'

My mind takes me back to all the awful things I said. 'I'm sorry if I was cruel,' I say, looking him in the eye, because even although I felt it all, there was no need for me to actually say it.

'I'm sorry too,' he says, and he holds my gaze.

A little moment hangs between us which is uncomfortably comfortable.

'You caught me when I was vulnerable,' I tell him, looking away, wishing I could find it in me to make myself vulnerable, to 'open my heart' as Zinnia suggested.

'You had every right to react the way you did. I did

247

something that hurt you, even though it was never my intention.'

And then it happens again, another moment between us, as if the sands are shifting.

'You should try to meet him again,' he says gently.

'Why?'

'You don't want to be left wondering, do you?'

I say nothing, watching him.

'After all, he does sound like a perfect gentleman, a romantic hero . . .' his eyes twinkle, and I can't quite tell if he's mocking me or not. 'Just like the guy from *You've Got Mail* . . . what was his name?'

'Joe Fox,' I say, before I can stop myself.

'That's right. Joe Fox. But wait. Joe Fox wasn't always the good guy, was he? Wasn't he also the anti-hero . . .?'

'Enough—' I begin, confused and frustrated that he's using something that meant so much to Mum and me to what, play with me?

I gather myself up then linger by the back door.

He puts up a hand to apologise, then gets up to leave.

'I hope you meet him soon,' he says, and this time it's he who brushes past me, and for a split second I feel something pass between us that makes me wish that he might not leave, that he might linger next to me a little longer.

'It would be a shame for you to miss out on meeting the one person who might just have that . . .' he pauses, and I feel that sensation again, as if I'd like him to move closer.

'How would you say?' he asks, smiling. Then he raises a finger as if remembering, 'I know – magic spark.'

Dear Mr PO Box,

Do you think we should try to meet again?
I'd like to, if you would . . .

CineGirl

32

JOAN

'I'm still not sure we should be doing this,' I say to Pamela as she pulls her Volkswagen into a side street off Goldhawk Road.

'Why not?' she asks, turning off the engine then reaching into the back seat for her flask and two cups which she places on the dashboard.

'It doesn't feel right. It's not our business.'

'Joan, the girl is stuck, she needs closure. She won't be able to move on until she's put this relationship to bed.'

'Yes,' I murmur, knowing Pamela is right, but still unable to shake the feeling of meddling, despite Jess having done something similar herself by placing the lonely heart to Joe.

'We've her best interest at heart,' she reassures me, rummaging in her handbag. She pulls out her phone and brings up a picture of Liam from Instagram that she's saved. 'This should help us identify him if we see him.'

'There must be a hundred Liam Andersons in London,' I say, implying that the odds of this Liam being Jess's ex-boyfriend are slim to nil.

'But not a hundred who are graphic designers,' she says, certain that we're waiting on the right man.

'No,' I reply, thinking back to how we got here.

Pamela had come round last week, to twist my arm some more about the trip to New York. When I'd stymied both that conversation *and* how I need to 'give closure to William in person, not just "ghost" him', she brought up the subject of Jess and Liam. I mentioned the fact that he was a graphic designer, and in no time at all she had dug out her phone and begun a search for 'Liam Anderson Graphic Designer London'.

Her search threw up someone who worked in Shepherd's Bush but, knowing we couldn't just turn up at a random person's work and accost him, she then narrowed her search by area and found an Instagram account by the name of @Anders-Li. There she discovered photos that showed a takeaway on a dashboard, the car's emblem and colour in the background, and when she zoomed in, she saw the name of the street where we're now parked. Her sleuthing astounded me, as did a person's complete lack of privacy or anonymity these days. I was thankful it wasn't like that when I was young.

'Have you made up your mind yet about coming with me to New York?' she asks.

'I've been thinking that I might,' I say. 'Actually, I've been thinking that I will.'

Pamela almost chokes on her coffee.

'Really?'

'Why not?' I say, not feeling the need to tell Pamela that since there is now no chance of me bumping into

Joseph, I have far less to fear. I realise that it was rather preposterous of me to imagine that I was ever going to bump into him in a city of several million souls, fear capable of doing strange things to a person. And it would be good to see the city again; it's more than likely unrecognisable, an entirely new adventure, little to remind me of my regrets. I've even given thought to contacting Kathleen.

'Good for you, Joan,' she says, bumping her coffee cup against mine, and she talks herself hoarse about all we might do: the museums, the parks, the shopping.

'I feel ridiculous,' I say, after sitting in the car for well over half an hour, our flask and a packet of biscuits on the dashboard, Pamela's phone with the photo of Liam in her phone holder.

'There!' shouts Pamela, rapidly handing me her coffee, putting on her seatbelt and starting the car.

'What did you see?' I ask, not having spotted anything.

'The car. The black Mercedes A Class. Registration SH53 FEI,' she says, pulling her car out of the parking space and making a quick right turn on to Goldhawk Road, me catching the subsequent avalanche of coffee and biscuits.

Pamela weaves her way in and out of the traffic, reminding me of the road race films Edward used to watch as a little boy on a Sunday afternoon, while I cling to the grab handle of the door.

'There,' I shout, when I see him turn left in front of a bin lorry, surprising myself at how involved I am in it all.

'Good spot,' cries Pamela, her hands gripping the steering wheel tightly as she makes the turn.

'He took a right, the second one down,' I say, and

Pamela follows, slowing as she enters the residential street, the Mercedes being parked a hundred metres in front of us. 'Go slowly, let him get out of the car.'

Pamela crawls down the street, coming to a standstill when we see the man blip the car shut and stroll into a terraced house.

What's strange is that the man doesn't look like the person I'd imagined at all, a ruthless, hardened criminal; in reality he looks rather average, indistinguishable, even meek.

There's no time like the present, I tell myself, when I arrive home to find Jess sitting on the veranda, deep in thought.

'A penny for your troubles,' I say, taking a seat next to her.

She shakes her head as if physically shaking her problems away. 'How was your day out with Pamela?'

I could offer some general comment, 'very pleasant', 'good to spend time with her' something that gives nothing away nor tells a lie, but the prospect of not telling Jess about Liam, knowing what she's been through, just doesn't sit comfortably.

'You mustn't be cross with me,' I say, fearing her reaction, and she turns with a puzzled, slightly amused expression, as if she can think of nothing I could do that would cause her offence. 'It's Pamela's doing really,' I add, entirely unfairly, keen to pass responsibility. 'We found Liam.'

Jess stares at me, a look of consternation on her face, as if I've just said something completely unfathomable.

'What do you mean?' she asks eventually, probably

presuming there must be some other explanation than the most obvious one.

'Pamela searched for him online, and we found him.' I hand her the address that I've written on the back of a small piece of biscuit packet.

She holds the bit of cardboard in her hand as if it holds the code to a missile.

'How?' she asks quietly, handing the card back to me.

I explain about Pamela's internet search through to the final car pursuit.

And just as I think she might flare up in anger, she does the opposite: she starts laughing.

'You and Pamela? On a stakeout?' she asks, her eyes shining.

'Yes,' I confirm, pleased that the idea amuses her.

She confides that she and Liam got together after the loss of her mother, when she felt 'helpless' and in need of 'care and attention' which he gave her in spades. And she explains about the flat she was buying, that he was to share with her, but two days before completion, he intersected the deposit.

'Hence why I answered your advert,' she says. 'After he took the money he disappeared. He changed all his contact details, social media; there was no trace of him anywhere.'

'Did you tell the police?' I ask, the similarities in our stories not lost on me.

'I thought about it, but something stopped me. I felt ashamed, numb, I suppose. I planned to over time, but you know how it is.'

'Secrets become buried,' I whisper, knowing her pain

254

all too well, realising now that the life I saw on her Instagram wasn't the whole story.

Thankfully, Jess is too caught up in her own emotions to notice mine rising.

'I'm sorry I didn't tell you until now. I was worried you might not understand, or judge me,' she shrugs. 'It shook me up badly. Ever since, all I've wanted is security, and to learn to trust again.'

'Perhaps you need to understand why he did it first. To face the pain, as you did with your mother's videos. Better to know than not,' I say, wishing I'd had the strength to do the same in my life.

Jess doesn't respond.

'She'd want you to, no? Only then can you move forward.'

I press the address into her hand, and this time she accepts it.

Dear CineGirl,

I'd love to meet, but I'm a little busy at the moment. Can you wait for a week or two? I promise we'll see each other just as soon as I'm able. For now, be strong, and embrace change.

Mr PO Box

33

JESS

Without my fitness app, I've lost count of how many miles I've run since the cinema closed, or how many different versions of my life I've imagined. But this morning, as I run along the South Bank, weaving my way through the meandering tourists and appreciating the sun dancing on the Thames, all I can think about is Ed and that thing he said, 'It would be a shame to miss out on meeting the one person who might just have that . . . magic spark.' When he first said it, I had nothing more than an intuition that I'd heard it before in a film maybe, or that he'd said it at some point, or that maybe it was something I'd said. And then it hit me, when I was out running, that Mr PO Box had written it in one of his letters, and what a weird coincidence that was.

I've run and I've run. Past and round the estate, thinking of Mum and what might have happened if she hadn't got sick, if I hadn't hooked up with Liam, and what she would tell me to do now that the flat and the cinema are gone. Like Debs, she would have told me to go after the thing I wanted, to be brave. But for once in my life, I'm all out of bravery.

I've run past the cinema, all boarded up, lifeless, and wondered about what would have happened if I'd worked even harder to find a buyer, when work will start on the place, and how long it will take. I've run through streets old and new, trying desperately to unravel the past and in doing so find the thread to my future.

And at the end of every run I've returned to Joan's, each time remembering the day Debs dropped me off when I was so sure that it was a new beginning, rather than the end of so many things as it's turned out to be.

Now, running under the edifice that is Waterloo Bridge, on my way to meet Cormac for a stroll along the river, I hear someone call, 'Hey, slow down!'

I look around, the voice directed at me, and as I do, I see someone wave, sitting on a café chair outside the British Film Institute.

It's Ed.

'Hi,' he says, looking casual in his T-shirt and jeans with an old cardigan staving off the chill of the shade.

'Hi,' I say, uncertain whether to go over. It feels a lot like our first meeting at the house, but different. Several months of desire and hatred and, now what: courtesy, friendship, no more Mr Arsehole?

He pulls out the chair next to him, pats it.

'What are you doing here?' I ask, joining him, thinking the BFI an unlikely place for someone who's just single-handedly shut down a historic, independent cinema.

'Educating myself,' he smiles wryly, beckoning for a waiter to come over.

I order a juice.

'What's with all the running? Mum said you're running for hours every day.'

'Guess I'm trying to figure out my future,' I say, glad to hear that he and Joan are talking, taking steps forward.

'Or running from your past?'

I shrug, knowing there's probably something in what he says.

'What is it you're after?' he asks, and oddly I don't even have to think.

'The core stuff: home, relationship, career. The things that bring everyone happiness.'

Ed's brow crinkles, making him look like a cute puppy dog.

'What about your passions?' he asks.

Now I scrunch my face in confusion.

'What are you passionate about?' he presses.

'Film,' I answer.

'Well, there you have it. Do that.'

'It's not that simple,' I shrug, kind of defensive.

'Sure it is. Kathleen Kelly had a bookshop, it closed, she became a writer. You ran a cinema, it closed, you become a . . .' he prompts me to answer.

'A producer.'

'That's the dream?'

I nod.

'Then follow that. I promise you, Jess, once you do, all the other stuff will fall into place.'

'How can you be so sure?' I ask, thinking of Mr PO Box and how he offered pretty much the same advice, and Debs. 'You hardly come over as the king of passion yourself.'

'Maybe not, but I'm working on it. And I do know that you have to think things into being.'

'What are you passionate about then?' I ask, turning the tables.

He shrugs, and it feels, just as it was at the coffee shop, that there's something he's not saying.

The arrival of my drink distracts us, and while I'm drinking he tells me that Zinnia popped into I-work the other day and left her number with Mariko. He scribbles it from his phone onto a napkin for me.

'She wants you to call her.'

'Thanks,' I say, grateful to have her details, having missed her this last month.

'You're welcome,' he replies warmly, affectionately even, if I'm reading him right.

We sit for a while, people watching, until I grow cold.

'Would you like to walk a while?' he asks.

'I'm meant to be meeting someone,' I reply. Then, figuring I haven't seen Cormac walk past, and that we'll be headed in the right direction anyway, I say, 'Sure, why not?'

Ed offers me his cardi and I accept, hoping he doesn't notice how the warmth of the wool on my skin and the faint aromatic scent of cologne that clings to the fibres, sends goosebumps all over my body.

'Are you meeting *him*?' he asks, when we're wandering past the Royal Festival Hall, me scanning the terrace for Cormac.

'Who?'

'Your lonely heart guy.'

'Oh. No,' I reply, slightly taken aback. For the first time in a while, Mr PO Box isn't front and centre in my mind. 'I'm meeting someone else, someone I'm sort of seeing.'

'Sort of seeing?' he enquires.

'I don't know. It's nice, he's great, we see each other about once a week, he wants more . . .' I consider what I want but I still haven't figured it out. 'I'm not on the same page as him, yet.'

'Because of the lonely heart guy?'

I look at Ed, wondering how it is that he seems to know more about my love-life than I do.

'You know, I never had you down as intuitive,' I say, as we continue walking.

'Thanks very much,' he laughs dryly.

'To be fair, you haven't given me much to work with.'

'True,' he agrees. 'I can be a bit of a closed book.'

'Ed, Guantanamo Bay has easier access than you!'

He laughs, then stops at a little newsstand by the London Eye, decked out with Union Jack bunting. 'Don't be afraid to meet him, Jess. He'd be mad not to be as crazy about you as you are about him.'

'Thanks,' I say, touched by his kindness, wondering how best to ask Mr PO Box out again without coming off as desperate.

As I'm looking around for Cormac and waiting for Ed to pay for a copy of *The Economist*, I notice, folded and stashed away at the bottom of the paper rack, *The New York Times International Edition*.

'This, please,' I say, waving the paper at the stallholder, who's hidden behind a bank of glossy magazines.

Ed walks on but, longing to see if Joseph has replied, I call him to come back, to sit on the bench looking out over the river for a while.

'What's so important?' he asks, as I manhandle the paper into position, turning and folding and tucking until I eventually have a manageable version of the classifieds section in front of me.

'Just a little project I'm working on,' I tell him, scanning the columns, not sure he's ready to hear that I'm looking for his mother's lost love and that I've been scouring the classifieds each day, just in case.

'Huh,' he says, crossing an ankle casually over his knee, an arm stretched casually along the length of the bench behind me. He casts his eyes out across the river while I scour the paper.

And then I see it. A neat little advert, just three simple lines. But enough to momentarily stop my heart beating.

JNY19, I'D LOVE TO REMINISCE
NYC anytime, anywhere.
JO22 xx

34

JOAN

I made it, I think proudly to myself as I arrive at the coffee shop on Holland Park Avenue Jess suggested I try. She told me it was 'welcoming and traditional' and all the things she knew I'd like, but most importantly, it was the route that mattered, the walk from home to the Avenue that I had to retrace and conquer alone, to truly move forward. And conquer it I did. No more clinging to walls, or trembling limbs or tightening chest. And while my heart rate is faster than usual as I wait to be served, that's down to the brisk walk, not because of panic. Even my hip throbs less, it no longer burning in its socket the way it did before Jess moved in and she got me out walking again, even doing some gentle yoga.

Having placed my order, I sit in the window on a lovely French rattan chair and take out my phone. Without hesitation I connect to the café's Wi-Fi and bring up the *Telegraph* subscription I signed up for, anything to distract me from the conversation I'm about to have with William. It's been fifty years since I ended a relationship, and five weeks since I last saw William; my heart may have recovered from the walk, but it's now beating hard from nerves.

'You need to tell him in person, Joan,' I hear Pamela tell me. *'Enough excuses. You may be a thoroughly Modern Millie these days, but you haven't lost your manners.'*

'Yes, yes,' I'd agreed, though it took me several more days to find the courage to message him to ask to meet. When I did, he replied immediately, with flower and heart emojis and a profusion of words that made me dread our meeting even more.

Unable to concentrate on the 'newspaper', I tap on Facebook instead, my finger hovering above the unopened message Kathleen sent me almost three months ago. With a sharp intake of breath, I tap on it.

> Joan, hello from NYC! How wonderful to see you on Facebook. I've searched for you often over the years. I'd love to reconnect, hear all about how life worked out for you. Please do get in touch. Your old friend, Kathleen

Reading her words, I scold myself for not opening the message earlier. Her note sounds exactly like the woman whom I called my best friend for over two decades. Someone loyal and sweet and true. Someone I have no reason to fear.

I hesitate, as I start my reply, uncertain how to summarise thirty-five years of life into a few short sentences.

Dear Kathleen, I begin, reminding myself of what I told

Jess, to start with the simple, small things and work from there. *Greetings from Notting Hill!*

I'm considering what to write next when I become aware of someone standing at the opposite side of the table.

'William,' I say, looking up and fumbling with my phone, lost as I was in another world, or at least another part of my life.

'Joan,' he beams.

I stand to greet him.

'Don't get up,' he fusses, bending to kiss me on the cheek, then he hands me a breath-taking selection of flowers. My nerves turn to guilt.

'How are you?' he asks, after I've thanked him profusely and he's ordered a flat white. He sits opposite me, leaning in.

'Quite well,' I tell him, rather underplaying the highs and lows of the last five weeks.

'You look marvellous,' he replies, his eyes shining warmly.

'Thank you,' I say, sitting a little further back.

'I've thought of you a lot.'

'Yes,' I say, laughing gently, implying that his messages made no secret of that.

'Have I overdone it?' he asks, still smiling. 'Bombarded you with messages and affection?'

I use the arrival of his coffee to gather myself.

'Not at all,' I fib, not wanting to hurt his feelings but knowing I must be cruel to be kind. 'But perhaps it feels as if the relationship should be one of friendship, rather than anything more.'

'I'd very much like there to be more,' he says, and his eyes glisten.

I pause for long enough, holding my nerve, that the shine begins to fade.

'I enjoyed both our meetings, very much,' I clarify as he edges away from the table. 'And I'm most grateful to you for encouraging me out and about after a difficult few years.'

'But?' he asks bravely.

I fiddle with the handle of my cup, thinking of what Pamela said about Jess, about needing to put her relationship with Liam to bed, aware that I need to do the same. 'It seems one cannot enter a relationship without first addressing those that came before.'

'Indeed,' he says, smiling through the disappointment. 'But let it be said, should you change your mind, I'll be right here, waiting.'

'Thank you,' I smile, grateful for his kindness, wondering if I'll ever have it in me to fully revisit the past.

35

JESS

My heart hammers heavily in my chest as I wait for Liam to answer his door. Pretty much every inch of me wants to turn and run, to not face the past and the heartache and shame, but I know, deep down, that if I don't confront him, I'll never move on. I'll be stuck here for ever, wondering why.

'Jess!' he says, on opening the door, and I swear the blood drains so rapidly from his thin face that there's a risk he could pass out.

'Liam,' I say, my voice nervy and breathy but my posture strengthening as I realise that he looks more frightened than I feel.

'How did you . . .?' He runs a hand over his short mousy hair.

I cast him a look of 'Really, you're the one asking questions?'

'Right,' he says, and he opens the door wider, inviting me in.

In the hallway, I squeeze past two bikes. Liam shows me into the living room, where two old sofas surround a tiled gas fireplace. Damp laundry hangs everywhere, filling the room with an unpleasant smell not dissimilar to wet dog.

'Coffee?' he asks, gesturing for me to sit down.

'No thanks,' I reply, pretty sure the mugs won't be that clean.

I sit at the far end of the smaller sofa, my hands shoved in the pockets of my gilet; he sits at the furthest end of the larger sofa.

'I figured you'd find me one day,' he says.

'And you didn't think it would be better to call?'

He looks at his feet, clad in socks I recognise, ones that I put in his stocking the Christmas before last having spent ages deciding which ones to buy in Selfridges.

'I picked up the phone so many times.'

'What stopped you?'

He pauses. Swallows hard. 'Shame.'

'Shame?' I ask, baffled, wondering why *he* would be feeling shame.

His turquoise eyes, ones I used to gaze into, dreaming my life away, scan my face.

'I've thought so many times about what you must have thought . . .' he tails off, as if this is his demon, not mine.

'*You've* thought. What about me, Liam? What do you think I've been doing?' I stare at him, willing him to answer, but he doesn't. 'You stole everything from me: my money, my home, my security and future. But more than that, you stole my confidence, my trust. Everything.'

I push my hands even further into my pockets even though there's nowhere deeper for them to go. 'You turned me into a ghost of myself.'

For a moment, as Liam stares at the floor, ashen, it seems as if my words mean nothing. That he has no remorse for what he did or compassion for how he left me. But then I notice that his eyes are full of tears, and I see the man I fell in love with, the man I knew, not the man I've created in my head: a scam artist, a fraudster, a monster who played me for everything I had.

As the tears spill down his cheeks, it occurs to me that he is not living the life I assumed he was: a fancy car, an expensive watch, a swanky pad in the city. And it hits me that something has happened beyond my imaginings.

'What happened, Liam? Why did you do it?'

He wipes his face, rubbing his hands down over his pallid cheeks.

'I was in debt,' he says quietly, man enough to look me straight in the eye. 'Serious debt.'

'How?' I ask, trying to think back to what he had then that would indicate he was overspending, but I come up with nothing.

'Little things, really: drinks, dinners, weekends away, a purple sofa . . .' he says, and I'm reminded of having to cancel the order, when he left me without a home.

I pause, wondering how any of that could amount to almost thirty thousand pounds. A thousand pounds a month for almost three years.

'I loved you so much, Jess,' he stops, corrects himself, '*love* you so much. I went out of my way to make sure you wanted for nothing. But it got out of hand: debt collectors, letters, phone calls. Several guys came to the flat. It was terrifying.'

'But what about your job?' I ask. 'You had a good salary, nice perks.'

'All of which went on rent, bills, travel, food. It wasn't enough for me to impress you.'

'I don't understand.' I feel my brow crease. 'I never wanted things. I only ever wanted you.'

He scoffs. Closes his eyes. Breathes deeply. 'I didn't think I was enough.'

We sit quietly while I try to make sense of him not being the villain I'd created in my mind, that he's the same person I knew then. It's just that he made one big mistake, and it hits me, that's his shame, not mine.

'I wanted to give you the world, but when I couldn't, when the opportunity came to intersect the flat deposit and pay everything off,' he pauses. 'I don't know, I barely understand it myself. I stayed late at work one night, creating a counterfeit letter, one that looked exactly like the solicitor's letterhead just with different account details, an account you didn't know I had. It felt like the only route out. Even though I knew it would break you. Break me. Break us.'

I release a long, heavy sigh, and wipe my eyes of tears.

'I can't imagine the pain I caused you,' he says, with an expression that burns with honesty. A look of longing and regret that tells me everything I need to know. This is the true version of events. A world away from what I'd created in my head.

'It's been almost the worst point of my life,' I tell him, knowing that he understands nothing could match the loss of Mum.

'I wish I could undo it all,' he whispers.

I think of my year at Debs' house, of all the laughter and life her little family provided, and now Joan and our adventures together. And for the first time, I realise, even if I could wave a wand and undo it all, I wouldn't.

'Life would have been nice for us both in that flat, with our jobs and friends,' I say. 'But that would have been it, I think. I'm not sure we would have moved each other forward. I reckon we might have stagnated, and begun to resent each other.'

He looks at me as if this isn't something he's ever thought, and I see it from his point of view. Living here in a dank house share, probably with two other guys, the life we had planned together was far better than this. I begin to feel sorry for him. And the realisation creeps over me that Liam did me the greatest favour, cutting me loose, forcing me to start over, to create a new version of my life, one that is already ten times better, and feels as if it might be about to get a whole lot better still.

'I wish you the best, Liam,' I say, getting up from the couch. He remains seated. 'And for what it's worth, I forgive you. You owe me nothing.'

Dear Mr PO Box,

*Forgive me if this comes across as too keen,
but are you able to meet?*

CineGirl

Dear CineGirl,

Soon! I promise.

Mr PO Box

36

JOAN

'Joan? Are you home? I need to tell you something,' Jess calls from the hallway, not having found me downstairs.

'Joan?' she calls again, her footsteps bounding up the stairs, until she reaches the middle landing, where I hear her stop.

'In here,' I call tentatively, no one ever having joined me in the nursery before. Parker couldn't bring himself to come in, and I always kept Edward out, dreading the questions he might ask.

'Hi,' she says, then her tone changes from excited to tentative, no doubt confused by the sight of an old lady sitting on a rocking chair in a nursery, dabbing her eyes. 'What's going on?'

As she enters the room, it hits me that Joy wouldn't have been much older than Jess is now. Thirty-five. I was forty-four at the time I had her, 'too old to be having another child', one doctor had told me, 'you're asking for complications.' But I'd longed for a second, hoped for a girl, and been beside myself with happiness when the scan confirmed we were having one.

'Let's call her Joy,' I'd said to Parker that evening, and he'd agreed, he having chosen Edward's name, and seeing that Joy was already etched on my heart.

I look at Jess, who's sitting cross-legged on the floor, and wonder what Joy would have looked like now. Would her hair be thin like mine or thick like Parker's? Her eyes were just like mine. Parker said it the moment she was born, 'She'll be beautiful, just like her mother.' Not that I ever was, but I imagine Joy would have been, and it was kind of Parker to try in that moment, the pregnancy having brought us closer.

'Joan?'

I sit quietly a moment longer, fiddling with a corner of my cotton handkerchief. And then I explain, unnecessarily, how I couldn't put out anything of Joy's after her death, that to have done so would have been to erase almost everything I had left of my baby girl.

And then I say it. The secret I've kept entirely to myself for thirty-seven years spills out of me.

'Parker wasn't Edward's father.'

Jess's brow furrows deeply; my hands turn cold.

'I don't understand,' she whispers.

'It's Joseph. Joe is Edward's father. That night I told you about . . . at the Barbican.'

She's quiet, absorbing what I've said, probably formulating which question to ask first.

'Does Ed know?'

I shake my head.

'Joseph?'

'If he suspected, he never said. Or not that I know of,' I add, thinking of all those unopened letters.

She's quiet again, her head bobbing slightly.

I wonder if now is the time to tell her that Joe has passed.

'What about Parker, did he know?'

'No,' I answer, thinking back to that time, when we'd been trying for years to conceive our first child. 'Back then, men rarely attended ante-natal appointments. I was able to fudge the dates enough that he wouldn't have known.'

'Did you know straight away, when you learnt you were pregnant, that the baby was Joseph's?'

'I couldn't be a hundred percent sure,' I say, not wanting to share my guile of sleeping with my husband the night he returned two days later. 'But when Edward arrived and I saw his eyes, so like Joe's, inky and deep, I knew. Nothing had ever been clearer.'

She ponders what I've just told her then asks, 'And you never told Joseph, or thought about leaving Parker?'

'I thought about it more often than I care to remember. But there were so many reasons not to, far more than there were to do so. There was the initial joy of Edward after so many years trying for a child; then Parker wasn't particularly well for the first year of Edward's life, he had a lot of stress at work, and the time was never right. The shame it would have brought on my husband was too much, and my family would have disowned me; and then there was the fact that I knew Joe never wanted children, that as much as he desired me, he didn't want a wife and child. And I knew if I went back to him, he might reject us, as I rejected him.'

Jess pauses for a moment, her eyes teeming with thoughts. 'And you've lived with this secret without telling *anyone* for thirty-seven years?'

'I know it seems shocking, but, as you know, life has a way of burying secrets. First there was the shock of being a mother, being robbed of the life you knew, of becoming a new version of yourself. Then there was Joy's death and Parker leaving, then the battle of being a single mother, grieving parent and teacher. Hit after hit heaped more layers on the secret, until there was almost nothing to be seen of it, other than the occasional look or expression from Edward that would throw me right back to the memory of that night at the Barbican and the utter relief, and guilt, that came from it. That's the reason I suffered the panic attacks, the reason I became stuck in the house for so long after my last pupil left; the great tower I'd been stacking up all those years collapsed on top of me, and I couldn't get out from under it.'

'What made now feel like the time to reveal it?' Jess asks.

'Parker's death, and Edward's heartbreak at never having known his father. And, of course, all the chat of Joe, and your search for him.'

I nibble my lip, uncertain if I'll ever have the courage to tell Edward that not only did he miss knowing Parker; he's now missed the opportunity to know his real father too.

'Forgive me,' I say, having indulged my thoughts too long. 'You wanted to tell me something, what was it?'

Jess scoops up her hair. 'It's not important, Joan. It'll keep,' she smiles almost knowingly . . .

37

JESS

As much I was desperate to tell Joan about Joseph being alive and well, that he'd replied to my advert, I couldn't bring myself to say it in that moment. I figured with her emotions being so fragile that she might not receive the news well, that I'd back her into a corner. So I decided to sit on it, to wait until the time was right to tell her about Joseph's reply to my advert, and also to show her his letter of regrets. Instead, we spoke about Liam, and how grateful I was to her and Pamela for tracking him down, and ultimately putting my demons to rest. But all of that feels like another world away, as I wait for Zinnia to answer her front door – a bright pink door on a four-storey Notting Hill townhouse.

'Jess!' she cries, flinging her arms up in the air then wrapping them round me, and it feels so good to be back together. 'How are you?' She clutches my arms, examines every inch of me, from my cropped long-sleeve top to my high-waisted shorts. 'You look thin. Too thin. Come in and let me feed you.'

She leads me into the hall, her bold, vintage kaftan flowing behind her, the walls full of gilt-framed paintings and brightly coloured shelves crammed with books. From the hall she leads me into the 'parlour' at the front, a room which looks out over the street and into one of the lush private neighbourhood gardens.

'Take a seat,' she says, pointing at an ornate armchair, re-upholstered in shocking pink velvet. 'Let me bring you refreshments.'

Zinnia disappears into the hall, giving me a chance to take in my surroundings. The room is huge and painted rose pink with dark framed artwork covering almost every inch of wall. There's furniture everywhere: chaises longues in Liberty prints, oriental armoires, quirky side tables and lamps of every colour. My trainers look out of place on the thick antique rug and my high street fashion, reflected back at me in a gold mirror framed with gilded peacocks, looks cheap. I could sit here all day and still not take it all in.

'Tell me how you've been,' she says on her return, placing a tray of iced tea and two bowls of peaches and ice cream on the table between us before sitting down.

'So-so,' I admit. 'I'm still struggling with losing the cinema. Maybe once it's up and running as an I-work I'll feel better, but with it just sitting there, all boarded up, it's hard to move on.'

'In my experience, these things take time. I promise, you won't feel this way for ever,' she says, handing me a dainty emerald glass bowl. 'Have you seen Mariko?'

I tell her that I bumped into her the other day when I was out running. 'She told me Daniel's exhibition has been pulled. The space Charlie had booked won't be open for a while still and he can't find another at short notice.'

'It'll all work out!' says Zinnia, through a mouthful of ice cream. 'He has talent, that boy. That particular door has closed, but another bigger and better one will open.'

'Let's hope so,' I nod, contemplating if I'll ever find my door.

'What's happening with you and that Irish character? What did you call him, Connor?'

'Cormac,' I giggle, having missed Zinnia's straight-talking ways.

'Right, Cormac.'

I tell her we've been seeing each other, that he's keen to define our relationship, me less so. I leave out the part about him not showing up the other day and having been on radio silence since, which is so unlike him.

'No sex appeal?' she asks. 'No oomph?'

'Not really,' I say, feeling guilty for admitting it, but she's right, Cormac, like Liam, neither sets my world on fire nor challenges me. For all his likeability, I know he's never going to be 'the one'.

'When I met my husband, I was courting someone else. But then I met him and, boom! It was like two stars colliding. There was no mistaking it. When it happens, you'll know.'

'How?' I want to ask but don't because Zinnia has already moved on.

'Now, I had something important for you,' she mutters, getting up to look for it. I'm left thinking about how Ed was so sure I should meet Mr PO Box, but how I can't imagine anyone giving me the feels the way Ed did when we first met.

Zinnia finds what she's looking for in an old writing bureau and returns, handing me a vintage postcard of Laurel and Hardy. 'Call this number and ask for Phil.'

'Who's Phil?'

'He's an old friend, a film producer. Very successful,' she says, a knobbly finger raised to mark the point. 'You tell him Zinnia sent you. He'll make sure you're looked after.'

I leave Zinnia's walking on air, buoyed by her energy; I even stop at a red phone box to call Phil to set up a meeting. In no time I've arrived at Hyde Park for Oscar's birthday party, which Charlie kindly invited Debs and me to join. I'm walking into the Diana Memorial Playground where I catch sight of Charlie and Marina supervising the kids on the pirate ship, and Debs, sitting next to Ed on a bench, which feels both strange and surprisingly normal.

'Should you be here?' I ask, stooping to hug her. Even her face looks puffy now.

'Day release for good behaviour,' she grins, clearly delighted to be out of her bed and house.

'Hi,' says Ed, standing to gently kiss me on the cheek, his hand placed lightly on my upper arm, giving Debs the chance to give me a 'what the hell is this?' look. And I shoot her one back that says, 'weird, right?' 'You look all lit up inside.'

I explain about Zinnia's film contact, how he'd be happy to consider me for a Production Assistant role, that we've set a date to meet.

'Oh my God, Jess!' shrieks Debs. 'That's like a total gift from upstairs.'

'I know, right?' I beam.

'Does being a Production Assistant feel right?' asks Ed.

'It would mean a route into becoming a producer without having to pay to study for years,' I say, pretty stoked about the idea.

'And you'd like that, more than being the manager at the cinema?'

I sit for a minute, mulling it over, watching Oscar and Debs' kids walking the rope bridges together.

'I can't believe I'm saying it, but I think so. I think producing is where my heart's at.'

'Jeez, Jess, haven't I been saying this for ages!' cries Debs.

'I know, I know, but there's been a lot going on,' I say, which feels like the understatement of the century. 'And besides, there's no guarantee I'll get the job. It's just an introduction.'

Debs gets up to check in on the kids, leaving me alone with Ed on the bench.

'Did you reach out to your lonely heart guy?' he asks, right off the bat.

'He told me, "soon".'

'Did he indeed,' he smiles knowingly, a smile that transforms his face. 'And how do you feel about that?'

'I'm cool with it. I trust him. Whenever he's ready.'

A moment sits with us, not uncomfortably this time.

'I was thinking about what you said the other day about me being a closed book,' he offers.

'Were you?' I ask, kind of liking that he would take something I said to heart, which seems so unlike him.

'Mum and I never spoke much growing up, about anything really, but especially not my dad or little sister.' He scrutinises his nails. 'It was easier not to bring them up, never knowing how they might affect her mood. Since I was tiny, I've kept myself busy on purpose, to avoid the silences.'

'I can't imagine,' I say, my heart aching for him, particularly knowing what I know. 'Mum and I spoke about everything.'

'Joan's always pushed things under the rug, told the stories she's wanted to be true, stories that have become her reality. And with me going to boys' school most of my life, I was never destined to be the best communicator!' He laughs, but his eyes, full of anguish, tell me he doesn't find it funny. 'I can't imagine what it would be to have a mother who I could talk with openly.'

'But you guys are doing a bit better, right? Since the funeral?' I ask, realising for the first time how lonely Ed's upbringing must have been, with a mother so closed off from the world, fighting to survive. It's no wonder he has so many barriers.

'We're trying, and that feels even more important now. But I'm not certain a lifetime of secrets is all that easy to unpick.'

He looks at me with a resigned smile.

I fight the urge to tell him about Joseph.

'I have a feeling Joan was the best mother she could be, under the circumstances.'

'I don't blame her for being as she was; it made me who I am,' he says. 'I just wish I'd known my father. Not knowing him left a gaping hole inside me. The only way

283

I know how to fill it is through keeping busy, trying to be the man I believe he was, even though it doesn't really make me happy.' He pauses, casts his gaze out over the playground. 'Sometimes I wonder who I might have been if they'd not lost Joy and stayed together, that there's someone else I could have been.'

I let his thoughts land, thinking of my own father, and how, given I feel so much like Mum, he rarely enters my consciousness.

'Do you share these things with Izzy?' I ask.

'How do you know about Izzy?'

'We met, remember, on Coronation Day, plus Joan told me about her.'

'Right,' he says with a roll of his eyes. 'But if Mum had listened, she'd know that Izzy and I aren't together any longer. We're just friends.'

'What happened?' I ask, trying to ignore the flutter in my stomach, and wondering who the someone is who's been helping him through the loss of Parker, if not Izzy.

'Izzy is someone who should fit me – do you know what I mean? She's ambitious, beautiful, has a great family. There's nothing about her that's "wrong", and because of that we've been on and off for years.'

'Are you now fully "off"?' I ask, thinking about the conversation I had with Mr PO Box about the wrong person fitting at the right time, and vice versa, and it occurs to me that he too has spoken about a different version of himself.

Ed stops. Turns to me. Scans my eyes.

'Completely.'

My eyes ask him why.

284

'Someone else came into my life, and I knew immediately that Izzy couldn't be perfect for me, because the other someone was.'

Neither one of us speaks for a few seconds, he lost in thought, me lost in the depth of his eyes.

'Did you get with the other someone?' I say, snapping myself out of my daze.

'Not yet,' he smiles kind of sadly though his eyes sparkle. 'You know, I'm kind of enjoying spending—'

Ed is cut off when I spot Debs stumble and then throw up in the sand around the pirate ship.

'Debs,' I yell, running to her. I help her to the floor.

Marina joins us, feeling for Debs' pulse. 'She needs to go to the hospital.'

'I'll get my car,' says Ed, running off, and even though it's totally not allowed, he appears minutes later with his car parked at the entrance to the play park, the back door flung open.

'We'll stay here with the kids,' says Charlie, and I hesitate, thinking they should probably come with me, but Marina insists:

'It's fine, Jess. We've food and drinks and sunscreen. They'll barely notice she's gone.'

Ed drives as I watch Debs, while calling Mike on her phone.

'He's an hour away,' I say, having told Mike we're en route to St Mary's.

'I'll let Charlie know when we're there,' Ed says, navigating urgently through the traffic of the Bayswater Road and on to Sussex Gardens.

We arrive at the entrance to A&E within minutes, Ed

285

dropping us both and telling me he'll be in as soon as he's managed to find a parking spot. I grab an abandoned wheelchair and put Debs in it, pushing her up the long ramp.

Before I can even stop at reception, a passing nurse clocks Debs and takes us straight to a bay. Within moments a doctor in scrubs arrives to assess her.

'We need to deliver the baby,' he says without an ounce of hesitation.

'Her husband is less than an hour away.'

'It can't wait that long,' he says, with a look that tells me this has to happen now.

Ed arrives just as Debs is being wheeled off for her C-section.

'How is she?' he asks.

'Not great,' I tell him, feeling the tears coming, and before I know what's happening, he's holding me, my tears soaking his thin T-shirt, my cheek pressed against his chest.

'I need to let Mike know what's happening,' I say, pulling away, blotting my eyes with the back of my hand, trying to gain some composure.

'Sure,' he says, as we walk towards the theatres together, me messaging Mike from Debs' phone, Ed with his arm round my shoulder.

It's not long until Mike finds us. We leave him to wait for Debs, while Ed and I go and collect the kids to take them home. As we're driving back to the park, both of us quiet, Ed says to me, 'Charlie told me he had to cancel Daniel's exhibition.'

'Right,' I reply vaguely, my thoughts still with Debs.

'I was thinking, work on the Portland is delayed. How about he uses that as an exhibition space instead?'

For a moment I think that I must be dreaming: Debs being unwell, Ed racing us to the hospital, and now he's offering to help Daniel too?

'Are you serious?' I ask, looking at his classical profile as he drives.

He turns briefly towards me, his features as strong and soulful as the day I first met him, and my breath catches the way it had then too.

'Anything for you,' he says slowly, as he pulls up again outside the play park.

'Thank you,' I say, unable or unwilling to break his gaze.

'It's my pleasure,' he says, leaning in towards me, reaching a hand softly to my face, and for a brief moment I'm certain we're going to kiss until there's a bang on the window, which startles me, and I turn to find Ash with his face squashed against it, his tongue licking the glass.

38

JOAN

'How are they?' I ask when Jess returns from taking a phone call from Mike in the hall. She pulls out a chair at the kitchen table and I pour us both a glass of wine.

'Debs is recovering. The baby's in neonate intensive care.'

'I'm so sorry, Jess. You must be dreadfully worried.'

'It's Mike I feel sorry for. There's nothing he can do but wait.'

As I join her at the table I'm hit with a sudden flash-back of when Parker came to visit me after the death of Joy. How he never spoke, or held my hand. He just sat beside me, completely bereft. His role of protector, stolen from him.

'In my experience the father takes things far harder,' I say.

She looks up, her eyes on mine. 'Forgive me,' she says, 'this must be painful for you, too.'

'The circumstances are different,' I reassure her, though she's right, it is painful knowing something of the desperation Debs and Mike must be feeling. 'Joy's birth was straightforward. She was well, supposedly.'

I go on to tell Jess about Joy being born in the morning, an easy labour, only a few hours long, and that we'd spent the afternoon gazing into each other's eyes. Parker brought Edward in to meet his sister early that evening, and I'd seen him afresh. Even though he was only two, he looked, comparatively, grown; a person in his own right, and someone who was as much a part of me as my own beating heart. I couldn't remember loving Edward more, even Parker, and now we had Joy.

'What happened?' she asks quietly.

'Parker and Edward left, I slept. Joy was attended to through the night by the midwives. Something they did back then, to allow the mother to rest before months of sleepless nights set in.

'The following day I spent the whole day with Joy, chatting with the other new mums on the ward and sharing stories. It was idyllic really. Meals brought to our bedsides, tiny babies asleep, companionship.

'We went to sleep that night around nine. Joy woke and I told the midwife I'd like to tend to her myself. No need for them to check on me . . .'

I drift off, uncertain if I can tell the rest of the story. A story I've never told.

'In the morning,' I begin then stop to gather myself. Jess places her hand on mine. 'In the morning, she was gone,' I whisper, swallowing back a surge of grief and pinching the bridge of my nose.

I concentrate on my breathing, and shake off the inevitable tears.

'She had a seizure in the night while I slept.' I pause, wrestling with my emotions. 'I had told the midwives not to check on her, that I would do it, that I'd look after her.'

Jess grips my hand. 'You couldn't have known, Joan.'

'If they'd checked in the night, they might have noticed in time to save her.'

'No,' she says, shaking her head.

'We don't know, Jess. Nobody can ever know.'

'And you've had to live with that,' she says quietly.

'I've learnt to live with it in my own way. Told myself the stories that eased my guilt, that she knew nothing of it. But deep down, I know there is no knowing if she suffered. That's the most painful part of all.'

I pause for a moment, realising that it must be difficult to hear my story, as it is to recount it.

'Knowing is much easier to live with than not knowing, don't you think? I'm glad you now know what happened with Liam.'

'I wish I'd confronted him when it happened, and saved myself a lot of agonising,' she admits.

'You have no reason to feel ashamed.'

'I know that now. Thank you, Joan.'

'In many ways, losing Parker, imagining how our life might have been together as a family of four, has made me realise that no version of a life is perfect. At least the ways things are, Joy is forever perfect in my mind.'

I'm mulling over how I wish I could say the same of my relationship with Edward, when Humphrey releases a long, loud yawn.

'Are we boring you?' I ask him and Jess laughs, both of us relaxing.

'I'm not sure if now is the right time, but . . . in the spirit of knowing,' Jess says, reaching into her backpack and pulling out a folded newspaper.

She slides the paper to me and points with a jewelled nail at the little three-line advert.

JNY19, I'D LOVE TO REMINISCE
NYC anytime, anywhere.
JO22 xx

'But this can't be,' I say, struggling to understand what's in front of me.

'Joseph replied, Joan. There's an open door, if you want it.'

I lift my phone from the table and go to the tab I haven't been able to close since first seeing it. 'Joe passed last year,' I tell her, handing her the phone.

'What?' she says, and she begins typing, muttering about how she knows she's 'breaking the pact', but searching and scrolling regardless, until she finds what she's looking for.

'Posted two days ago. Proof that he's still alive,' she says, showing me a video of Joe, alive and well, playing his guitar on stage in a packed bar. 'The obituary must have been for another Joseph Blume.'

'Oh my,' I say, my breath catching, staring first at the video and then at the advert, the tips of my fingers tingling. A relief, the likes of which I've never felt before, washes over me, followed by fear rising through me at the prospect of New York City, and how Joe might react to all I have to tell should we meet.

'Would you like to be alone?' Jess asks.

'Perhaps that would be best,' I say, my eyes focused solely on the few sparing words of his advert, which somehow manage to embody his free spirit entirely.

'For what it's worth,' she says, getting up from the table. 'I think it's time you saw him.'

'Yes,' I whisper, as she leaves.

On hearing Jess's bedroom door click shut, I look at my phone again.

'Facebook,' I mutter, scanning the little icons on the screen, my heart racing frantically, then opening the message I've drafted to Kathleen.

'Perhaps Jess is right,' I say to myself. 'Perhaps it is time that I caught up with the past. Put the last fifty years to rest, if for no other reason than Edward.'

Dear Kathleen,

Greetings from Notting Hill!

I'm planning a trip to NYC and would very much like to see you.

Are you in touch with Joseph?

Joan

Joan,

I can't tell you how happy it makes
me to hear from you, and to learn
that you're coming to the city!

It's been such a long time since I saw Joseph,
he moved just over a year ago now,
but I can try to reach out to him.

When do you arrive?

K x

Kathleen,

We arrive on August 5th.

J x

Joan,

Send me your flight details.
I'll collect you from the airport.

K x

August 2023

Dear CineGirl,

Would you like to meet this Saturday, 12.30 p.m.? Do you know the Meeting Place statue at St Pancras? I thought we could meet there, stroll along the canal, maybe have something to eat at Coal Drop Yard.

  I hope you can make it.

Mr PO Box

39

JESS

Cormac and I both knew something was off just by the nature of how we arranged to meet. I set it up instead of him, in an unexciting café, at mid-morning, when neither of us would want to eat, just knock back a brew. And though we both knew it was the end on the phone, neither of us said anything, politely playing the game.

'I'm sorry again that I didn't show at the RFH,' he opens, kissing me on the cheek rather than the lips.

'It's fine,' I say casually as we sit at a Formica table. He explained over the phone that he got stuck on the Tube. 'I bumped into Ed while I was down there.'

His brow wrinkles. 'Cinema Ed?'

'Yeah,' I answer, my tone implying we're no longer total enemies.

'Are you telling me you're frenemies now?' he asks, kind of delightedly.

I hesitate, one, because I've no real idea what's going on with Ed, and two, because I don't want to make Cormac feel bad.

His phone pings between us. He looks down.

'Who is that?' I ask, realising that more often than not when we've been together that same alert has gone off repeatedly.

He sighs, clearly preparing himself to confess something. 'My ex,' he says, not proudly.

I urge him to go on.

'We split up a few months before I met you. Things had gotten kind of heavy. We needed to figure out what we felt for each other, so we decided to take a break, see other people. If I'm honest,' he says, looking up sorrowfully, 'I guess I put some of that on you.'

'Like you were trying on clothes, to see if they fit?' I ask, and he laughs.

'Because you hope they might fit, right? Because you want to figure out if there's something more comfortable, something that makes you feel more "you".'

'Did your old clothes turn out to be the comfiest?'

He scrunches his nose and nods. 'I'm sorry, Jess. I never meant to drag you into this.'

'It's all good,' I say, sitting back in my chair, gently playing with my mug of tea. 'If I'm honest, I think I've been doing something similar.'

'How so?'

I explain about Liam and needing to find a way back into dating, and how I confused Cormac's steadiness for something else. And I tell him about Mr PO Box, and now, most confusingly of all, Ed.

'Sounds like you're more confused than I was,' he smiles.

'Call it quits, while we're ahead?'

He reaches across the table and places a kiss on my lips, drawing away with a look full of warmth, of regret but also of finality.

'I'll miss you, Jess Harris,' he says, clasping my hand.

'I'll miss you, too.'

'Remember,' he says, releasing his grasp, 'love is never straightforward. On paper my ex shouldn't work at all, but despite her flaws, which are many, she's still "the one".'

'That one person you can't imagine existing without,' I say more to myself than to him, my mind flitting between Mr PO Box and Ed.

'Are you doing OK?' asks Ed, after I've given him an update on how Debs and her beautiful baby daughter are home and doing much better, *and* how I just broke up with Cormac.

'I'm meeting Mr PO Box tomorrow, so the timing was right,' I tell him, hoping he'll pick up on the hesitation in my voice that tells him I'm in a total muddle.

'Where are you meeting him?'

'The Meeting Statue at King's Cross,' I say, and he nods approvingly, paying for a bag of cherries from an organic Kent farmer at the market.

'Romantic,' he says.

'I think so,' I reply, unable to tell what he's thinking, but not wanting to bring up the near kiss in the car, in case I somehow misread the signals. After we collected the kids, the topic was off the table, their incessant chatter not giving us a chance. And with Mike and Debs at the hospital, I had no choice but to stay at Debs' to make the kids dinner, even though I wanted more than any-thing to be with Ed.

'I wonder what he's like . . .' Ed ponders.

'He could be anyone,' I say, a bubble of nervous excite-ment growing in my stomach, conscious for the first time that Mr PO Box could be any one of the guys strolling through the market right now.

'He could even be someone you know,' Ed says gently.

'I doubt that,' I laugh. 'What would the odds be?'

He scratches his chin. 'Well . . . London has a popula-tion of what, nine or ten million?'

'I guess.'

'Half of whom are men, so let's call that five million, maybe a tenth of whom are in their thirties, and only half of those are single. What does that make?'

'Two hundred and fifty thousand.'

'Well, there you have it. The odds of you knowing him are about 1 in 250,000.'

'So, pretty unlikely then.'

'Pretty unlikely,' he nods, a little hush falling between us as we walk through the stalls. 'How many single guys do you know in the city?'

I think for a moment. 'I only know you, and Daniel!'

'Huh,' he says, and he eyes an old ink well and foun-tain pen, considers it for a while. 'Then it will be a wonderful surprise!'

'Yes it will,' I say, a small doubt creeping in.

'Are you excited?'

'I am,' I answer cautiously, not wanting him to think that I've forgotten his kindness with Debs, not feeling quite as excited as I might if it hadn't been for *that* moment between us.

'He's got you hooked,' he smiles, eating a cherry.

'I guess he has,' I say, and I think of Joan and how hooked she's been on Joseph all her life.

'Ed, are you aware of your mum's ex, Joseph?'

He shakes his head. 'I knew there was someone before my father but nothing more than that. Like I said, Mum and I aren't really ones for heart-to-hearts.'

'I've been searching for him, via the classifieds,' I tell him. 'And he's been in touch.'

'What does Mum think about that?' he asks, giving nothing away about how he feels about it.

'I've a feeling that she really wants to see him again, to either pick up where they left off, or to be able to close that chapter of her life, but I'm not sure she's decided yet.' I don't mention that I've replied to Joseph, to cover all bases, suggesting a time and place for them to meet during her trip. 'Joan and I have been talking a lot recently about how it's better to know things in life than not. To be armed with all the facts, no matter how hard that is,' I say, preparing the ground should Joan share with Ed the identity of his real father.

'A second chance,' he says deftly.

'Exactly.'

'I'd give anything for one of those.'

'You mean with your dad?'

'In part,' he says, stopping under the canopy of an antique bookstore. 'But something else too . . .'

'What?' I ask, roaming his eyes for some sense of what

he's alluding to, aware that my chest is rising and falling more heavily than it normally does.

'Do you ever think about what might have happened if I'd just met you as Joan's son, and not as the "evil emperor" of I-work?'

I think back to the first time we met at the cinema and how I thought he was the most heart-achingly gorgeous guy I'd ever seen.

'I would have asked you out,' he says, reaching to replace one of my stray curls.

'But that would have been awkward,' I say, not moving. 'If it didn't work out, I mean. We'd have been stuck having to see each other at the house.'

'It would have worked,' he says, his eyes locking on mine.

'How do you know?' I ask, pushing myself not to run, to remain in the moment, to allow myself to open my heart.

'I just know, the way you know,' he says slowly, and then, ever so gently, he brings his lips to mine.

My brow twitches in confusion as Ed kisses me softly, and I wonder if this is my moment, when I'll know the way Zinnia said I would. But how can it be? Just when I'm on the cusp of meeting Mr PO Box, the man whose heart I've fallen for, Ed, the most infuriating but gorgeous man on the planet, is kissing me . . .

'I should go,' I say, pulling away, when the confusion in my mind grows too loud.

'Wait,' he says, reaching for my hand. 'Please forgive me for closing the cinema.'

'Ed, you put me out of a job and destroyed one of London's oldest cinemas.'

300

'But you're in a better place now . . . the knot of life isn't so tight.'

'Where did you . . .' I falter, then stop.

He looks at me enquiringly, willing me to continue.

'I gotta go,' I say, walking away from him, leaving him standing among the stalls and tourists, my heart telling me one thing, my head in a spin.

40

JOAN

'Happy Birthday to You,' sings Jess, not only singing but playing the piano, too, when I arrive downstairs. 'Happy Birthday to You. Happy Birthday Dearest Jo-oan. Happy Birthday to You!'

'Thank you!' I say, clapping my hands together and marvelling at the balloons Jess has festooned about the place, and the 'Happy Birthday' garland she's hung over the mirror. In all my eighty years, no one has ever gifted me a room full of balloons.

'Happy Birthday, Joan,' she says, patting the stool next to her, where there's a gift with my name on it.

'Jess, you shouldn't have,' I say, though inwardly I'm delighted.

'It's not very much. Just something for your trip.'

I open it carefully, having no idea what's inside, trying but failing to push the anxiety that now surrounds the trip to the back of my mind, not having slept a wink since discovering Joe is alive. I've worried myself sick about whether Kathleen will be able to contact him or not, knowing it's now too late to place a reply in the paper.

'A bum bag, just like yours!' I say delightedly, when I unveil the bright little bag.

'Do you like it?'

'I love it!' I say, putting it round the waist of my soft 'waffle' trousers which Jess and I picked out together in town, my first jaunt to Regent Street in years.

'I got it for your trip,' she says, squeezing me. 'It looks cute on you!'

'And you learnt to play "Happy Birthday". You're spoiling me.'

'I've also been practising something else.' She slides out *It's Easy to Play Beethoven*, opening it at *Ode to Joy*. 'I thought it might be nice to celebrate Joy's memory by playing it together, rather than to mourn. What do you think?' she asks tentatively.

'I haven't played in such a long time,' I say uncertainly.

'But it wouldn't hurt to try, right?'

She wiggles her stool along a little, to make room for mine, and starts playing the left hand. I can tell from her concentration that it would mean a lot to her for me to join in, so falteringly I raise my right hand to the keyboard and begin.

It takes me completely by surprise, how quickly it all comes back, and before I know it, the two of us are in full swing, me with goosepimples peppering my arms, just as they had been when I played at the Carnegie Hall for the first time with Joe watching on from the wings.

'One more time?' she asks, turning to me and grinning,

and inwardly I marvel at how far she's come with her piano playing over the last few months, at what extraordinary things can happen when we let go of habits and distractions. And not only that, but how remarkable it is that we both not only survived our challenge but flourished.

'Why not!' I reply, delighting in the joy she's brought to the house and how far she's brought me out of myself. The simple act of playing the piano for pleasure feels momentous in the scheme of how things were.

'This is an unexpected surprise,' says Edward, arriving soon after, when Jess and I have moved on to other beginners' repertoire. Jess makes a momentary mistake on his arrival but is clearly thrilled at the sensation of duetting, and I'm even more thrilled by her enjoyment. He places a cake box on the bureau.

'I didn't hear you come in,' I say, still playing, not wanting to break the moment, until Edward comes over and opens his arms to embrace me where I'm seated.

'Happy Birthday, Mum,' he says, hugging me, his strength cradling my frailty. It's all I can do not to burst into tears.

'Thank you,' I say, as he moves away slowly, and I try to compose myself by focusing on the music, finding my way back into the piece that Jess has continued to play.

Edward sits in the armchair by the doors to the garden, watching us both, his eyes more on Jess than on me. And as he does, a broad smile spreads across his face, one I haven't seen in a long time, if ever, his eyes luminous like Joe's.

We play a little longer, to Jess's first audience, until her fingers tire and she decides it's time for her run. Edward applauds us both as she gets up, and she does a funny little curtsey. And then, just before she heads upstairs to change, she nods towards Edward, her eyes focused on mine, and I know exactly what she's suggesting: that I tell him about Joseph.

'A slice of cake in the garden?' I suggest, and he accepts.

Outside we chat casually for a time, he mostly about work, and me about my trip to New York later this afternoon despite my worries about Joe.

'I can't believe you're taking a trip abroad,' he says, eating his cake on the bench next to the back door. 'How long's it been?'

I'm embarrassed to tell him I haven't left the country since before he was born, though I suspect he knows, that the last plane I was on was with Parker, to attend a rather dreary conference in Frankfurt where I traipsed round the city with all the other bored wives while he talked business. I spent the whole trip trying not to think about the last time I'd been to the city, with Joe in 1970. That visit had been the opposite in every way: we'd woken late, eaten cake for lunch, and schnitzel and beer for supper, before Joseph performed into the wee small hours.

'It's all Pamela and Jess's doing,' I tell him.

'You should take some credit, Mum. You've come a long way these last few months.'

'Yes, I suppose you're right.'

'But why New York? It's not the most likely destination for an octogenarian.'

I pause, wanting to rush in and tell him everything, from meeting Joseph when I was nineteen, to having to give him up, to our liaison nine months before he was born. But I know it would be too much, so I start with small steps.

'You know I spent my twenties in New York.'

'Vaguely,' he says. 'Is it a trip down memory lane?'

'Or an opportunity to explore a second chance,' I suggest carefully.

'At what?'

Again, I hesitate, unsure how much he can absorb on top of the loss of Parker.

'I lived in New York with a boyfriend, before your father,' I say, annoyed with myself once more for referring to Joe as if he was nothing more than a teenage crush. 'More than a boyfriend really . . . we were very much in love.'

I swallow back a surge of emotion, knowing what I must tell him.

'Really?' he says, a look of intrigue in his eyes which enables me to go further.

I tell him about our relationship, how the family disapproved and how I ended up marrying Parker instead.

'But you don't regret marrying Dad, do you?'

This time I really hesitate, considering how to say, *yes, I have regrets*.

'Oh my God,' he says slowly, when my delay in responding provides him with the answer he needs.

'Times were very different,' I'm quick to say. 'Attitudes were changing, but not that rapidly. The decision to marry your father was not entirely my own.'

He pauses for a moment, thinking. 'You told me Dad left because of Joy. Are you telling me he left because of you after all?'

306

'No,' I answer certainly. 'No, that's not it.'

'Then what?'

'We made a go of things, Edward. When Joy was born we were doing quite well. We might have continued to grow if it weren't for our loss as a family. Parker simply couldn't cope with that.'

'Mum, you have to stop calling him Parker,' he says. 'He was my father. Whether you like it or not, he was my dad.'

I don't say anything, but Ed is intuitive enough to know that in my saying nothing I am saying something.

'What aren't you telling me?' he asks, standing up, an awareness now growing that this goes much deeper than he initially thought.

I wait, trying to formulate the words, knowing there are none that will lessen the distress of what I have to tell him.

'Mum?' he asks, his voice breaking. And I know there's no going back.

I take a deep breath and exhale before telling him, 'Edward, Parker wasn't your father. Joseph is.'

41

JESS

I'm returning from my run, in need of a shower and a drink, when I see Ed walking quickly down the garden path.

'Hey,' I say, when our paths cross at the front gate.

'Hey,' he says coolly, barely looking at me, his face gaunt.

'What's up?' I ask, sensing something's off, and I wonder if it's me, if he's miffed that I ran off so soon after we kissed.

He walks east towards the Tube, and I follow.

'Mum just told me about my dad,' he says, walking so fast I can only just keep up.

I sidestep a woman coming towards us. 'I wondered when she would.'

Ed stops sharply, his eyes ablaze. 'You knew?'

'I—' I begin, unable to think fast enough to backtrack, mad at myself for not thinking. He takes off again, turning south on to Pembridge Road.

'You knew and you never told me?' he says, when we're

308

shoulder to shoulder again, weaving our way in and out of the tourists milling towards Portobello.

'It wasn't my secret to tell.'

He stops again, his eyes narrow and sharp. 'You didn't think that was something I should know, that I might be entitled to know who my real father is? You knew I'd been looking for him.'

A wave of guilt runs through me, even though I know I couldn't have betrayed Joan.

'This whole thing's a mess, Jess. And it's all your making.'

'How do you figure that?'

'All your meddling with my mother! I may have wanted to find my father, but not like this. It's all your fault.'

'That's not fair,' I retaliate, as he moves on again. 'Without me, you may never have found out who your father was.'

He stops abruptly. 'I should have trusted my instincts about you,' he says, his whole body tight with anger. 'From the start, I knew you were out to use my mother, that all you ever wanted was a free ride.'

The sting of the verbal slap hits hard. It numbs me.

Ed looks away, knowing he's gone too far.

I should leave but something holds me back.

He runs his hands through his hair furiously, then exhales, gathers himself, the fight beginning to drain.

'I told her it's him or me,' he utters, almost hauntedly.

'Shit, Ed,' I say, my own fury lessening. Despite the row, I can't help feeling sorry for him.

He looks skywards, inhales sharply, physically fighting

his tears, before saying, 'I have to go.' And he turns away from me, away from his mother, then disappears into the crowds.

Despite the run-in with Ed, I still manage to arrive early at St Pancras Station. I pace restlessly up and down the Grand Terrace, trying to focus on my breathing, dividing my time between staring through the glass screen to the Eurostar trains below, and taking laps round the nine-metre-tall statue of a man and woman kissing.

'Great shout,' I think, gazing up at the bronze embrace, impressed but unsurprised that Mr PO Box should think of something so romantic, so reminiscent of *Brief Encounter*, one of my all-time favourite love stories.

I pace some more, fussing with my dress, waiting for Mr PO Box, and thinking of Ed.

I think about how things have been between us recently – his concern for me and his advice, his kindness towards Debs and Daniel – and of how Joan told me once that 'he has a good heart', and his loyalty to Charlie. And I think too of all the coincidences that have happened between us: him being Joan's son, him buying the cinema, of him using the phrase 'magic spark' and 'knot of life', and how he seems to know more about how I feel about Mr PO Box than I do. And as I wonder how it is that he knows what he knows, I find myself distracted by the thought of our kiss and then, of our argument, and I wish above all else that it had never happened.

As I look at the huge clock on the wall, reading twelve-forty, I wonder if I'm angry at Ed, or if I feel sorry for him, or guilty for not telling him about Joseph, or if it's a

310

big jumble of the three that all the analysing in the world won't unpick right now.

Eventually, I sit at the base of the statue and try not to worry about Ed, or Mr PO Box being late. I remember Joan telling me how she often had to wait for Joseph to arrive, so I do the same, watching the passers-by, most of them on their phones, and I reflect on the last few months and how far both Joan and I have come. Four months ago, I couldn't have waited two minutes without digging out my phone and mindlessly scrolling; now I can pass whole swathes of time without it.

By the time I check the clock again, it's one-thirty, and I know in my heart that the man I'd hoped might turn out to be my own romantic hero, isn't coming.

42

JOAN

'Jess, thank goodness,' says Pamela, who's been prowling around the kitchen and garden for the last half an hour. 'Maybe you can talk some sense into her.'

'What's going on?' Jess asks, putting down her keys on the table where I'm sitting. She looks out of sorts, rattled in some way.

'She says she can't go to New York after all,' declares Pamela, as if I've just pulled out of the NATO treaty rather than a short break.

'Why not?' Jess asks supportively, sitting down next to me.

'I spoke to Edward,' I begin, and Jess inhales in a way that suggests she already knows.

'I saw him,' she confirms.

'How was he?'

Her head moves from side to side, 'As well as you might expect, under the circumstances.'

'He doesn't want me to go. He needs time,' I tell her,

the image of Edward's shock, his eyes so full of fury, imprinted in my mind.

'Can somebody please tell me what's going on?' Pamela interrupts, pulling out a seat at the table and joining us, though I can tell she's anything but ready to sit still. She keeps looking at her watch, no doubt wondering just how much longer she has before she categorically has to leave for the airport.

I give Jess the nod to explain about Joseph, her finding him after all these years, and how he's also Edward's father.

'Joan Armitage, you never cease to amaze me!' says Pamela, without any indication of judgement, possibly, dare I say it, with even a hint of respect.

'Now do you see why I can't possibly go to New York? How could I betray Edward's wishes at a time like this? He forbade me to go.'

'Joan,' says Jess, wriggling a little in her chair. 'Ed's a grown man. You don't have to protect him any more. This is your life. You have to put yourself first, not your son.'

I smile at Jess's naïvety. 'One day you'll be a mother and know.' At which Pamela clears her throat.

'As a mother,' she says, 'I'm afraid I have to agree with Jess. It's time to live your life for you, Joan, not for Edward.'

'Pamela, you can't be serious,' I say. 'Try standing in my shoes for a moment. If your girls found out their father wasn't who they'd thought he was a short time after he'd passed, wouldn't you have gone out of your way to protect them? Edward needs time to process the news, and until he does, I can't possibly attempt to see Joseph.'

'But by going, by trying to see him, you'd be laying the foundations for Ed to have a relationship with his real father – that would be an act of support, not betrayal,' says Jess.

I rub my forehead, knowing there is truth in what Jess says, and wanting Edward to know Joseph so badly, but unable to see past the obvious: 'How could Joseph possibly forgive my betrayals? First, I leave him, and then I withhold the truth about his son from him for thirty-seven years. That's unforgivable. What if he already knows, and in all those unopened letters he's been chiding me, berating me?'

Jess gets up from the table and returns a moment later with a letter. A letter I recognise with its pale pink envelope and Joe's handwriting.

'Open it,' she says, and I do.

My Dearest Joany,

Of all the letters I've written to you over the last sixty years, I believe this to be the most important. Allow me to tell you three things:

'May I?' Pamela asks, and I hand it to her, trembling, unable to absorb what I've just read.

Pamela reads the letter over several times then hands it back to me. 'If I may say,' she begins, rather less abrasively than usual. 'It's not often we're given second chances in life. If I had the chance to bring back Derek,' her voice catches at the mention of her husband's name, 'I wouldn't think twice.'

I clutch her hand for support, then Jess squeezes mine; our own little circle of friendship.

'Joan, you've worked really hard for this trip,' says Jess. 'If you don't go now, try to make amends, when will you?'

'She's right, Joan,' Pamela agrees. 'It's just like we said when we were talking about a lodger. If not now, when? And look how that turned out.'

We both look to Jess, so radiant at the table, the beautiful rose between two cabbages. I find it almost impossible to put into words how much she's come to mean to me, as close to Joy as I'll ever know.

'But who's to say I can even find him? We've left it too late to post an advert,' I say, my thoughts beginning to soften. 'Kathleen wasn't certain in her message that she could reach him; she says he's moved after all. It's been a long time since they saw each other.'

'I already set something up for you,' smiles Jess, and she reaches into her bag and pulls out a copy of *The New York Times*. 'Look.'

JO22 MEET JNY19
Radio City Music Hall 8 p.m.
Aug 5th

My finger sits below the little advert for longer than I know, a rush of excitement and nerves coursing through me, followed by a stillness, a feeling of my old self, the version of Joan I once was, returning.

43

JESS

As soon as Pamela and Joan drive off in their taxi to the airport, I hot-foot it with Humphrey to Debs.

'What happened to you?' Debs asks, after I've let myself in, Mike being out with the kids.

'It happened again,' I say, throwing myself on to the corner sofa, where Debs is parked in the corner, nursing the little one; Humphrey lies down at her feet. It's impossible to believe that only a week ago, Debs had collapsed and the little one was holed up in intensive care, hooked up to a ventilator. 'PO Box stood me up.'

'You're shitting me?' she says, covering the baby's ears.

'Nope! I waited for over an hour.'

'Bloody hell, Jess. Why would he do that?'

'Maybe Pamela was right,' I groan, laying my head on the back of the sofa and staring at the ceiling. 'Maybe he isn't who he says he is.'

'It doesn't make any sense: all of those letters; all that time . . .'

'I honestly thought he was going to be the one. That

one person who was sweet and kind and even hotter than Ed.'

'Hun, I'm so sorry,' she says, reaching out an arm, even though there's no way she can hug me while nursing.

'And that's not all,' I continue. 'I had a bust-up with Ed.'

'How come?'

I explain about Joan telling Ed about Joseph. 'He thinks I meddled, that it's my fault the way he found out.'

'He's hurt,' she says in a way that tells me not to worry about it, but I can't help it; I can think of nothing else. 'He just found out his father isn't who he thought, *and* that he's alive. And, forgive me for saying, but you did search for Joseph without Joan's consent, so in a way he's got a point; you are the catalyst behind it all.'

'You're right,' I sigh, wondering where Ed is and how he's feeling, if he really believes I took advantage of Joan. 'Truth be told, I feel bad for him. It's like a total role reversal – I'm mad with PO Box, and thinking only about Ed.'

Debs laughs, with no malice, at my misfortune.

I roll my head round to look at her. 'He kissed me, you know.'

'When?'

'Yesterday.'

'What was it like?'

'Surprisingly tender.'

Debs watches me for a moment, trying to read me. I've a feeling she can sense I ran off.

'It would be cool if you could find someone who has the same sensitivity as Mr PO Box and the insane

317

hotness of Ed,' she says, placing her baby girl over her shoulder to wind.

'Never going to happen,' I laugh, though I wish that it would. 'Turns out there is no magic in real life. I'm destined to be on my own for ever.'

I'm too exhausted from the day to chat any more about me, so instead I ask how Debs is doing.

'I'm much better now we're home. The boys are being amazing. I've got the girl I always wanted. The family feels complete.'

'I'm happy for you, Debs,' I tell her, watching her lay the baby down in the crib beside the sofa. 'Have you thought of a name?'

She finishes tucking the baby in, making sure there's no sign that she'll wake again soon, then snuggles back into the sofa.

'We were thinking about Jessica Joy,' she says, and I well up immediately. 'In recognition of the best friend a woman can have, and to honour Joan's loss. Do you think she'd mind?'

I shake my head, lost for words, then reach over to squeeze Debs as tight as her post-partum body will allow.

44

JOAN

'Joan Armitage,' says Kathleen, embracing me wholeheartedly. Her energy, unchanged after almost four decades, seeps into me and softens the discomfort my body feels after a long flight. I begin to release her, but she holds me tighter, closer than anyone has held me in a very long time. 'Where have you been all this time?' she asks, releasing me, holding me at arm's length, and scrutinising my every line.

'It's been too long,' I say, admiring her hair, which was always strong and thick, and it remains so now even though the colour has gone. The grey accentuates her dark, gentle eyes, and enhances her olive skin.

She clutches my elbows. 'Yes, it has.'

'This is my neighbour and good friend, Pamela,' I say, only then remembering my manners, Pamela having had the good grace to keep an eye on the luggage rather than our reunion.

'Lovely to meet you, Pamela,' says Kathleen, and she embraces Pamela too, who stiffens, patting Kathleen woodenly on the back.

'Joe messaged this morning to let me know about your rendezvous, so we'd better get going!' rallies Kathleen, not realising that this is the first confirmation of our meeting.

Pamela places a hand on my back, and a calmness spreads over me, a feeling akin to the peace I used to get when I began a piano recital after experiencing all-consuming nerves for hours beforehand.

After collecting our luggage, Kathleen escorts us to her car. I try hard to 'stay in the moment' as Jess would put it, to focus on the delight of being together with Kathleen again, or how it will feel to see Joe, rather than the regret of the missing years.

'Peter and I were just discussing how long it's been,' says Kathleen, when she's navigated her way out of the car park and network of surrounding roads and on to the freeway towards the city. 'I saw you after Edward was born, but after that . . .'

'Almost forty years,' I say, gazing out of the car window. 'How things have changed.'

'I don't suppose much of this was here when you left,' says Pamela.

'I don't recognise any of it.'

'Some days I don't recognise myself in the mirror, let alone the buildings and roads,' laughs Kathleen, and Pamela and I join her.

'I never can mesh the physical changes with the spirit that remains as youthful as when I was twenty-one,' says Pamela.

Kathleen nods sagely, and I wonder what they mean. It always feels to me as if my spirit has aged even faster than my physical being.

'Is Peter well?'

'Not bad. He's enjoying being back in his hometown. I'm not sure London ever really compared. Most days he walks for hours, absorbing the changes, revelling in the millennials and Gen-Zers! He's fallen back in love with the place.'

'Who can blame him?' I say, watching the large suburban homes turn to the projects and then to the glorious brownstones of Brooklyn.

And then, when I'm least expecting it, the freeway opens up and there in front of me is Manhattan, magnificent and breath-taking as ever, the place I loved to call home. I find it almost impossible to imagine that somewhere, in amongst all the buildings, is Joe, preparing to meet me.

'There she is, ladies,' cries Kathleen. 'New York City in all her glory!'

'Wow,' says Pamela. In the mirror I see her visibly moved by the sight, her face close against the back-passenger window like a young child. One of her hands is placed on the back of my chair and I reach up to hold it, knowing she must be thinking of Derek, and wishing he were here too.

We drive on, parallel to the island, catching fleeting glimpses of the Statue of Liberty, drawing ever closer to the Brooklyn Bridge, the pulse of the city coming back to me.

'I thought I'd drive you the long way round, give you a bit of a trip down memory lane. We don't want to arrive too early,' says Kathleen, as she winds her way south to the Financial District where Joseph and I would occasionally stroll to Battery Park and gaze out at the statue and remind ourselves of our own freedom.

And we drive past the Freedom Tower, neither it nor the Twin Towers there in my day, and I'm reminded afresh of how much time has passed, how much loss there has been for so many.

'Do you remember drinks in Jack's Tavern?' Kathleen asks, when we pass a bar in SoHo, where the four of us used to meet when Kathleen and Peter visited from London.

'I do indeed,' I say, recalling how Joe and I used to stumble home afterwards, basking in our love.

Before I know it, we're upon Washington Square Park, at the bottom of 5th Avenue, with its majestic stone arch, where Joe and I would often meet when coming from different parts of the city to walk home together.

I want to press pause, and then rewind the years.

I must have lost myself in my memories because next thing I know, Kathleen is indicating and slowing to pull into a residential street, one that fleetingly stops my heart.

'Here we are,' she says, finding a place to pull over on beautiful Perry Street, narrow and tree-lined with brownstone houses, where Joe and I lived together for five glorious years. 'It's only recently that Joseph moved, not wanting the stairs to become a problem. I've been remiss in not sending his latest letter that he sent some months back; I imagine his new address is in there.

'None of us are getting any younger,' I hear Kathleen continue, but it sounds far off in the distance, my rising emotions drowning out everything else.

It takes me unaware when I feel tears spilling down my cheeks.

Pamela reaches over to place her hands on my shoulders. Kathleen holds my hand softly.

'Why didn't he stop me that night? Ask me to marry him as he planned?' I sob, unable to fathom that fifty years have passed when the street looks and feels as if it were only yesterday.

Neither of them answer.

'Why not propose when he found out I was going to marry? He wrote. Why not say?'

'I think he felt it would come across as an act of desperation, rather than one of love,' says Kathleen gently.

'If not then, why not the night we met—' I realise I'm confiding something Kathleen doesn't know.

My feelings overwhelm me, and I struggle to catch my breath.

'It's OK, Joan. Just breathe,' says Pamela, sensing the possibility of a panic attack. 'Remember the way I taught you: four lines of a square. When you're ready, you can tell her.'

I close my eyes, follow Pamela's instructions: in along one side, out down another, in along another side, out going up.

'Edward wasn't Parker's,' I begin, opening my eyes, and to my surprise, Kathleen nods.

'I could tell by his eyes,' she smiles supportively, her own eyes full of compassion. 'They were all Joseph.'

I smile back at her, my tears lessening. 'I was so afraid to contact you,' I confide. 'The one person who had a link to Joe, the one person who I thought might know my secret.'

'It was always safe with me,' she says.

'You never told Joe?' I ask, fearing the answer.

'It wasn't for me to tell,' she replies, patting my hand. 'But, for what it's worth, I think he would want to know. More than that, I think he would be delighted to know.'

'I'm so afraid, Kathleen,' I say, and it takes me back fifty-five years when I confided in her about leaving home to live with Joseph. She was equally supportive then. 'Edward forbade me to see him. What if I lose Edward too, and I'm left without either of them?'

'Joseph's only regret is not marrying you, of not giving you children,' she says, blotting a tear for me with a tissue, peering deep into my eyes. 'I really don't see anything but good coming from this.'

'I agree!' says Pamela, gripping my shoulder.

'But I can't,' I say, any sense of calm I had is gone, my fear finally getting the better of me, and I wish, wholeheartedly, that I'd stayed at home.

45

JESS

It gives me goosebumps to round the bend and see the cinema in front of me, all lit up again with the canopy reading:

Daniel Corvel: Urban Landscapes
Opening Night

The foyer is busy with people milling around, absorbing Daniel's artwork, which has been hung and lit so beautifully by Charlie.

'Jess,' says Daniel, greeting me with a kiss on the cheek, something he's never done before.

'Your work looks amazing, Daniel,' I say, immediately noticing how composed and self-assured he seems, in stark contrast to the person he always was while working at the cinema.

'It's going great,' he says, and Charlie joins us, placing a hand on Daniel's shoulder.

'Better than great,' he adds. 'Check out how many red dots there are.'

I scan the painting labels and notice that over half have sold already. 'I love how the theme of the exhibition ties so well with the empty building. Almost symbiotic,' I say, admiring a piece he's done, photo sharp, of a graffitied wall and an abandoned bike propped up against it.

'You've Ed to thank for that,' says Charlie, drinking from a glass of champagne. 'It was his idea, Daniel's work lending itself so well to the space, not mine.'

'Is he here?' I ask, looking around, anxious about how he'll receive me after this morning's run-in.

Charlie tells me that he's downstairs so I head down to the bar, full of people mingling, with waiting staff circulating with trays of fine canapés and glasses of champagne.

'Jess!' squeals Mariko when she sees me, waving me over to where she, Gary and Clive are huddled together, deep in conversation. Mariko squeezes me within an inch of my life.

'How are you, Jess?' asks Gary, offering me a bony hug, clearly several glasses in.

'Better for seeing you guys,' I say, and Clive air-kisses me three ways, Lulu, tucked under his arm, preventing a hug. 'How is everyone?'

The three of them exchange looks I can't read, as if they've a secret I'm not in on.

'Out of work for now, but doing OK,' Gary answers.

'Not loving I-work but enjoying managing,' says Mariko. She speaks stiffly, as if choosing her words carefully.

'And I'm in love with retirement,' sings Clive. 'Lulu and I have booked our first cruise to the Med.'

I can tell Clive is about to launch into his cruise plans, so it's a relief when Debs and Mike arrive, Debs looking glorious in a fifties tea dress that skims over her post-delivery bump.

'You made it!' I say, hugging them both.

'Grandparents – yay!' laughs Debs, doing a little thrill-wave with her hands.

'Congratulations!' says Mike, and I cock him an uncertain look. 'On completing the offline challenge,' he prompts.

My mouth falls open. 'I can't believe I didn't remember!'

'What!' cries Debs. 'Are you mad? I've been on a countdown all week.'

'She called you as soon as she woke up this morning,' confirms Mike.

'But your phone was off,' she adds. 'Where is it?'

'Still in the understairs cupboard,' I confess.

Debs looks at me despairingly. 'Jess, you cannot stay offline a moment longer. I can't cope with you not being available 24/7.'

'Jess, please, if not for Debs then for me,' laughs Mike. 'You've no idea how much more Debs talks when you're not contactable!'

'Rude!' laughs Debs, and she slaps him playfully with her clutch bag.

'For you,' I say to Debs, 'but only you. I like being offline; it's been good for me.' My eyes wander towards Ed where he's chatting to Zinnia in the corner.

Ed looks over as I'm thinking how frustratingly handsome he is, and our eyes meet. Neither of us looks away. He raises his glass to me, his eyes sparkling.

327

Before I can redirect my attention, he excuses himself from Zinnia and walks towards me. I drain a glass of champagne from a passing tray.

'Jess,' he says, and despite our dancing eyes, I can still feel this morning's argument standing between us.

'Thanks for doing this for Daniel. It was kind of you.'

'It's a good turnout,' he replies, and I wonder if, like me, he'd like to bypass the small talk.

'I'm sorry about this morning,' I say, swallowing hard. 'I can see why you'd think I've been interfering. But I promise, I just wanted the best for Joan. I couldn't possibly have known Joseph would turn out to be your father.'

'I'm the one who should be apologising,' he smiles tenderly, and my muscles relax. 'I was hurt, in shock. I needed a scapegoat. I'm sorry that was you.'

'Thank you,' I say, our eyes flickering, the rest of the room beginning to fade.

'You're the best thing that's ever happened to my mother, Jess. I know that. She knows that. Hell, even Pamela knows that.'

I laugh, thankful for his humour.

'Part of me was jealous, insecure: that Joan would prefer you to me,' he adds.

'I'm sorry you felt that way. And I'm sorry too that I didn't tell you about your dad.'

He shrugs. 'Like you said, it wasn't your secret to tell. You were being loyal. I get that. It's for me to sort out with Mum. Really I should be thanking you.'

'Don't be too hard on her,' I say, worried for Joan, for them both. 'I know you're hurt, but you have to let her live her life, give her the chance to love again.'

'Maybe I need to do the same for me too,' he says, and he takes me by the hand, leads me into the office.

'What's going on?' I ask, searching his dark eyes, his pupils wide in the dim light.

'Jess, there's something I need to tell you. Something I should have explained a while ago.'

I watch quizzically as he pulls something from his back pocket, beneath the flap of his jacket.

He hands me a bundle of letters bound with red ribbon.

'These are . . .' I start but can't finish.

I stare at the collection of envelopes in my hand, all of them recognisable, all of them written by me.

'Ed, where did you . . .'

'Some prefer to call me Mr PO Box,' he says quietly.

'Oh my God,' I say slowly, backing up a bit, my hands tingling.

'Are you pleased?' he asks, his eyes scanning mine.

'I'm shocked,' I say, leaning up against a collection of old coats, not sure what to think. 'Not that I hadn't thought about it, because all those hints . . .'

It's then that I remember him talking about Joe Fox not only being the romantic hero of *You've Got Mail* but the anti-hero too, and I realise he was trying to tell me then, or pave the way to now.

'I wondered if you'd picked up on those.'

'I convinced myself they were just coincidences,' I whisper.

'I think we're all out of coincidences, don't you?' he says, drawing closer. 'You working at the cinema, me being Joan's son . . .'

'How did you figure out my handle?' I ask, so many questions racing through my head.

'That morning when we met at the house, Mum let the cat out of the bag about you posting in the lonely hearts. She said your name was CineGirl. Then, when Debs mentioned your handle was inspired by *You've Got Mail*, I couldn't resist writing to you, like NY152 did to Shopgirl.'

'So you knew it was me?'

'Yes,' he admits, and I pause, not sure what to feel. Four months ago I would have been livid at the deception, but now, after all that's happened, the closure and trust and security found, I don't find myself feeling angry at all.

'I probably should have thought it through a bit more,' he says slightly nervously. He backs off, takes a seat on the swivel chair. 'I only did it because I wanted to get to know you better. I wanted you to know the real me, not work Ed, with the serious persona.'

'Like Parker,' I say, sitting on the little office bench opposite him, and he nods, 'the man you thought you were meant to be.'

'I didn't want you to just see work Ed or Joan's son, with all his barriers up. I wanted you to know that within me was someone else, the man, I suppose, nature always intended me to be.'

'The son of a passionately romantic musician?'

He shrugs, smiles. 'I guess.'

And I smile too, flattered that he should go to such lengths for me.

'The whole thing was just too tempting . . . me looking to buy your beloved cinema, you so against it. The symmetry and romance. I even tried to replicate some of the scenes from the film.'

'You did?' I laugh.

'It started with the coffee shop – you were expecting Mr PO Box and I showed up instead. I'd planned to tell you who I was that day, but you were still so mad at me, the timing was off, until now.'

'Debs did point that was a weird coincidence,' I say, remembering how furious I was with him at the time, how far in the past that seems now.

'And then there were the flowers I brought to your house, trying to win you round, and the date at the market . . . and then we were meant to meet at the station.' He looks at his shoes, then directly at me. 'I'm sorry I didn't show up – I was so angry with Mum – I wanted it to be your real-life end of movie moment.'

'I love that you tried,' I say, tailing off.

'But?' he asks, his forehead knitted.

'I'm still not sure I can forgive you for closing the cinema,' I say, uncertain I'll ever be able to move past it. 'It was never about my job, Ed. It was about losing the place that felt like home and family. There were so many other sites you could have bought.'

'What if I told you I could reverse the decision?' he asks, his face relaxing, his eyes twinkling.

'How do you mean?'

'What if I told you the other person is still interested, that it's all arranged?'

'He pulled out ages ago,' I say, thinking about the hedge fund guy Clive thought might bid. 'It all came to nothing.'

'Not "he", "she",' he says, and he gets up, offers me his hand and takes me back out to the bar, where he finds Zinnia.

'I don't understand,' I say to them both.

'I told you I was looking for a sideline,' says Zinnia. 'The TikTok campaign was fun, but now it's time for something bigger.'

'I . . .' I begin, only just joining the dots. 'Are you saying what I think you're saying?'

'Zinnia is the new owner of the Portland Cinema,' confirms Ed.

'How?' I ask, now totally bamboozled.

'We've been planning it for months,' says Zinnia proudly.

'Since your media day, where I saw just how much it meant to you. I knew you'd never forgive me if I turned it into another I-work,' says Ed, his eyes burning with sincerity.

'But how can you afford this?' I ask Zinnia.

'I'm rich!' she says. 'My husband's family established one of the big film studios. I just needed some time to release the funds.'

'Hence why we didn't start work on the place, and it being boarded up for so long,' says Ed.

'I can't believe any of this,' I say, my head in overdrive, though Zinnia having an old friend who's a big film producer now makes much more sense. 'The only thing is . . .' I begin tentatively, not wanting to burst anyone's bubble.

'Is that you got the Production Assistant job?' asks Ed.

'Thanks to you guys,' I nod, Phil having called on my way back from Debs' this afternoon to offer me the job with Working Title. Humphrey and I celebrated with a bone and a Starbucks. 'How did you know that?'

'Phil called to tell me,' smiles Zinnia.

'So we've sorted that too,' Ed says, gesturing to Mariko who joins us with Gary.

'Meet the new manager of the Portland, and your projectionist.'

'Get out of town,' I scream, hugging them both instantly, knowing that this will give Gary his new home, and Mariko her shot at managing somewhere she's passionate about. I think of all the things she'll bring to the place that Clive never did: more exhibitions, talks and events, weddings, and location hire, and how amazing she'll be at promoting everything through her socials.

'Why don't you both go outside and talk things over,' says Zinnia to me with a wink.

'Let's,' says Ed, and after one final squeeze of Mariko, both of us brimming with excitement, I follow him upstairs and outside.

'You know Mr PO Box told me once that his "true self might one day find his way out",' I say, as we both take a seat on the bench, me thinking back through his letters. 'Maybe this is the start of that happening.'

'I hope so,' he says.

'Get to know your father, Ed, and the three of you to know each other. You've come this far already . . .'

'I'll try,' he says earnestly, and I believe him.

'Good,' I say, nudging closer.

'Happy?' he asks, a full moon high above us.

'Very,' I say, and he places his arm along the bench.

'I'm happy for Mariko and Gary, and Zinnia too; happy for me that I get to follow my passion, my dream job.'

'I'm glad, Jess.'

'I can't believe you'd give up a bit of I-work for me,' I say, gazing up at the sky.

'How else was I going to prove how much you mean to me?'

I turn my head to look at him. He looks back at me, his eyes full of the moon.

'You asked me on the South Bank what I'm passionate about and I couldn't tell you then, but I can now,' he says. 'I'm passionate about you, Jess Harris. Always have been, always will be,' he says, and I remember what he said at the playground about how Izzy couldn't be perfect for him because someone else was. I realise that person was always me: "bubbly, self-assured, kind". 'I want nothing more than to be with you, if you'll have me?' He wraps an arm warmly around me.

'Who is "me"?' I ask, scanning his dark, deep eyes. 'Ed Armitage or Mr PO Box?'

'Who do you want me to be?'

'Both,' I grin, loving them equally, thrilled that I've found the impossible: the sensitivity, loyalty and kindness of Mr PO Box, and the insane hotness of Ed.

'Good. Because one can't exist without the other,' he says, in such a way that tells me he's not only talking about himself, but also us.

And then he kisses me, sweeter and more soulful than any movie, and it feels just as Zinnia said it would, like two stars colliding: magic sparks flying everywhere.

46

JOAN

In the end, a parking attendant came along, and Kathleen had no choice but to move on. We're driving through midtown, the moon beginning to rise above the city, when my phone rings. 'Edward Armitage' flashes on the screen. My stomach lurches.

'Guess who I'm with?' he grins, seemingly not angry at all, the videocall remarkably clear given we're an ocean apart. He moves the camera further away so I can see.

'Hi Joan,' Jess waves, grinning.

'We've news,' says Ed, and they kiss tenderly.

'I had a notion you might,' I smile, delighted for them both, despite my worries.

'And that's not all,' says Jess. 'Ed is Mr PO Box!'

Ed moves the camera rapidly back and forth to create a dramatic effect, causing Jess to laugh. 'Can you believe that, Joan? Ed is Mr PO Box!'

'Extraordinary,' I say, admiring them both. What I don't say is that it doesn't surprise me, that I always knew he was a romantic at heart, just like his father.

'And all because of our challenge, Joan. Without me going offline and you going online, I wouldn't have fallen for Ed-slash-Mr PO Box, and you wouldn't be on your way to meet Joseph.'

'About that, Mum . . .' says Edward.

I hold my breath, his face now serious, causing him to look so like Parker. It surprises me, not for the first time, how a man can look so like someone who isn't a blood relation.

'I didn't mean to storm out the way I did, or say what I said,' he explains. 'I'm sorry, Mum. Of course you must see him.'

'I'm not sure I—' I begin, not wanting to disappoint Jess, but feeling I haven't the physical or emotional strength to go through with the meeting.

But Ed doesn't let me finish. 'You need to do this for you, Mum, but also for us. Go find him. Tell him the truth. Find your happiness.'

For all my fear, I still want to clasp my hands around his handsome face, his eyes now as soft and rich as Joe's. 'Are you sure?' I ask, my resolve rising.

'I'm certain. Tell him I can't wait to meet him.'

'Then I will,' I say, on an outward breath, spurred on by their courage and youthful enthusiasm.

'You'll be great, Joan,' calls Jess, as the video begins to pixelate, and the connection is lost.

Kathleen manages to pull up outside the entrance to the Radio City Music Hall, leaving Pamela and me to navigate our way to the elevator to the roof terrace.

'Hang in there, Joan,' says Pamela, checking her

appearance in the mirror of the elevator. I'm unable to do anything other than stare forward and think of my breathing. To make sense of what is about to happen would be impossible, so I don't try, I simply allow my body to take the necessary motions.

'Here we are,' she says brightly, though her voice is tight, no doubt nervous for me.

'I'm not sure I can,' I say, as the door slides open, my newfound determination wavering. I find myself hoping the door might close and enable me to go back to the certainty of my past rather than out towards an unknown future.

'One more step, Joan,' says Pamela, positioning herself against the door to prevent it from closing, and offering me her hand.

Even in my state of anxiety, I can still see Pamela's good-hearted guile. Stopping the doors from closing means I'd have to push her to break free, which she knows I wouldn't do.

'It's rather beautiful out here,' she says, and foolishly I'm duped into looking.

Pamela is right, the garden is beautiful. Soft planting is lit from below in contrast to the skyscrapers overhead. And everywhere people are clustered around tables, chattering and drinking, and enjoying the night air.

Before I've noticed, Pamela has led me from the elevator and out, towards a low bench on a curved path, just out of sight of the entrance.

'Perhaps he's here already,' I say, my heart rate dangerously high.

'I'll go take a look.'

'How will you know if it's him?'

Pamela laughs. 'Joan, there's not a person here under forty. I'm certain I'll be able to identify someone in his eighties as Joseph.'

'Righto,' I say, allowing her to go, feeling suddenly inconsequential, conscious that each person, behind every window of each skyscraper above, has a love story of their own.

I sit and breathe, unable to do anything more.

'No luck, I'm afraid,' she says, returning.

She must see my face drop with disappointment because she adds, 'You know how it is in the city, it takes an age to get from A to B, particularly at our age.'

'Yes,' I say, hoping that this is it, and not that he's had second thoughts.

A moment later, my phone pings, and I look to discover a message from Kathleen. Five simple words:

He is on his way

I inhale sharply, grip the wood of the bench, physically bracing myself for the moment I've waited a lifetime for. I'm trying to gather myself when a voice I know better than my own, sends a tingle running through me from the top of my head to the tips of my toes.

'Hello, Joany,' he says, and I look up to see Joseph, as mesmerising and handsome as he was that first night at Ronnie Scott's, walking towards me. And then he's standing in front of me, Joseph Blume. My Joe. As real as the tears that tumble down my cheeks.

'Sorry to keep you waiting,' he says, reaching out and catching a teardrop with his thumb.

'That's OK,' I say, a smile I haven't smiled in decades spreading over my face. 'What's a few minutes of waiting, after a lifetime of longing?'

And then, as if I am dreaming, he sits beside me and opens a small box.

'I kept this ring all these years, Joany. Now that I've found my way back to you, I have no intention of losing you again.'

He puts his arms around me, and I fall heart and soul into him.

I have so much to say, about Edward, about the journey that has led to this moment, but I don't want to move from his arms.

He looks down at me with those dark sensuous eyes and gently lifts my chin before placing a kiss on my lips that both rewinds the years and ignites my spirit.

'Now,' he says, smiling, his face aglow, 'let's start the end of our story.'

ACKNOWLEDGEMENTS

A big thank you to Juliet Pickering, my incredible, hard-working agent whose patience knows no bounds. She believed in this book from my first scrappy pitch to the final draft. Thank you for enabling me to do what I love.

To Sherise Hobbs at Headline Publishing. What can I say? It was a dream come true to have the opportunity to work with you, and the reality proved better than the dream. Thank you for your expert guidance, endless enthusiasm, and sheer love of romance. Together we made this book.

And to Priyal Agrawal: a quiet romantic. Poised, gracious and marvellously efficient. It's been a joy to work with you.

To the rest of the dream book team at Headline, including but not limited to: Caroline Young, who nailed the cover; Sarah Bance, for fixing the stuff I probably should know but don't, and the brilliant rights team, always so ahead of the curve, I thank you all.

Jess and Joan, and their journey, were shaped by so many conversations with friends along the way. Thanks go to: Anneke, whose spirit and dedication inspired and informed; Jane, who sparked the swap idea and helped bring Joan back to life (and for generally being someone I admire and adore); Lindsey, for all the tea and scones, support, and generously gifting me part of her story, and Jana, for being so constant in her friendship, and for sharing a nugget of romance.

To Liz at the bank who inadvertently fixed a plot hole – thank you! And to David for being better at maths than I am.

My thanks to Lesley, Dani and Helen Z, who all listened for longer than any friend should have to. And thanks too, to the many strong (slightly older) women in my life who inspired me along the way: Jeni A, Ann and Judy, to mention a few.

And last but never least, my family. To my parents for their tireless support, for my son and all his radiance, and to Peter, for knowing when to listen, knowing when to advise, and most importantly, knowing when to leave me in peace – I thank you.

AUTHOR'S NOTE

Dear Reader,

The Library of Lost Love is a novel I felt compelled to write; I needed to write a book that would demonstrate to me, and to you, that there is an alternative to this fast-paced, often lonely world we live in.

The initial idea was simply two women, Jess and Joan, women of differing age, moving in together to combat costs and loneliness. Then came the idea of them switching from online to offline, and vice versa. It was only after that, when I had the idea of the lonely hearts column and the letter writing, that the idea of their love lives entwining came to mind.

As the novel took shape, the lost art of letter writing came to the fore. I grew fascinated by how the process of not only writing a letter but also of waiting for the response, developed a patience, a quietness, a greater focus within Jess. And it also interested me how the emotions connected with these very personal tangible objects, sometimes scented or bearing traces of their journey, affected Joan's decision-making.

The letters became more than a device within the book, the distance they create (both time and physical) made safe places for the characters to voice words they might not have in person or by other means. The letters began to impact directly on the characters' journeys.

After reading *The Library of Lost Love* I hope that you the reader will feel compelled to start writing your own letters, be they to friends, family or lovers. In doing so I hope that you too will find, as Jess does, your own sense of quiet contentment, in the midst of this hectic world.

Sincerely,

Norie Clarke